Twelve Curious Deaths in France

by

John Goldsmith

Print Edition 2014

Licensed by Marble City Publishing

Copyright © 2014 John Goldsmith

First published by Marble City Publishing in 2014

ISBN 10 1-908943-40-8

ISBN 13 978-1-908943-40-8

FOR ANTHEA

and

FOR THEO

CONTENTS

INTRODUCTION

BY MICHEL WALRANGIS

I am convinced that it was actually my colleague who compared our first meeting to two dogs sniffing round each other in a park. He swears that the analogy was in fact mine. My memory is admittedly somewhat hazy but it seems to me that the image is very much more in his style.

This is how it happened. I had recently completed the first draft of a screenplay. The producer was anxious to attract American investment into the project and as a result had agreed (without consulting me) to bring an English-speaking writer on board to "assist" me in writing the second draft. I was, rather naturally, taken aback and not a little offended when I learned of this – and in any case I am by nature suspicious. This, I think, is due to my family background. For many generations my ancestors were minor landowners in a part of the world that now belongs to Belgium but had, during the centuries, been fought over and disputed almost incessantly by the European powers. The Comtes Walrangis had been obliged to shift their allegiance between the Spanish, the French, the Dutch and various German Princes, Electors and so on with bewildering frequency. After the Franco-Prussian war my great-grandfather decided to call it a day, sell his properties, definitively opt for French citizenship and move to Paris. But I digress.

The film I had written was a piece of historical fiction, based on the works of Alexandre Dumas, featuring the young D'Artagnan. The villain of the piece was the Bishop of Luçon, political adviser to the Queen-Mother, Marie de' Medici. The Bishop was, of course, known later to history as Cardinal Richelieu, famed as possibly the most devious political animal of them all. Much of the action turned on the intrigues swirling round the marriage of the young French King, Louis XIII, with Anne of Austria. I was convinced that the wretched Americans would want to cut out a great deal of the politics and pump up the action: sword-fights, ambushes, kidnaps and so on. I was both right and wrong.

My colleague and I met for the first time in a very grand restaurant in Paris. (The producers were paying.) This was a little stratagem of mine. I thought that this unknown American screen-writer might be intimidated by the imposing décor and the immense, leather-bound, menu. Imagine my surprise when I discovered that the potential enemy was not only English and spoke fluent French, but was on first-name terms with the maître d'hôtel! I was, I confess, disconcerted. It took some time, and several glasses of champagne, to dispel the tension between us and produce a more relaxed atmosphere. It then turned out that the Americans did indeed want to cut out much of "the politics" – so I was right about that – but that my new collaborator was completely opposed to this line – so I was wrong. His point was – and I quote: "Action has to spring from something real, otherwise it's just a lot of flashing blades and thundering hooves."

As a result of that lunch we became not just allies in a war against Hollywood but firm friends. We worked together very intensely for several months. I learned a great deal of technique. I came to appreciate, as well, the value of humour in telling a story and building a character. In the end we produced an excellent screenplay. I quote again: "It's lean, it's mean, it romps along and it sings."

My confidence in our friendship grew to such an extent that one day I showed him the collection of stories I had been gathering over the years. He was most taken with them and offered not only to translate them into English but to provide explanatory notes. I accepted his offer with all possible enthusiasm.

Now, my friend has declared that "nobody ever reads Introductions." If he had said "very few people ever read Introductions" I might have been inclined to agree. But "nobody?" A gross exaggeration. (To which he is unfortunately rather prone.) And you, dear reader, have just made my case!

Editor's note: The film never got made.

TWELVE CURIOUS DEATHS IN FRANCE

DECLAN MCCLAIRE

Michel Bourrez and my Dad go back a long way, to the 1970's, when they did their *Service militaire* together (I escaped it by a couple of years, thank God!) After the army their paths diverged – my Dad took over the family farm from his father, Michel went into the police – but they kept in touch. Then Michel got a job in Tarbes, which is only thirty kilometres from our place, and he and his wife and two kids would often come over at weekends, especially in the summer. We'd splash about in the secret lake my Dad had made in the woods below the house and the two old men – they seemed old to me then! – would reminisce about their days in the army, how they first met in the canteen, recognizing each other's accents and discovering that Michel was from the Hautes-Pyrénées and Dad from the Gers; how they both ran up against a brutish sergeant from Lille called Dieux, inevitably nicknamed Dieu Tout Puissant; the agonies of boredom and cold they suffered on sentry-duty in some Godforgotten garrison town in the North East. Even as a kid I suspected that there were other shared adventures they considered unsuitable for exposure to women and children and this was confirmed later by Michel's son, René, who became one of my best friends. The stories, mostly about women and drink, are actually not that interesting.

I've noticed that old friends are to some extent also rivals. They can't quite help comparing their relative progress in life: how much money they're making, what car they're driving, how their kids are doing at school and so on. Was it entirely a coincidence that soon after Michel was promoted to Inspector my Dad bought a race-horse?

I'm rambling. But then I can afford to ramble. Since my Editor has spiked this story, the best story I've so far come across in my admittedly short journalistic career, I have the freedom to tell it in my own way – and I intend to make the most of it.

A few months after I got my DUT and landed my current job with the *Dépêche*, Michel asked me out to lunch. He told me that there was a long-established line of communication – that's how he tactfully put it – between the police and the press. A policeman was often in a position to tip off a favoured reporter about an interesting story before his rivals could get on to it. The payback was simply that the reporter would share his information with the police. "You see witnesses are often intimidated when we interview them," Michel said. "They're defensive, nervous, suspicious. They clam up. They're usually much more open with a reporter – especially if he's sympathetic, you know, a good listener. Let them gabble on and you can get their whole damned life-stories out of them and though most of it'll be irrelevant, sometimes little details slip out that can be helpful to an enquiry."

This was something that none of my teachers at IUT had told me about. Perhaps they don't know. But it made sense to me. I'd already discovered that most people actually like talking to a reporter. It flatters them. It makes them feel important. Madame Y is going to have her name in the paper! (I always make sure I have the spelling of a person's name and above all their *age* dead accurate!) And in my case, as a humble CLP, I didn't even have an official press card to unsettle the ultra-nervous interviewee. Of course, France is full of, you could almost say France functions *because of*, such little unofficial systems. You're stopped for speeding. A discreet phone-call to your friend the Mayor and – abracadabra! – file erased.

Over the next couple of years the "system" worked well. Michel scratched my back and I scratched Michel's, to our mutual advantage. Then early one morning in April, about eight when I was lying in bed, half-asleep, next to my girl-friend Julie, my mobile rang. It was Michel. He told me he had something very interesting for me. A foreign kid, Irish they thought, had died earlier that morning in bizarre circumstances in Lourdes. In the grotto itself. Right underneath the statue of the Blessed Virgin! Cause of death as yet uncertain but possibly drug-related.

The drive to Lourdes from Marciac, where Julie and I rent an apartment, usually takes around forty-five minutes. I did it in thirty-eight, getting flashed by the speed camera on the Route de Bordeaux as I headed into Tarbes. Michel had given me the name and address, in Lourdes, of one of the voluntary helpers who had been working in the Shrine that morning and had witnessed the event. I wanted to get to him as quickly as possible.

Ivan Arosteguy lived in Lourdes, in a small apartment in a modern block near the station. He was seventy-two years old, a widower, a devout Catholic. He was short, slightly built, dressed in grey flannel trousers, an old tweed jacket, a shirt and tie. His manner matched his clothes: it was rather formal, very polite, slightly reserved. His hair, carefully cut and brushed, was mostly grey and his face was narrow, lean and very lined, with a sharp, pointed nose. His eyes were kindly, intelligent – and watchful. I decided right away to be completely frank with him. I told him that a friend in the police in Tarbes had told me about the incident that morning, that it was bound to be widely reported and that I was anxious to get the facts right.

"You're after a scoop," he said. But with a little smile.

"Of course," I replied.

He thought for a moment then invited me in. I followed him down a short passage, past a lot of religious pictures, into a small kitchen. He offered me a cup of coffee and as he brewed it up, he started to interview *me*. This happens oftener than you'd think, especially with the more intelligent and circumspect type of person. I told him that

I'd studied journalism at the ITU Michel de Montaigne in Bordeaux, mentioned a few stories I'd written for the *Dépêche* that he might have seen (he said he remembered a couple of them but I think he was just being polite) and generally described the sort of work a CLP does. By the time the coffee was ready I'd managed to swing the focus round to him. I asked him about his name (an old trick when a name is unusual) and he told me that his grandmother on his mother's side had been Russian. His father's family, however, were of Basque origin. He had worked all his life in the insurance business, had retired at sixty-five and lost his wife three years ago. There was a married daughter living in Biarrtitz and a son, in Paris, in insurance, like his father. He had five grand-children. He had worked as a volunteer at the Shrine since his retirement.

He explained what he did. It was basically a mild form of crowd control, ushering pilgrims into the Shrine of the Grotto in an orderly fashion and making sure that there was a minimum of coming and going during the celebration of a Mass. I thought it would be useful to establish a bit of Catholic cred and told him that I used to serve at Mass in our local church.

"Do you still attend Mass?" he asked with another hint of a smile. Reverting to honesty, I admitted that I hardly ever did.

"People have a wrong idea about Lourdes," he said. "They think that terminally ill people come here in the hope of a miraculous cure. I suppose there are a few who do, but the majority come not to prolong but to complete their lives. It's a *pilgrimage*. That's the essence of it." He paused for a moment, then: "But what you really want to know is what happened this morning." Another pause. "Well, I'll tell you."

That morning he had, as he often did, volunteered to supervise the first Mass of the day, which started at 6.45 am. He emphasised that this was not out of any particular

8

devotion to duty but for selfish reasons. "They open the gates at five o'clock," he said, "but there's hardly anybody about at that hour. There's a peace about the place, an increased sense of its mystery, that I love." The Mass was to be said for a party of Japanese pilgrims. There were about fifty of them, led by a Japanese priest. The service was in Japanese. Arosteguy, of course, didn't understand a word of it but that didn't matter to him. "The Mass is the Mass in any language," he said. "One can follow it, become absorbed in it."

It was during the first reading that he noticed a young man running towards the Grotto from the direction of the water taps. To see someone running was in itself unusual but what immediately struck him was that the boy was wearing only a tee shirt and jeans. "It was a cold morning, very damp and misty and I thought he should have a coat on."

What happened next happened so fast that Arosteguy could do nothing about it. The kid vaulted over one of the movable metal barriers that define the worship area and – still running – pushed his way past the Japanese pilgrims, who were sitting for the reading, threw himself down on his knees beneath the floodlit statue of Our Lady that stands high up in a niche in the rock to the right hands side of the grotto itself and began to cross himself, again and again, while repeating over and over, in English: "Thank you, Mother, thank you, Mother, thank you, Mother."

The Japanese pilgrims were staring, the reader had stopped reading, the Priest was gaping and Arosteguy realized that he had to do something. He walked as quickly as possible, without breaking into a run, towards the kid. "I was working out what I should do," Arosteguy said. "I speak very little English but I had understood what the boy was saying and I was trying to remember what 'Please come with me' is in English."

His plan was to get the boy to his feet and persuade him to move quietly out of the area. He was hoping that the boy could speak a little French. But before he could do anything, the boy suddenly collapsed. He fell forward and slightly to one side and by the time Arosteguy got to him he was lying completely still on the ground.

"I felt at once," Arosteguy said, "that it was a very serious situation. I knelt down beside him and it seemed to me that he wasn't breathing." At this point, Arosteguy's colleague joined him. They had both had training in First Aid, but Arosteguy felt it best that his colleague should apply it while he went to telephone the emergency services. When he returned to the scene he found that the Mass had been abandoned. Two local policemen were now in charge. The boy's body had been covered with a blanket and Arosteguy's colleague told him that he was dead.

"There was really nothing more that I could do, apart from giving my name and making a short statement to the police, but for some reason I didn't want to leave the Shrine until the ambulance had arrived."

The ambulance came a few minutes later and the boy's body was taken away to the *Nôtre Dame de Lourdes* hospital up the hill. "I went into the Basilica to pray for the repose of the soul of this young man whose name I didn't even know – and then I came home." There was another of his long pauses, then he added: "A death inevitably stirs up memories of other deaths."

One of the tricks of this trade is sensing accurately when people have come to the end of what they are willing or able to say. Then you have a choice between pressing them, which can be dangerous and counter-productive, or leaving them in peace for a while and coming back later. I got a strong feeling that Arosteguy didn't want to talk any more, that he wanted to be left alone.

I said: "Well, look, thank you, I think I've got all I need. It must have been very upsetting for you."

"Yes," he said. "There was something – disturbing about it. Very disturbing."

Thanking him for the coffee, I stood up.

"Could I ask you something?" he said. "If you find out any more, would you telephone me?"

"Of course."

"I'd like to know his name – and anything else you could tell me."

I had switched off my mobile before knocking on Arosteguy's door and as I walked back to my car, I switched it back on. There was a message from Michel asking me to call him back as soon as possible.

Michel had new information. The kid's name was Declan McLaire. He was eighteen. He had been staying at an hotel in the rue Sainte Marie with a group of Irish pilgrims. The leader of the group was a Father Eamonn O'Dowd. Declan McLaire had left the hotel the night before some time after eleven o'clock. So far they had found nobody who could account for his movements between then and early the following morning when he'd appeared at the Shrine. The exact cause of death was still unknown.

Driving in Lourdes is a nightmare, to say nothing of parking, so I left the Twingo in the *souterrain* in the Place Peyremale at the top of the town and walked down through the maze of twisting streets, past the innumerable shops selling the usual Catholic junk, over the river, to the rue Sainte Marie.

The hotel was a Three Star establishment that looked as if it had been recently refurbished. I went in and asked for Father O'Dowd. The girl behind the desk said he was out. She didn't know where he'd gone or when he'd be back. I'd met her type many times before: the bored, underpaid, unhelpful hotel receptionist. She obviously knew what had happened but equally obviously wasn't about to be of any help to me, so I didn't bother to ask her any questions. I thought the most likely place to find Father O'Dowd would up at the hospital, so I thanked her politely and left.

It was as I stepped back into the street that I had my little moment of inspiration. Opposite the hotel was a bank. It had a hole-in-the-wall. Tacked up in the window of an empty shop right beside it was a big yellow poster advertising a local night club called the Kosatti. I imagined that I was Declan McLaire, eighteen, sneaking out of the hotel, looking for some fun. Money would be the first thing and if I didn't have a lot on me I might well step across the road and get some cash out of the dispenser. If I did, I couldn't miss that big, yellow poster. Maybe I wouldn't miss it anyway. Maybe I'd clocked it before. It was a hunch, but a hunch worth pursuing, I thought. The night club was in the Esplanade du Paradis, not more than a ten minute walk away. I set off. I hadn't been going more than a minute or two when my mobile rang. It was Michel. He sounded excited. There had been a development. Somebody – one of the Japanese pilgrims presumably – had videoed the incident at the Shrine and had posted it on YouTube. Talk about the world of instant communication!

I turned round and headed back up to the Place Peyremale. I had my laptop in the boot of the Twingo – I never go anywhere without it – and as I walked, fast, I worked out a strategy. Presumably there were hotspots in Lourdes but I didn't know where they were and I didn't want to waste any time finding out. Better to drive to the airport at Ossun where I knew there was public Wifi. It was only ten minutes down the road.

Ossun used to be this quaint little 1930's airport but a few years ago they rebuilt the whole thing and now it's a pretty cool-looking glass and steel structure. I sat down in the bar on the upper floor, fired up my laptop and logged on. Michel had been a bit hazy about finding the relevant YouTube video but it was dead easy. I just did a search for "Lourdes" and there it was, top of the list. The thumbnail showed the blurred face of a kid with a mop of black hair – Declan McLaire presumably – and to the right of it was the heading "Kid goes crazy at Lourdes." The information line below told me that the clip had already garnered two stars and had been posted three hours ago by a user called *sakiboi*. I clicked on the thumbnail. Declan sprang to life. His face was huge in the screen. He was pushing right past the guy with the camcorder. He looked wild. It occurred to me that sakiboi must have been filming the Mass from the start but had cut out all the earlier stuff. He was no mean cameraman, sakiboi. You could tell that immediately after Declan was past him, he stood up to get a clearer view and he kept adjusting the zoom to keep the moving figure in shot as he stumbled past startled old Japanese ladies and gentlemen, past the altar and the pyramid of flaming candles towards the brightly lit statue up in the wall of the grotto.

Because it was still dark, and the only meaningful sources of light were the candles and the floodlights on the statue, the image was grainy and fuzzy but I could see the action fairly well. It was exactly as M. Arosteguy had described it to me. Declan fell to his knees below the statue. Although his back was towards the camera, I could make out his movements as he repeatedly crossed himself and I could hear his voice screaming out "Thank you, Mother" again and again. I don't want to offend anybody but it reminded me of some guy in a Rugby stadium cheering on his team. Then I saw Arosteguy himself hurrying towards Declan and Declan keeled over and Arosteguy knelt beside him. And that was it. The video stopped.

Knowing what I knew, that Declan was dead, I was shocked. It took me a moment to get over it. I downloaded the video onto my desktop, turned off the laptop and headed back to the car.

The Esplanade du Paradis had an edge-of-town feel. The shops and apartments looked out across open land to the river. You could see fields and the mountains beyond. The Kosatti club was a squat, chunky building with dull red walls. As I approached, laptop under my arm, I suddenly realized that the place would probably be closed.

They wouldn't open up till the evening. On the other hand, it was about half past eleven by now and there might be somebody about. I tried the street door and found it was open. I stepped inside. The huge bar, which smelt of stale cigarette smoke and damp, at first seemed completely deserted but then I heard somebody cough and weaving my way through the bare-topped tables and neatly arranged chairs I saw a guy sitting at a table near the service entrance. He was going through a stack of papers – invoices I presumed – and tapping at a calculator. A cigarette in an ashtray was sending up a curl of smoke.

Raymond Beder turned out to be the manager. He was thirty-eight, mother French, father Algerian. I introduced myself and briefly told him about the story I was working on. His attitude was wary. A faint memory came back to me about the Kosatti, a piece that had appeared in the *Dépêche*, to do with under-age drinking. To reassure Beder, I told him that I was following up a pure hunch, that my only interest was in trying to put together what happened to this Irish kid between leaving his hotel and ending up at the Shrine, that in all probability he wouldn't be able to help me. But just in case ...

I opened up my laptop, switched it on, waited for the desktop to load up then clicked on the YouTube icon. As Declan's miniature face appeared I was watching Beder closely. I saw a flicker of recognition.

"Yes," said Beder. "He was here."

I guess the same phenomenon occurs in all walks of life: the feeling that for once the tide is running in your direction, that things are panning out, that you're on a roll. It's a great feeling.

"I had to throw him and his friends out," Beder went on. "He was drunk, making a lot of noise, upsetting the other kids. I told Andrew to calm him down or I'd have to throw him out. There was an argument. I told them all to fuck off."

I wanted to ask him who "Andrew" was but Beder

wanted to see the video, so I played it for him. He lit a fresh cigarette as he watched and when the clip ended he said: "You say he's dead. Shit. I'm sorry." Then I asked him about Andrew. Beder told me that Andrew was English but his parents lived in France. They were rich, had some sort of château. He and his friends, mostly English, were regular clients. He'd never seen Declan McLaire before and had no idea how Andrew knew him. Maybe they'd met up in the club. I asked him about Declan's condition. "You say he was drunk."

"He seemed that way. The bar staff told me he was on vodka. He seemed to have plenty of money."

"Drugs?"

Beder became wary again. "We have a very strict policy on drugs," he said. "We don't allow any dealing." I assured him that I'd make that clear in any article I wrote, adding that I wouldn't mention the club by name if he objected. "But he might have got something outside," I said. "Taz, for instance?" Beder thought that, yes, taz might have been involved.

The next step was obviously Andrew, but here we hit a problem. Beder knew him only as Andrew. He didn't know his surname or where exactly his parents' château was and he couldn't think of anybody to ask.

When I was a kid there were hardly any English living in our part of the world. Now there seem to be thousands. They're all over the place. There was even one in our village, a very nice woman called Rosanna, who'd bought a barn from my Uncle Georges and converted it. She and my parents got on well – she often came round to buy eggs and honey – and as I walked back to the car I thought maybe she could help. I rang home, got my mother and she gave me Rosanna's number. I rang Rosanna. She was in. She doesn't speak the greatest French – though it's a hell of a lot better than my English – but we managed to communicate. I told her what I knew about "Andrew" but it didn't ring any bells. However, she offered to ring a friend of hers, another Englishwoman, who, she said, knew everybody there was to know in the ex-pat community. I waited in the car. About ten minutes later, Rosanna rang me back. She said there was an English couple called Hawthorne – she spelt it out for me – who had a big house near a village called Troncens ... and a son called Andrew.

I felt the tide flowing my way again because Troncens is only a few kilometres from Marciac, where I live. It's up in the hills and has a ruined castle you can see for miles. By now it was getting on for midday and I was tempted to swing by the apartment and have some lunch – I was hungry – but something told me to press on. It was a good thing I did.

It took me an hour to get to Troncens, via Tarbes and Rabastens and another ten minutes to find the Hawthorne's place. It wasn't a château. It was a big old farmhouse to which two towers, with conical roofs, had been added, one at each end, some time in the late 19th century I guessed. I admit that the entrance gates, the drive and the grounds, with huge cedars and horse chestnuts, were impressive, but subtract the towers and you'd have nothing much bigger or better than the house I was brought up in.

Near the house, the drive divided, one branch leading towards the front entrance, the other, under an arch – another later addition – to the yard and outbuildings. I didn't want to park right in front of the house so I drove under the arch into the yard. A silver Range Rover Sport was stationary near the back entrance. A man, a woman and a girl were standing by the car. The two front doors were open and one of the rear ones. The family were obviously about to set off – for lunch, I assumed – and were waiting for someone.

"Andrew," the woman shouted impatiently. "Come on."

My English was just about good enough to understand this. I quickly switched off my engine, picked up my laptop and got out of the car. The man – Mr. Hawthorne – was staring at me. He looked to be around fifty, tall, running to fat. The two most notable things that struck me about him were the blinding yellow corduroy trousers he was wearing and the look in his eye. His attitude was suspicious and hostile.

"Can I help you?" he said, in French. His accent was terrible. His wife dived in, again in French. "We're going out," she said. "We're late." Her accent was impeccable. I realized that she *was* French. I apologized for bothering them, introduced myself, said I was a local correspondent for the *Dépêche*. I was *very* polite.

"What's this about?" asked Mrs. Hawthorne, her manner now as guarded and edgy as her husband's. I thought she was a few years younger than him. She was also tall. She was wearing a very chic silk head-scarf. I began to describe the incident at the Shrine – without revealing that Declan McLaire was dead – but before I could get very far a kid shambled out of the house. He was tall, skinny, with long blond hair falling all over his pale, washed-out face. His eyes looked like dried glue. He hadn't shaved. He was a walking wreck.

Andrew Hawthorne eyed me blearily. "What's going on?" he said, in a French as perfect as his mother's.

This gave me the opportunity I'd been waiting for. I opened up my laptop – it was becoming a sort of passport to information in this enquiry – rested it on the bonnet of the Range Rover, earning myself another glare from Mr. Hawthorne, and hit the appropriate keys. Up popped Declan's face.

"I think you met him last night," I said to Andrew. "I was just telling your parents that he turned up in Lourdes early this morning, in the Shrine. He collapsed. I'm afraid he's dead."

Brutal, maybe, but effective. Andrew looked shattered. "Fuck," he said, in English. But it was a word I understood.

"What happened?" Andrew continued. He looked very shaky.

"We don't know. He just collapsed."

"God, I'm really sorry."

Now Mr. Hawthorne said something, in English, that I didn't follow and suddenly they all started talking at once, in English. I recognized the word "police" but basically I was lost. Mrs. Hawthorne must have realized this because she reverted to French and asked me if the police were involved. I realized that I had to go very carefully here. Mr. Hawthorne's attitude was becoming more and more hostile and defensive. I felt he was on the point of telling me to leave. I said that at the moment the police didn't know of their son's connexion to the incident but that, probably, when they were informed, they would want to take a statement from him.

"Did someone in the police tip you off about this?" Mrs. Hawthorne asked. A Frenchwoman who knew her France!

"Yes," I said.

Mr. Hawthorne got in on the act again at this point and they all started speaking English and the conversation was getting heated when Andrew said, in French, and more to me than to his parents: "Look, we met up with this guy in the Kosatti, we got talking, we went on to the Frégate, then the O2, then, I don't know what happened, we lost him. That's all I know."

The Frégate was another club in Lourdes, just out of town, on the lake. The O2 was the big club on the *rocade* in Tarbes. It all seemed logical. But what interested me was that Andrew had failed to mention that he and his friends had been kicked out of the Kosatti.

"Yes, I went to the Kosatti," I said. "I talked to the manager." I paused deliberately, then: "What I'm interested in is where Declan went after the O2."

I was trying to convey to Andrew: your secret's safe with me. He may have had the world's worst hangover but he was still alert enough to pick up the signal.

"I don't know," he said. "The last I saw of him he was talking to a guy called Cagou."

"Who?" said Mrs. Hawthorne. "Who's Cagou?"

"Just somebody who's around," Andrew said. And waited to see if I would honour our unstated pact. I did.

"I think I know who you mean," I said. "He's got a band, hasn't he?" Andrew just nodded. Mrs. Hawthorne seemed satisfied. She wasn't to know that I'd just told a thumping great lie to save her son from any further embarrassing questions.

Cagou didn't have a band. He was a small-time drug dealer and pimp, well known to the police and, of course, to local reporters.

I had what I needed now. I just wanted to get out of there but I wasn't quite sure how to make a graceful exit. Mr. Hawthorne came to my rescue. He said something in English to his wife. She turned to me and said that if they were going to talk to anyone about this they preferred to talk to the police. I said I quite understood. I gave her my card and said that if they changed their minds they could ring me at any time. Then I closed up the laptop and headed back to the car. As I got in they were arguing about whether to go to lunch or not.

I put a couple of kilometres between me and the Hawthorne's place then pulled off the road and called Michel. I told him everything I'd found out. He was impressed! We discussed the next move. Should I try to track down Cagou and interview him?

"I don't want you anywhere near that little bastard and his friends. He wouldn't talk to you anyway. We know where to find him. We'll have a word with him. Well done. You've saved us a hell of a lot of time and legwork."

I drove home. Julie had already left for her shift at the *Maison de Retraite* where she works. I got myself something to eat and sat down to write up my notes. My mobile rang. It was Andrew Hawthorne. He was at home, alone, having swerved round having lunch out with his family. He said he was really chewed up about what had happened to Declan. He hadn't really taken it in when I'd told him. He wanted to talk. I didn't discourage him! And I hit the "record" key.

"He was sort of weird," Andrew said. "It was the way he walked. It was like he was on stilts or something. We kind of assumed he'd already had a shitload to drink but in retrospect I don't think it was that. I don't know what it was. Anyway he just came up and started talking. He didn't speak any French. He'd heard us talking English. He was hyper. Couldn't stop talking. He was really funny. He scored a couple of taz off me. Then he kind of got out of control, tried to dance and fell about all over the place. It was kind of embarrassing but we couldn't stop him and Ray came up and told him to calm down and he totally lost it, told Ray to fuck off and Robert kind of stood up for Dec and Ray threw us out.

"I kind of felt like calling it a night but Dec said fuck it, he had a shitload of money and wanted to party all night and there had to be another club we could go to, so we piled into my car and drove up to the Frégate. It was kind of dead and Robert said why not the O2 so we headed up to Tarbes. Dec was sitting next to me. He said he wanted drugs – taz, skunk, coke, everything. We got to the O2. You know they've refurbed recently? I thought it kind of sucked, anyway I'm not into techno but Dec was in seventh fucking heaven. He kept hitting on me about drugs and Cagou was there so I told Dec that Cagou was the man but watch yourself with him. Dec said he didn't give a fuck and went off to cut a deal with Cagou and that was kind of the last I saw of him.

"When he didn't come back I kind of looked around for him but the place was heaving and anyway it was like two in the morning and I wanted to go home so we left. Robert said Cagou probably fixed Dec up with a girl. I didn't know Cagou was into that but Robert said for sure he was and back at the Kosatti Dec had been asking him about getting a girl so it kind of made sense."

Fascinating. But then came the real reason why Andrew had called me. His parents, he said, were already giving him a hard time. A few months ago he'd agreed to stop smoking dope in exchange for a car. They suspected that he was reneging on the deal. They didn't approve of his friend Robert. They were convinced that he was leading Andrew astray. "Classic," Andrew said. "Blame everybody but your own boy." He admitted that he was indeed smoking some dope but "moderately" and that he'd lied to his parents about it. What was worrying him now was the possible police enquiry. What kind of questions would they ask? Would his parents be involved?

I said I thought the police would primarily be interested in establishing Declan's movements so that they could provide the facts for the inquest into his death. I asked Andrew how old he was. He said he was nineteen. I said that in that case I didn't think his parents would have to be involved. I suggested that he didn't mention the taz he'd given to Declan. I certainly wouldn't mention it in my article. If Declan's death did in fact turn out to be drug-related the focus would be on Cagou, not on him. He sounded very relieved. I took the opportunity to press him a little harder on Declan's emotional state.

"From what you've told me," I said, "it sounds as if he was already on something when you connected with him in the Kosatti."

"Yeah, it was kind of like he was on speed," Andrew said. "But I'm not sure. It was more like he'd just been let out of gaol or something, I mean he was like really hyped up, kind of elated, you know? But what the fuck was he doing at Lourdes, I mean at the pilgrim thing?"

"He didn't tell you he was on a pilgrimage?"

"No. I assumed he was just on holiday or something. That is *really* weird."

We talked a bit more. I told him to feel free to call me

any time if he needed advice. Just before ringing off he asked me about the YouTube video. I told him what the link was. The conversation ended.

About five minutes later, when I was writing my notes, my mobile rang again. It was Andrew. He said he'd tried the YouTube link but had got nothing. "They must have taken it down," he said. I checked this right after he'd rung off and found that it was true. I thought it was strange. In fact I thought the whole chain of events I was uncovering was starting to feel strange, very strange indeed.

I didn't know what to do next. I felt a little frustrated that Michel had forbidden me to interview Cagou because he was obviously an important character in a story that seemed to be developing into something highly unusual. Then I remembered Father O'Dowd, the leader of the pilgrimage Declan had been on. I decided to go back to Lourdes and see if I could find him and get an interview.

I was heading into Tarbes, crawling past that damned speed camera on the Route de Bordeaux, when my mobile rang. It was Michel. I turned into the Intermarché car park so I could concentrate on the call. They'd interviewed Cagou, Michel told me. At first, he'd been uncooperative but thanks to the information I'd provided they'd been able to put some pressure on him. He denied supplying Declan with drugs but admitted that he'd given him the name, phone number and address of a girl in Tarbes called Lenya. A colleague of Michel's had interviewed her. Declan had arrived at her place around three in the morning and had stayed till about twenty past six when he'd left in a taxi.

"Lenya, I assume, is what I assume she is," I said to Michel.

"Exactly."

He had more information. The preliminary autopsy on Declan had established that he died of heart failure brought on by a cocktail of alcohol and drugs combined with physical exhaustion.

"Fuck," I said.

"Yeah," said Michel. "But listen to this. This is the bizarre bit. It seems he was in a wheelchair."

"A *what*?"

"A wheelchair. He was paralyzed."

"I don't understand," I said. "He *wasn't*."

"I don't understand either. It doesn't make any sense. We've tried to get hold of the priest who's leading the pilgrimage but he's been unavailable all day, we haven't been able to talk to him." I said that I was heading for Lourdes in order to interview him. "Good luck," said Michel. "If you find him let me know what he has to say."

I parked in the Place Peyremale and walked down to the hotel in the rue Sainte Marie. I was thinking that there had to have been some sort of misunderstanding. Declan might have been in a wheelchair for some reason but certainly not because he was paralyzed. Michel must have got that wrong. Declan could have been suffering from some sort of disability – that would tie in with what Andrew Hawthorne had told me, that he looked as if he was "walking on stilts" – but paralyzed? Impossible.

Michel had wished me luck. Well, my luck was in. As I entered the hotel, the first person I saw was a very fat, very bald man in a black suit and clerical collar. He was half sitting on the arm of the little sofa in the reception area, talking quietly but very urgently on a mobile phone, in English.

Eamonn O'Dowd. It had to be.

Behind the desk was the same unhelpful girl I had encountered that morning. She was eyeing me. I ignored her. I waited for Father O'Dowd to finish his conversation and when he did, a few moments later, I went over to him.

In my atrocious English I asked him if he was Father O'Dowd and if he spoke French. He replied, in French, that yes he did. There was a sheen of sweat on his forehead and bald pate. He looked exhausted and harassed, a man who was having a terrible day. He was already eyeing me in a very hostile way and when I introduced myself his face went hard and blank.

"I can't talk to you," he said. "I've got nothing to say to the press." His accent was heavy but his command of French seemed solid.

This was a situation I had to handle *very* carefully.

"I understand," I said. "It must be a very distressing situation for you. It's just that I've been following up on the story and I can tell you where Declan went and what he did."

There was a flicker of a smile, an ironic, almost a self-mocking smile. "I'm not sure I want to know," said Father O'Dowd. He sighed. He looked away.

"I've been talking to some people he was with last night," I said.

O'Dowd's eyes flicked back to me. Again there was that little smile. "Curiosity always gets the better of one, doesn't it? In any case, I need a drink."

I followed him into the room behind the reception area where breakfast was served to the residents. After a moment the receptionist came in. O'Dowd asked her for a beer and I said I'd have the same. Her manner was surly. We sat down at one of the tables. I told O'Dowd everything I knew. I didn't leave anything out. He listened in silence. He didn't ask any questions. It was hard to tell how he was reacting. His face gave very little away. I had expected that as a priest he would be shocked by the drink and drugs and especially by the girl, but there were no obvious signs of surprise or disapproval.

The receptionist came in with two bottles of beer and two glasses. O'Dowd poured his beer and drank the lot in two tremendous swallows. "D'you think I dare ask her for another?" he said. His face was deadpan but I couldn't help smiling.

"I wouldn't risk it," I said. "Have mine."

"I couldn't do that."

"I don't really want it," I said and pushed the bottle

towards him. He took it, filled his glass and took a sip.

"I don't know what to say to you," he said after a moment. "I don't understand what's happened – at least I think I do but I don't want to believe it. I've known Declan since he was born. I baptized him. His parents were both active in the Church. Two years ago there was a terrible accident, a car accident. Declan's father and mother were both killed. Declan suffered a spinal injury, a serious injury. He was paralyzed from the waist down. He's been in a wheelchair ever since."

His mobile phone rang. He answered it, said something in English, then cupped his palm over the phone and said to me: "I'm sorry. I've got to take this. It's going to be rather a long one." I rose, thanked him, said I'd be in touch and left him to his phone call.

I stepped out into the street. It was dark now. The lights over the entrance to the hotel had been switched on. They were shining on the window of the empty shop next to the bank. The yellow poster seemed to be glowing. My thoughts were in a turmoil. How could you reconcile the undoubted fact that Declan had been paralyzed from the waist down with the equally undoubted fact that last night he had walked into the Kosatti club, had *danced*, for God's sake, then gone on to shag a prostitute in Tarbes?

I felt a desperate need to talk to someone about it. Julie would still be at work and for some reason I didn't want to call Michel. Then I had a thought.

Ivan Arosteguy ushered me into his little kitchen and offered me a glass of wine. We sat down. I laid out the whole chain of events for him: Michel's initial call, Ivan's own testimony, Raymond Beder's contribution, Andrew Hawthorne, Cagou, Lenya, Eamonn O'Dowd's final revelation. I finished. Arosteguy was silent. He was gently swilling the wine in his glass. He put the glass down.

"It's clear," he said, "that what we're dealing with here is a miracle. There was a miraculous cure." He looked up at me and obviously read my thoughts. "They happen," he went on. "They are very rare, of course. Since the first appearance of the Blessed Virgin to Bernadette in 1858 the Church has officially recognized only sixty-seven miracles. But there have been many thousands of inexplicable cures. This boy was given a very great gift from God. He used it – in the way he used it."

I found myself imagining that I was Declan, in the same way that I had earlier in the day when I first saw the Kosatti poster. It's about eleven o'clock, I'm alone in my room, lying in bed, when suddenly I become aware of an extraordinary change coming over my lower body. *I can feel my legs.* I can feel the feathery touch of the duvet on them. I reach down and pinch myself just above my knee. There's *sensation*. I pinch harder. I feel something wonderful, a slight pain. Now I pull the duvet off and very gingerly swing my legs over the side of the bed and place my feet on the floor. Another wonder. I can actually feel the pile of the carpet against the soles of my feet. I wriggle my toes. I dig them into the carpet. Now, very, very carefully, I stand up. I find that my legs, thin and wasted as they are, actually support my weight. I take a tentative step forward. It works. I can walk. I can *walk*. To make sure that this isn't a dream I walk up and down the little room. I switch the light on and off. I realize that it's true, *I can fucking walk again*. I'm a good Catholic boy, I'm on a pilgrimage to Lourdes, there's no doubt in my mind that a miracle has happened. What do I do? Walk, yes *walk* down the corridor to Father O'Dowd's room? Knock on his door? Proclaim the miracle to him? What would happen then? At first he would be would be utterly amazed. Then he would want us to pray together. In the morning he would inform his Bishop in Ireland. That would set off a whole chain of events because the Church investigates miracles rigorously, there are well-established procedures. There would be medical inspections, signed statements, publicity. I wouldn't be left alone for a moment. I would be *trapped*. No, I decide. All that will have to happen of course but it can wait. It can wait for one night, one night of freedom, one night during which I can make up for lost time, for two years of being wheeled around in that fucking chair, of being lifted in and out of cars, of being helped into the bath, being helped with the toilet, of being helped to dress, helped to undress, of being pummelled and manipulated by physiotherapists, of having every moment of every fucking day *supervised*. I get dressed. It's a fantastic feeling just being able to do that. I leave my room. The hotel is silent. Everybody's asleep. I walk down the stairs. I can hardly believe I'm doing it. I cross the reception area and let myself out into the street. I'm going to do everything tonight. I'm going to get gloriously drunk. I'm going to take every drug I can lay my hands on. Above all I'm going to do what I've never done before, what I've only ever been able to fantasise about in lonely, arid acts of masturbation, I'm going to make love to a girl. The bank, with its cash dispenser, is right there on the other side of the street. Next to it a yellow poster advertising the Kosatti club is glowing like the fucking Star over Bethlehem or the pillar of fire in the Egyptian desert.

I came out of my reverie. I glanced at Ivan Arosteguy. He was suddenly looking very old, very tired and – there's no other word – anguished. "There's a message here," he said. "But I don't know what it is."

*

Editor's note: I have met the author of this story. He is twenty-six. He wears the standard uniform of the up-and-coming young French professional: jeans, white tee-shirt and leather jacket – all designer. You would call him pleasant-looking rather than handsome. He has an open, frank, fresh, friendly look about him. His great gift, I think, is that he is very easy to talk to. The evidence for that is clear in his narrative. In it, he says, early on, that his editor spiked the story. In fact a very brief notice of Declan McLaire's death did appear in the *Dépêche*. It was five lines tucked into the bottom right hand corner of a page mostly occupied by advertisements.

A formal inquest into Declan McLaire's death was apparently held in Ireland many months later. It was never reported in the Irish press. When I asked my collaborator why he thought there had been a cover-up, Michel replied: "I don't think you could call it a cover-up exactly. It's more a discreet silence. As to why: that rather attractive character, M. Arosteguy gives you the reason. There was a message there – but nobody can work out what it is."

HENRI CHAPPEMORT

Henri Chappemort was born in 1884 in Douloureux L'Eglise, a small market town in the centre of the plain of Picardy, that flat tract of land in North West France that even its natives admit is quite the dullest place in the country, if not in the whole of Europe.

Climb up to the belfry of the hideous 19th century basilica and all you will see for miles around is a vast expanse of level fields with hardly a copse, a stream or a valley to relieve the eye. The town itself is completely uninteresting. It consists of a grid-pattern of streets, none of them wide enough to be dignified with the name *boulevard*, none so narrow as to constitute anything as exciting as an alley, but all just wide enough to make crossing them hazardous.

Henri's father had a hat-shop and had done well enough out of it to have bought himself a seat on the Town Council, a small country house, and membership of a Freemasonic Lodge. Henri's birth took place in his parents' bedroom above the shop, during a violent storm, which prevented the doctor from attending. It was a very difficult birth and for three or four days the baby's life was despaired of. The infant survived, however. It was the mother who died.

So it was that at less than a week old, Henri lost the one person who might have given him that unconditional love so vital to the healthy development of human character.

There was nothing of that sort to be expected from the father. After the loss of his wife – who was still being spoken of in Douloureux, at least up until the Great War, as the very soul of cheerful good-heartedness – M.

Chappemort could hardly bear to look at his son and when he could not avoid it, did so with an air of chilly repugnance bordering on hatred.

Henri was the most unpopular boy at school. Even the masters despised him, in spite of the fact that he possessed a certain intelligence, a degree of application, and a nascent love of literature. He was the butt of cruel jokes and the victim of innumerable pranks. Once, when he was about twelve, his schoolmates dared him to walk across the millstream on a narrow plank. Unaware that they had already sawn almost completely through the centre of the plank, Henri set out boldly. The plank collapsed under him, he fell into the stream and the swift current was carrying him into the jaws of the slowly-turning millwheel – and certain death – when the miller, unaware of what was going on outside, happened to throw the brake-lever. Henri emerged from the stream soaked, battered, breathless but alive.

Henri's universal unpopularity had a single cause. He spoke his mind. He had absolutely no notion of those slight compromises with actual feelings and opinions, those little, tactful half-lies, without which any form of social intercourse must be supposed to be impossible. Whence came this devastating – and disastrous – candour is a mystery. His mother had a reputation for forthrightness, certainly, but it sprang from a spirit of no-nonsense honesty that did not repel people but on the contrary made them warm to her. His father, whose business was to sell expensive and unsuitable headgear to plain women of modest means, was a master of insincerity.

It was assumed by the town, and by Henri himself, that on leaving school he would join his father in the shop. M. Chappemort had no such idea. He told his son that he must fend for himself. He (M. Chappemort) would do nothing more for him. It was an invitation to candour that a nature such as Henri's could not resist. The roars of incoherent rage from M. Chappemort could be heard as far away as the butcher's at the end of the street. Henri left his father's house that day and they never spoke again.

If this candour of Henri's had been accompanied by anything approaching good looks, his habit of saying exactly what was in his mind might have been mistaken for wit. Alas, Henri was irredeemably ugly. His face was suggestive of an over-indulged pig, his hair was reddish and scanty (he was almost completely bald by the age of twenty-five) and his pale, clammy skin had the colour and consistency of a plucked chicken.

Where it wasn't spattered with large, brown freckles it erupted in all manner of warts and boils.

Henri found it extremely difficult to get a job. Prospective employers, looking for politeness and acquiescence, found instead a disconcerting directness combined with a strong tendency to contradict. Eventually he was taken on at a lime-kiln. The work was so supremely dirty, dangerous, and badly paid that they were glad to find anybody who'd do it. Henri rented a damp attic room in a house that contained a rancorous family of fifteen who stopped shouting at each other only to cough or snore.

On his eighteenth birthday, Henri decided that the time had come to be initiated into the mysteries and pleasures of sex. He made an appointment with the local prostitute, a Madame Chatebite. But when he took off his clothes, Madame Chatebite fell into such paroxysms of laughter at the sight of his endowment that she had to send out to the chemist for a physic.

Utterly humiliated, Henri decided to kill himself. He bought a revolver and some ammunition and went out into a lonely field. He loaded the gun, put it to his head and pulled the trigger. Nothing happened. The gunsmith had cheated him. He had sold him a weapon that was mechanically faulty and ammunition that had been stored in a leaky outhouse. The owner of the land, by chance passing at that moment, took Henri for a poacher and immediately had him arrested.

So dark, cold and noisome was the cell in which Henri passed that night and so bright, warm and fresh was the day into which he emerged, blinking, next morning that he decided that, after all, life – even his miserable, lonely life – was worth living.

Five years later his father died as a result of complications following some slight injuries sustained during a Masonic ritual. Under the beneficent laws of France, which take no account of family feuds, Henri inherited all his property.

He moved back into the shop and tried to make a go of it. Unfortunately, the extreme candour with which he would comment on a customer's choice of hat, and indeed upon her personal appearance in general, soon drove his father's carefully nurtured clientele elsewhere. Creditors pressed in on him, the local Bank Manager, eager to take revenge for certain remarks Henri had made about his wife's tendency to flirt during Mass, saw his chance and foreclosed. Henri was forced to sell the shop – and at a sacrificial price, since France was in the grip of an economic crisis at the time. He decided to retire to his country house and grow vegetables.

The house his late father had bought was a very good house indeed. It was some three miles out of town and stood in a large garden, almost a park, in a suspicion of a valley, threaded by a muddy brook. Its situation, by local standards, was picturesque. Its honey-coloured stone, classical proportions, and mellow slate roof were a delight. It had been built towards the end of the 18th century by a local magnate as a love-nest, and that is in fact the purpose for which the late M. Chappemort had mostly used it.

Henri arrived in a hired conveyance, with his few possessions, to discover that the night before this gem of the *dix-huitième* had burned to the ground. It had not been insured.

Henri built himself a rudimentary sort of cottage, using

stones from the ruins, and planted his vegetable garden. He had very little money but once a week the daughter of a neighbouring farmer would deliver milk, eggs, and a chicken to his door. Her name was Heloïse Crevejeune, she was well over thirty, and had never succeeded in getting a husband owing to a pronounced squint, a hair lip, and an unmanageable stammer. Henri fell passionately in love with her and she with him. However, being a devout Catholic, she refused to share his bed until she had a ring on her finger.

They were married in the village church, a medieval building in a deplorable state of repair. It was a windy day. As they came out of the church , as man and wife, a tremendous gale, suddenly sweeping down from the North, dislodged one of the decayed sandstone gargoyles above the porch. It missed Henri by an inch but struck his wife on the crown of the head.

After the funeral, half mad with grief, Henri decided once more to end it all. He took a train to Pontneuf-en-Picardie, where an imposing suspension bridge had recently been built to carry the main road to Paris over the River Maldestin. He climbed to the topmost pinnacle of the central tower and hurled himself off.

As he plummeted, a barge, heading for the tannery up river, loaded with lambs' fleeces, was passing under the bridge and Henri fell directly into it, suffering only minor bruises. Lying snugly among the malodorous fleeces, he found himself thinking of Heloïse. He decided that he owed it to her memory to return to his vegetable garden and go every week to the village churchyard and lay flowers on her grave.

This he did with unfaltering regularity until the outbreak of the Great War. In September, 1914, the German offensive reached the outskirts of Douloureux L'Eglise. The French army put up a sturdy resistance and in the ensuing artillery duel, which lasted over a week, the village church, Heloïse's grave, Henri's cottage, and his carefully tended garden were all blown to atoms.

Henri joined the army. He volunteered for every dangerous mission in the hope that a German shell or sniper would put an end to his wretched existence but he never received so much as a scratch. On one occasion his entire platoon was mown down by German machine-guns but all he got was a few spatters of mud kicked up by stray bullets. He passed through the hell of Verdun, that charnel house in which a whole generation of French youth perished, with no greater threat to his health than a brief attack of dysentery.

The war over, he returned to Douloureux, to find that the only building left standing was the lugubrious basilica. He walked through the ruins of the town (later rebuilt in exactly the same style) into the country, and there discovered that his little bit of land, which had been fought over and captured and re-captured a hundred and one times in the last five years, was a waste of abandoned trenches and makeshift wooden crosses indicating where the fallen had received temporary burial. Never mind, he thought, I'll rebuild, I'll replant, I'll make a little shrine for Heloïse and place flowers in it every day. And so, no doubt, he would have done if the Ministry in Paris hadn't designated his few acres an Official War Cemetery.

Penniless now, Henri sought work in the large industrial town of Renonce-sur-Espoir. After weeks of trudging the pitiless pavé of this sulphurous conurbation he got a job as a sewerage worker. He spent his days wading through the waste products of his happier and more prosperous fellow citizens, his ears assailed with the shrieking of gigantic rats and his nose by unspeakable stenches. He spent his nights, alone, in a room that overlooked the railway marshalling yard. Once a year, on the anniversary of his wedding, he dined in solitary state at the *Bistro De Pression*.

The waitress there was a delightful young woman called Hélène Laniche. She was pretty, vivacious and exchanged racy banter with the customers, setting the place in a roar with saucy anecdotes and off-colour jokes. Henri thought she was adorable and the idea that her name, Hélène, was so much like that of his lost wife, Heloïse, always gave him a pang.

It was on the fourth of his annual visits that he and Hélène struck up a conversation. Henri found it so delightful, so refreshing, that a fortnight later he returned to the *bistro*. It seemed to him, though he could hardly believe it, that Hélène was singling him out for special attention. On the pittance he earned, he really couldn't afford to eat out more than once a month but by dint of existing on little more than bread and water during the week he contrived to go the *bistro* every Saturday.

A few months later, with the candour that had never deserted him, he told Hélène that he was in love with her and asked her to marry him. To his utter stupefaction – and almost unbearable joy – she accepted him.

By selling his watch and medals he managed to buy her a ring. A date for the marriage was agreed. Dressed in a decent suit, obtained through the sale of his fountain pen, type-writer and the little silver frame in which he had kept a photograph of Heloïse, he arrived at the Mairie at the appointed time.

Hélène was standing outside with a large crowd of regular customers from the *bistro*. As Henri drew near, reproaching himself for the thought that his bride might have gone to the trouble of dressing up for the occasion, Hélène burst into peals of uncontrollable laughter that took Henri instantly back to the flock wall-paper and mountainous bed of Madame Chatebite's establishment in Douloureux.

Hélène's laughter was contagious. Within seconds her companions were helplessly convulsed, as if they had all been struck simultaneously by some hitherto unknown laughing disease. "It was a bet," Hélène eventually managed to choke out amid fresh explosions. "I bet them all a thousand each I could get you to the *Mairie* before Assumption."

Henri returned to his room, stuffed the ill-fitting window with socks and underwear and the equally ill-fitting door with old newspapers and rags, turned on the gas and lay down on his bed. With the mantle hissing, he fell asleep. At about that moment, an industrial dispute at the gas-works, which had been simmering for some weeks, erupted into full-scale industrial action and the first thing the strikers did was to turn off the town's gas supply.

Henri now withdrew completely into himself. He never left his room except to go to work and to shop for bare essentials. Another war came, the Germans occupied the town. He hardly noticed it and certainly the Germans never noticed him. Soon after the war, he retired on a pitiful pension.

As the century sped forward, Renonce-sur-Espoir changed. The old factories closed down, industrial estates sprang up, tarmac replaced *pavé*. The building of a colossal nuclear power station brought fresh prosperity and intermittent demonstrations by Green activists. Henri knew little of it and cared less.

In 1970, in his eighty-sixth year, he was walking to the *pâtisserie* on the corner of his street when he suffered a heart attack. An ambulance was called, he was rushed to the new hospital on the edge of town, wired up to machines – and survived.

In 1996, at the age of one hundred and two, he had a second heart attack. Once again he was whisked to the hospital, wired up, and made a complete recovery.

During the years that followed, the usual accidents of extreme old age happened: the trippings over loose paving-stones, the fallings down stairs, bumpings into parking-meters, near-misses with speeding *mobylettes* and reversing taxis. Henri survived them all. And if, at this point the reader is beginning to feel that his story has been too extravagantly ironic to be credible, it can only be stated that every word of it is true. For candour compels me to admit that I, Henri Chappemort, am its author.

*

Editor's note: Earlier this year (2004) Henri Chappemort was officially declared to be the oldest person in France. The President announced that he was to be made a Chevalier of the Légion d'honneur at a banquet at the Élysées Palace. An official car was sent to bring him to Paris for the occasion. It collided, head-on, with a truck, between exits 9 and 8 on the A1 autoroute. His autobiographical sketch, published here for the first time, was discovered among his effects.

LA MORVANDELLE

Please understand, Monsieur, I never had anything to do with that sort of thing before my husband's death. I suppose one was aware of the existence of such places but one never thought about things like that and the people who came to our restaurant were not the types to discuss them – at least not in my presence.

It was a little *restaurant du coin* such as hardly exists now in Paris, unfortunately. My husband took it over from his mother, a widow, soon after we were married, and for thirty years we worked together, he in the kitchen, I at the *caisse*, Young Paul waiting on the tables. He must have been over fifty when we started but everybody called him Young Paul! We closed in August, of course, but otherwise we were open all the year round. That was the system then. Our clients were mainly elderly gentlemen, bachelors and widowers, who lived in the *quartier*, and they relied on us as on a family. Each had his own peg on which to hang his hat and coat, each had his own place at the large table in the window, and each, of course, his favourite dishes. We served lunch and dinner every day, including Sundays, public holidays and Christmas Day: soup, *entrée*, main course, cheese and dessert, all for eight francs fifty, *vin et pain compris*. Can you imagine? That was our price, Monsieur, until the late sixties when inflation forced us to raise it. And we made a comfortable living. The secret? So many people have asked me that! Let's just say it's not in the selling but in the buying.

There was another element in our success: my husband's cooking. I do not believe that outside the great restaurants you find such cooking today – and even in the so-called three-star establishments, where, thanks to the generosity of my dear Madame, I can well afford to eat from time to time, one can be disappointed. I recently lunched at a famous place a little way down the coast – I won't mention the name, but I think you know where I mean – and I swear to you that the so-called *bordelaise* sauce was thickened with flour! My husband would have been shocked. All his sauces were reduced, of course. He would have it no other way. Any fool can *boil*, he used to say, but it takes an artist to *simmer*. His *queue de boeuf* for example – one of my dear Madame's favourites. Twelve hours in the pot, Monsieur. And the result? One of the cheapest cuts of meat available at market transformed into a dish to delight the palate of the most exigent diner – the sauce rich and dark and glutinous, a world away from the watery messes one is forced to consume today.

My husband would always say that he owed his skill to his mother's teaching – but of course he had to say that. I never believed it. It was an inborn gift he had, like an ability to play the piano, or paint pictures. The result was that over the years our clientele came to include not just local residents or passing trade but people who would journey from all over Paris to sample his *cuisine*. I mean rich people and people famous in the worlds of the arts and politics. That was how I came to know my dear Madame.

It must have been in the early seventies that she first ate in the restaurant, in the company of a lady who was one of our regular "overseas visitors," as my husband used to call them, and extremely well-known in a certain field of the arts. I won't say which. Madame came to lunch. The dish of the day was *Lapin Morvandelle* and she went into ecstasies over it. I must say it was one my husband's most successful and popular dishes, another example of how one can turn the cheapest ingredients into something delicious, the secret in this case, if you insist, being the addition of *croutons* fried in butter.

After that, she lunched or dined with us at least once a

fortnight, usually alone, but sometimes with a female companion. She kept herself to herself, rarely joining in the conversation, which, in the evening, would often become general after my husband emerged from his kitchen. He liked to chat and joke with the customers, who were always eager to buy him a *cognac* or a *Chartreuse*. At times it was more like a club than a restaurant and you would find, for example, a retired *métro* worker, like old M. Taupon, arguing politics with Deputies and Senators or the Abbé Dupouy defending God against a famous philosopher. I rarely joined in the talk. It was my job to keep an accurate tally of the drinks consumed. But sometimes, when I had nothing immediately to do, I would have a little chat with Madame, about nothing very much – the weather, the news. On these occasions, my husband would always question me closely afterwards, wanting to know what we had talked about and whether I had picked up any clues about her.

She was a mystery to us, you see. My husband called her 'La Morvandelle' because of her penchant for his *Lapin Morvandelle*. It was obvious, from the way she dressed, that she had money – and taste. She wore a wedding ring and a magnificent diamond engagement ring but that told us little. If she had a husband he never came with her to the restaurant. Perhaps she was separated, or divorced, or a widow? There was no way of telling. Once, when her friend, the lady I mentioned earlier, came with some other people, my husband urged me to question her discreetly about 'La Morvandelle' but I refused. First, there is no such thing, in Paris at least, as "discreet" questioning and second, I had an instinct that it was precisely because we never pried into her affairs that Madame found our restaurant so congenial.

Some months later, the mystery deepened. Madame had rung to reserve a table for dinner, as she often – but not always – did. The restaurant was busy that evening. Apart from our regulars there were a number of "overseas visitors," including a famous politician and his wife. Madame arrived punctually. Just inside the door, where I had my *caisse*, she paused for a second, looking towards the table where the politician was sitting, then turned to me and said: "I've had a sudden dinner invitation. It's not far away so I thought I'd look in to cancel my table." With that, she left.

For the rest of the evening, I was distracted. I even made a mistake over a bill, something that hardly ever happened. I could not decide what to tell my husband. I could not conceal the fact that Madame had cancelled because he knew that she had made a reservation. On the other hand, I could perhaps suppress the fact that her sudden change of mind had clearly been caused by the sight of the politician and that her story of a sudden dinner invitation was a fabrication.

I did indeed try to conceal the truth from my husband after we closed but of course it was no good. He sensed immediately that I was hiding something and soon had the real story out of me. I remember the thoughtful expression in his eyes and the way he tapped the end of his cigarette on the edge of an ash-tray, even though there was no ash to fall. He said that perhaps we wouldn't see her again and when I asked him why he just shook his head. It didn't matter. After more than twenty years of marriage I could read his thoughts as easily as he could read mine. He thought that La Morvandelle was the politician's mistress and that we wouldn't see her again. "In any case," I said, "we won't say anything about it if we do see her again." He thought that the chances were that we wouldn't.

We did. Two or three weeks later, Madame reappeared. I made no reference to the previous incident, of course, and she continued to come regularly until, in 1987, my husband died.

It happened while we were on holiday. For many years we spent August with my mother-in-law, who had retired to a small house in the Oise, in the village where she had been born. On her death, my husband inherited the house and a certain amount of money. He assumed that we would go on spending our holidays in the village but for once I put my foot down. I have no taste at all for the countryside, Monsieur. Frankly, it bores me. There's nothing to do, nothing to see. My great joy has always been the sea-side. When I was a girl we always spent our holidays at the sea-side. It was a considerable sacrifice to my husband to sell his mother's house but he did it and we bought a small villa at Danville-sur-Mer. We went there every August. My husband acquired a boat and took to sea-fishing, which he greatly enjoyed. Most evenings he would cook the best of his catch, inventing wonderful new recipes. We even talked of leaving Paris and opening a sea-food restaurant in Danville. So many of our old gentlemen had died, you see. Of course, others had taken their places, but not so many. Only the Abbé Dupouy remained of the original group. Also, Young Paul had retired and our new waiter was turning out to be less congenial than we thought when we engaged him.

It was a Friday – a very hot day. My husband had spent the afternoon in his boat and returned at about six o'clock. He did complain of a slight headache from the glare of the sun and the sea but otherwise appeared perfectly well. He went straight to the kitchen to prepare the fish he had caught. I was on the terrace, watering the plants, when I heard a crash from the kitchen. I felt instinctively that something serious had happened. In thirty years I had never known him drop anything while cooking. With a knot of dull pain forming in my stomach, I ran from the terrace into the kitchen.

He was lying on his front on the floor, his arms clutched under his chest. Nearby lay the fish kettle. I knew at once that he was dead, that there was nothing I could do. His father had died in exactly the same way, you see, of a heart attack, and at about the same age, in his mid-fifties. There was some hereditary weakness in that family.

I am not capable of describing the emotions I felt at that moment, Monsieur – nor would I wish to. It's enough to say that in those first few seconds I realized that my life had changed forever, that nothing would ever be the same again. I didn't touch the body. I could not bring myself to do so at that point. It was only when the undertakers arrived to remove him that I was able to place one last kiss on his forehead.

Amidst all the formalities, one question was uppermost in my mind: what to do about a funeral? I should explain that I was brought up a good Catholic, as was my husband – in fact, that was how we met, at a dance laid on by a Catholic Youth organisation – but owing to the nature of our business and the hours we had to keep, we had rarely been able to attend Mass. I would go occasionally to an early service on a Sunday morning and of course whenever we stayed with my mother-in-law she insisted that we accompany her to the ten o'clock service – but I confess that I had never set foot inside the church at Danville. Would my husband have wanted a religious ceremony? We had never once discussed it. Was that what I wanted – and, if so, where was it to be held? In Danville? We knew hardly anybody. In Paris? It was mid-August. Nobody would be there. I found myself absolutely paralyzed. On my husband's side there was nobody to whom I could turn for advice. There were some cousins in the Oise, the children of his mother's sister, but we were not on good terms. On my own side, my parents were deceased and both my sisters were married and living a long way from Paris, one in Provence, the other in Bordeaux. There had been little contact with them since the loss of our parents. In the end I telephoned the Abbé Dupouy – I knew he would be in Paris.

I can't tell you what a comfort he was to me, Monsieur, how good it was to hear his voice. We talked for a long time. He offered to come to Danville – but of course I couldn't think of putting him to such trouble. In the end it was he who suggested that I should have my husband cremated – in Normandy – and that in September, when everyone was back in Paris, that there should be a service of remembrance in the parish church, which the Abbé offered to conduct himself.

Never will I forget that service, Monsieur. The number of people who came! It was astonishing. I could hardly take it in. So many of our clients – and others I hardly knew, such as the market people my husband had dealt with for so many years. The Abbé Dupouy spoke eloquently about my husband – a fine tribute. My dear Madame was there, of course, and she came to the restaurant for the reception afterwards.

That reception was the hardest part for me but I was determined to do it. I felt I had to offer hospitality. Anything less would have been to dishonour my husband's memory. Madame was one of the last to leave. Very discreetly she said she had something she wished to discuss with me and proposed that we should lunch together later in the week. I was surprised by this invitation, and rather embarrassed, but, out of curiosity I suppose, I agreed.

We met at a *brasserie* in a part of Paris that was unfamiliar to me. It was a noisy, crowded place and, frankly, the food was not of the standard I was used to – not that I'd had much appetite since my husband's death. Madame was very gracious, very tactful, full of sympathy. She asked me what my plans were and I told her that apart from closing the restaurant – I had not even thought about keeping it going, it was obviously impossible – I did not know what I was going to do or even where I would live. I should perhaps explain that we had occupied the apartment above the restaurant and that although the landlord had made no difficulty about terminating the lease it was doubtful that he would be prepared to let the apartment separately – even if I wished to go on living there.

"I think it would be a mistake," Madame said, "even if

the landlord is willing. Have you thought about Danville?"

I had, of course, but for some reason I felt reluctant about moving there permanently, even though I had calculated that with our savings and what remained of my husband's inheritance I could afford to live there without working, if I was very careful.

"Well," Madame said, "I need somebody to help me in my business and I think you would be ideal."

I said that I had no idea what her business was and I remember that she gave a little smile, then said that the best way would be to come and see for myself. It wasn't far.

We walked for a few minutes along the *boulevard* then turned into a side-street. There were a few expensive-looking shops but it was mainly residential. We came to one of the houses. Madame let herself in with a key and I followed her inside into a small vestibule furnished in very good style. She ushered me into a room on the right, a sort of office, with comfortable chairs, a sofa and a desk. A girl was sitting at the desk, smoking a cigarette. I later learned that her name was Sylvie – not her real name, of course. She was young, in her mid-twenties I estimated, very pretty and very well dressed. Madame asked her if there was anybody in the house and she said that nobody was expected until after six.

Even then, Monsieur, I did not guess the nature of Madame's business. It was only when she showed me into the room behind the office that it became clear. It was a bedroom, with an adjoining bathroom. There was an enormous four-poster bed. On the walls were mirrors. The window was heavily curtained. Built into a wall was a capacious wardrobe. I was shocked. So much so that I blurted out: "It's a brothel."

"Exactly," Madame replied, with perfect calm. "But of a very special kind."

She stepped to the wardrobe and opened it. Suspended on a wire on the inside of the door were numerous whips, canes and other such instruments. Behind, on coat-hangers, I could see a variety of clothing: uniforms of different kinds, garments made of leather and rubber.

"I'll show you the rest of the house," Madame said.

I followed her upstairs in a sort of daze. As I said before, I suppose I knew that such places existed but to find myself actually inside one and at the same time to realize that Madame was, well, what you tell me the English call a *Madame* – it was almost too much for me. She showed me the other rooms, six in all, on the three upper floors, each with a number on the door, as in a hotel, each with its own bathroom. They were all furnished in different styles – one as a doctor's surgery, another, very bare, with just a desk, a bench and a few chairs, as what Madame described as "an interrogation room," and so on – and all the time she talked in the most matter-of-fact way, telling me where she had bought various items of furniture, about the problems she was having with the central-heating system, the difficulty of finding a cleaning-woman with the necessary discretion.

As we came back downstairs, Madame offered to make me a cup of coffee – I can assure you, I had need of it! – but first, she said, we must complete the tour. By a little door under the staircase, we went down into the basement. The house was eighteenth century, Madame explained as we descended, but the cellars were much older. She switched on a light to reveal a vaulted stone chamber, not unlike the wine-cellar below the restaurant, except that this contained a rack, a great wheel, like a cartwheel, a wooden cross in the form of an X and other objects.

"Wonderfully authentic, isn't it?" I remember Madame saying – and adding that there was another cellar beyond but that they didn't use it. By this time I had become aware of a faint but familiar odour – not the damp, musty smell that you find in every cellar, but something else. I looked down and sure enough, in a corner, I saw mouse-droppings.

"You've got mice," I said.

They were a plague, she told me. One set traps, of course, but they never seemed to work. She showed me a trap, half-hidden behind the wheel. It was baited with a small piece of dried-out cheese. I explained that cheese was no good. You know it is a complete misconception, Monsieur, that mice like cheese. They don't. Bread, or a piece of cereal, or a raisin is much more effective. I said to Madame that the best defence against mice is a cat. She said that she was well aware of it but that it was impossible for her to keep a cat because so many people were allergic to them and she could not take such a risk with her clients' health. I said that it was for a similar reason that my husband and I had never kept one. It would not have been hygienic. For the same reason we had never been able to use poison.

In the little kitchen on the ground floor behind the stairs, Madame made me a cup of coffee and I described the long battle I had fought against mice and the techniques I had developed in baiting and placing traps. "All the more reason," she said, "why it would be so good if you would come and work here."

Before I could say anything, she explained that she needed somebody to answer the telephone and book appointments for clients – a potentially complicated matter if a specific girl was requested or if, as was often the case between ten o'clock at night and one in the morning, there was a heavy demand for the services provided by the house. Regulars were generally no problem, she said, but newcomers, especially first-timers, had to be handled with great tact and skill. They were often shy about saying precisely what they wanted and a wrong word or inflection could frighten them off. The hours, she admitted, were long, but the pay – well, I could hardly believe my ears when she told me what it was. And that didn't include tips – which, she said, were often generous in the extreme.

On the subject of sex, Monsieur, which I think we must

attack at this point, I will tell you now what I tried to convey to Madame that afternoon. My father, who had an ironmongery off the Rue Vaugirard, was extremely strict, as was my mother, who worked with him in the shop.

There were, of course, some adventures during our annual sea-side holidays, but they were very innocent. There was one boy, I remember, quite handsome and of a good family, who wanted me to go further than I was willing and kept pressing me. The solution was simple. I invited him to the *pension* where we were staying and introduced him to my father – and that was that! Accordingly, it was not until I married that I experienced full relations with the opposite sex. I will say no more than that it was a famous experience! Early on in our marriage my husband and I made the decision not to have children but this in no way inhibited the physical side of our conjugal life. On the other hand, as I explained to Madame, my experience, limited as it was to my marriage, hardly seemed to qualify me for the role she was proposing.

"Oh, that's of no importance at all," she said. What she was looking for, she explained, was efficiency, a sympathetic manner and, above all, discretion. From what she had observed of me in the restaurant, she felt that I had all those qualities – especially the last one. Some of her clients, she said, were extremely well-known – politicians, actors, industrialists – so discretion was absolutely essential. I was shocked. It had never occurred to me to associate a place like that with people prominent in public life.

In the kindest way, Madame invited me to think a little more deeply. Did I imagine that the so-called deviant tastes for which she catered were unknown in the higher circles? On the contrary. Men in positions of power and responsibility had pressures and tensions that could often, and best, be relieved in – certain ways. In that sense, what she offered was a sort of therapy. You smile a little cynically, Monsieur. But, you know, if you reflect on it you will see that it is true.

Madame hated the word "deviant." Here I am describing not so much what she said to me that afternoon but rather the opinions she expressed during the many discussions we had on the subject over the following years. She felt that 'deviant' implied some sort of 'norm' – whereas in fact, she maintained, human sexuality was as diverse as human personality. But of course society at large had always refused to acknowledge this – with the result that people were made to feel ashamed about their desires and were forced to suppress them, often with disastrous consequences for themselves and for others. Enabling men to realize their fantasies provided a vital safety valve. "Ah, the marriages that have been saved within these walls," I remember her exclaiming one night.

The girls who worked for her were selected not so much for their physical charms as for their acting ability. "The most important thing," Madame would say, "is that the experience, for the client, should be as authentic as possible. Any element of falseness can completely ruin it." Often, she would refer to her establishment as "the theatre" and to herself as "the producer." I can tell you, without of course naming any names, that several of the girls went on to successful careers as actresses.

Madame once confided to me that as a girl she herself had ambitions to go on the stage. That was about as much as I ever learned about her past. She never talked about her parents or her family, where she had been brought up, where she went to school, how she had entered her current profession – and naturally I never asked about these things. There were, of course, some clues: her accent was refined, her taste was impeccable, she was obviously a woman of good family and education – but I found I could enjoy an excellent professional relationship with her – more, a real friendship – without having to know anything beyond what she was willing to reveal about herself.

Her own role in the establishment? Your questions are always so much to the point! So far as I was aware it was entirely supervisory. I was never aware of her being directly involved with any client. She was – how can I put it? – aloof. What her activities had been in the past I cannot say, of course, because, as I have explained, it was never discussed, but in all the time I worked for her I never had a request for her personal services.

Well, Madame found a little flat for me in a modern block less than a ten-minute walk from "the theatre" and helped me to move in. In trying to decide what to do about the villa in Danville, I was surprised to learn that "the theatre" was closed in August in exactly the same way as the restaurant always had been and for the same reasons. I could therefore – if I wished – continue with the system my husband and I had devised for letting the place in June, July and September and shutting it up during the winter months. So I decided not to sell but wait to see if spending August next year in Danville without my husband would be bearable. As it turned out, it was. I found myself making a few friends – you among them, of course.

In the meantime I started out on my new life with Madame. Yes, at first, it was rather strange. I couldn't help being shocked – even disgusted – by some of the things the clients told me they wanted over the telephone. But I soon got over such feelings. I learned that the best way was to be as matter-of-fact about it all as possible, as if these men were ringing up to book a table and request a particular dish. By far the most difficult part of the job was what Madame called "the choreography." She had a rule that clients should never meet each other on the stairs or the landings if it could possibly be avoided. At busy times, this involved quite complicated liaison work on the internal telephone system and it was often necessary to engage a client in conversation in the office until all was ready for him. I met some very interesting people that way. It was really very pleasant. There was rarely any embarrassment. One would just chat about this and that. During quiet periods, I would make tea or coffee for the girls and we would gossip. Sometimes they'd talk to me about their problems and worries and I'd try to help. As Madame said, I became a bit of a mother to them all.

From the start I was determined to solve the problem of the mice. I was able to improve upon the techniques I had employed in the restaurant in that the use of poison was possible and the results astonished and delighted Madame. The only problem was the August holiday when the house was closed. I would return from Danville to find those wretched mice in possession again, just as in the restaurant, and would have to renew my campaign.

Life went on smoothly and regularly for several years. The girls came and went, of course – always new faces – and from time to time, Madame would buy and install new pieces of equipment. "We must keep up to date," she would often say, "we must keep up with the trends." And it was this, combined with the August closure, which led to the tragedy.

It must have been in May of that horrible year that Madame told me she had commissioned a new piece of equipment, to be installed in the second cellar, the one beyond the dungeon. First of all, artisans appeared to lay a new floor, put in electrical wiring, and plaster and paint the walls. It took some time because Madame would only let them work in the morning, when there were hardly any clients. Then one day when I arrived as usual at one o'clock I discovered that a van had arrived very early that morning with the new equipment and that its installation was almost complete. Soon after the men left, Madame invited me to go and view the "latest attraction" as she called it.

In the dungeon, I paused to check my mouse-traps but, for once, Madame showed some impatience and told me to leave them till later. She seemed unusually excited and eager for me to see what lay beyond the door. I followed her into the new room. It had been painted all over – walls, ceiling, even the floor – in a sort of metallic silver. A strange-looking mirror-glass booth had been built into one corner and in the centre stood an object that at first sight I took to be some kind of hospital operating table – but made of a shiny metal, like aluminium. To describe it more fully I would have to close my eyes and try to recreate it in my mind, which is exactly what I do not at all want to do because of the painful memories it would revive. It is surely enough to know that it was fitted with metal restraints and flexible arm-like devices.

"It's like something out of a science fiction film," I said.

Madame was delighted. "Exactly." I didn't understand. She saw this. "Alien abduction," she said. "It's all the rage in America and Germany. That's where I had this made."

All I could find to say was that it must have cost a lot of money. "A fortune!" she said cheerfully. She stepped to the booth in the corner and disappeared inside. A moment later the room started to go dim and I noticed, for the first time, that light fittings had been sunk into the ceiling, walls and floor. Some of these were coloured – red, blue, green, all sorts of colours – and were obviously controlled from inside the booth. For a few moments it was like a *Son et Lumière* except that instead of music there were rather frightening high-pitched whining and buzzing sounds. "Isn't it amazing?" Madame demanded, emerging from the booth. "It's all controlled from in there. The wires run under the floor." She stepped to the table and picked up a box attached to it by an electric flex. She explained that if a client wished to operate the device himself he could do so. "There's nothing like this in France," Madame said, "and only two in America. You wait. The phone won't stop ringing!"

Frankly, I was sceptical, Monsieur. Even in the light of the often very peculiar demands made by clients, this seemed too bizarre. I was wrong and Madame was right.

The phone did ring and suddenly it was all alien abduction, alien abduction, alien abduction. How did people find out? I can only assume by word of mouth. Today, of course, it would be the Internet but in those days it was only beginning.

August came round, the house was closed and I went to Danville as usual. That was the year, if you remember, that we bumped into each other in the Salon de Thé and discussed Pérec's triumph at the Olympics and got to know each other better.

I returned to Paris on 28th August and immediately rang Madame on her home number to confirm that I was back. There was no reply, only the answering machine, so I left a message. Yes, I was a little surprised because she always returned from her own holiday – with friends in the countryside – a few days before me. I certainly expected her to reply before the end of the day but there was no call and when I woke up next morning there was no message from her on my own machine.

At about nine o'clock that morning I rang her at home again and again got the answering machine. I was puzzled, no more than that and since we were due to meet anyway at "the theatre" at ten o'clock, not alarmed in any way. I assumed she must have gone out for an earlier appointment. Another possibility was that her answering machine was not working properly, something that often happens. I walked to "the theatre," arrived promptly at ten o'clock and let myself in with my key. It was always rather dark in the vestibule and I automatically reached out to switch on the light – only to find that the lever was already down. The bulb has gone, I thought. I remember standing still for a moment – I don't know why – and listening. I could hear faint sounds from the street outside but the house itself was completely silent and I realized that Madame had not arrived yet. Imagine my surprise, therefore, when as I stepped into the office I saw her bag on the desk – her black Gucci bag. So she was here. In one of the lavatories perhaps, or upstairs. Then I noticed something about the bag. It seemed to be covered with a fine film of dust. I went to turn on the light, to see better, but again the lever was down. I stepped to the desk and ran a finger over the surface of the bag and sure enough I saw a trail of shiny leather where my finger-tip had removed the dust.

It was the same as when I heard the crash from the kitchen the evening my husband died. I knew instinctively that something terrible had happened and that dull knot of pain formed in my stomach. I ran out of the office into the bedroom behind. It was empty and so was the bathroom. I ran into the kitchen – empty – then up the stairs and into every room. For some reason, as I entered each room and found it empty, I clicked the light switch up and down, up and down, though of course it was obvious that there was no electricity. Perhaps I already knew subconsciously where I would find Madame and this useless clicking of light switches was just a method of delaying the moment when I would have to go down into the cellars.

A torch was kept in a drawer in the kitchen. I took it and clicked it on. It was working. Feeling more and more distressed and ill, I opened the door onto the cellar stairs and immediately smelt a disgusting smell. It was fairly faint on the stairs but as I descended into the dungeon it grew stronger and I felt I was going to be sick. It was a nightmare, Monsieur. The beam of the torch throwing up shadows. The scuttle of mice. A nightmare. Later, I realized that I could have spared myself. It was obvious that Madame was down there somewhere, dead. I could have gone back up and called the police and let them find the body. Such a thing simply didn't occur to me at the time. Holding one hand to my face and nose, throwing the beam of the torch into the corners of the dungeon with the other, I groped my way towards the room beyond. The door was closed. I threw it open as quickly as possible, shone the torch into the room, saw her lying on that horrible device and then I fled.

After that, I was violently ill, upstairs, and found myself shaking and unable to move. Eventually, I managed to go back into the office. At the sight of Madame's bag I burst into uncontrollable tears and it was only after I managed to compose myself that I called the police.

You can imagine what happened next – an invasion of police, medical experts, photographers. It all seemed to pass as if it was happening on a stage or in a film. I was numb. I answered questions, made tea and coffee but – how can I describe the sensation? – it was as if somebody else was doing these things.

It was obvious what had happened. Madame had returned early from her holiday (in fact, the official enquiry later established that she had never left Paris) had gone to the house and placed herself in that abominable device unaware that mice had been eating at the electrical wiring. There was a short circuit. The power failed and she was trapped. Without electricity there was no way of freeing herself.

But why? Why had she gone there? That was the question that tormented me because the answer was inescapable. She had done it for her own gratification. It made no sense to me. I couldn't believe it. But there it was. There could be no other explanation.

It was only when I was at last allowed to go home that I was able to think about my own situation. Once again my life had been turned upside down. Worse, there was bound to be a scandal and my name would appear in the newspapers. The thought terrified me. Never before in my life, not even when my husband died, have I felt so wretched and desperate.

But as you have pointed out, there was no scandal. No report of the enquiry, which of course I was obliged to attend, ever appeared in a newspaper and, as I promised, here is the reason.

Maître D------.

He appeared the next day, a most charming, elegant man, and introduced himself as Madame's lawyer. It seemed that he had been handling her affairs for many years and he simply took over. "Leave everything to me," he said and naturally I was only too happy to comply. How he managed to keep such a strange, indeed sensational story out of the press I do not know. I did once mention it to him but he only smiled and said: "In France, everything is possible."

It was Maître D------ who informed me, some weeks later, that Madame had left me money in her Will. The taxes were fearful, of course, but even so the legacy enabled me to retire in comfort to Danville.

As you are aware, Monsieur, I keep myself very much to myself not so much because I don't enjoy the company of others but because I have learned that it is impossible truly to know another person. I thought I knew my dear Madame, I thought I understood her character, but the nature of her death showed me that my knowledge was superficial. That's the reason why, though I have some acquaintances here, I avoid forming deeper friendships.

Are you an exception to this rule? Well, I have always wanted to tell my story – I suppose a psychologist or someone of that sort would say that I needed to unburden myself of it – and when you told me about your project I decided to speak to you and permit you to tape the conversation on the terms that we have agreed. But although I have always found you a most agreeable and helpful neighbour I have no illusions. You might well betray me.

*

Editor's note: My collaborator, Michel Walrangis, has not, in fact, betrayed the anonymous narrator of this strange tale. She has read and approved the edited transcripts and, in the belief that enough time has passed to make it difficult, if not impossible, to identify any of the characters in it, has agreed to its publication.

VOLTAIRE (AND HIS RESURRECTION)

At the beginning of the year 1778, certain subtle changes in the political weather in France opened up the possibility that Voltaire might be able to return to Paris from his exile in Ferney, just over the Swiss border, without risk to his life or liberty.

Accordingly, on February 3rd, his niece, Mme Denis, set off to test the temperature, accompanied by her cronies, the Marquis and Marquise de Villette. Voltaire himself promised to stay at Ferney and await their report. But within hours of their departure he had changed his mind. After a morning spent dealing with the day-to-day business of his estate – reducing a rent here, advancing a loan there, offering sage advice on everything from winter crops to flighty wives – he announced to his secretary, Wagnière, over lunch, that he intended to leave for Paris as soon possible.

The faithful Wagnière was astounded and alarmed. "What of the risk to your life?" he asked, his glass poised between table and lip, visions of *lettres de cachet*, the sabres of the Royal Guard, and the slimy stone of a cell in the Bastille racing through his mind.

"My dear Wagnière," Voltaire replied, "I spent twenty minutes in the privy this morning and passed less urine than the wine in that glass you are holding. Are you about to propose a toast, by the way?"

"What? No – no."

"Then drink, my dear fellow, drink." Wagnière drained his glass in a gulp. "Nature," the old man continued, "has already given sentence. It is only by a daily act of will that I contrive a stay of execution. I don't want to die in

Switzerland. It would give quite the wrong impression. I want to die in Paris."

"But – but if they arrested you!"

"I should have time and leisure to put the finishing touches to my essay on the *Prix de la justice et de l'humanité*. Where better to perfect a new criminal code than a prison cell? It would be a delightful irony!"

Two days later, Wagnière helped his master into the great coach-and-six and they took the road to Paris. Travelling via Nantua, Bourg-en-Bresse, Dijon and Joigny, they arrived in the French capital on 19th February and drove straight to the Marquis de Villette's house on the corner of the *rue de Beaune* and the *Quai des Théatins*.

Within hours the house was besieged by friends and well-wishers. Within a day, the news of the great writer's arrival had spread throughout Paris and whenever Voltaire ventured abroad, his carriage was mobbed by ecstatic crowds. A sort of fever ran through the city. It was as if the unlettered rabble of workers and artisans sensed that the power of the words that had flowed unceasingly from the pen of the pale, frail, stick-thin old gentleman they cheered whenever they caught sight of him, the words that few if any of them had ever read or were capable of reading, would one day bring about their liberation.

At Versailles, Louis XVI sulked and grumbled. Like the Paris crowds, he too sensed – but more dimly – that something extraordinary was happening, that the very presence of this devilish old scribbler in his capital was unleashing forces that all the apparatus of absolute monarchy might be unable to combat.

When it was reported to him that Voltaire had been received at the *Comédie française* to wild applause, that his bust had been placed on the stage and crowned – *crowned* – with a laurel wreath, and that certain prominent members of the aristocracy had not only been present but had joined in the thunderous accolades, he flew into a rage. He summoned his Ministers and demanded action.

When they told him that, in the present circumstances, there was nothing to be done, he relapsed into sulks.

The State is often reduced to such paralysis, the Church – never. His Eminence the Cardinal Archbishop of Paris had been observing Voltaire's triumphs with growing alarm. When he learned, through spies in the Marquis de Villette's household, that the Enemy of Christ was a dying man, he decided that urgent measures must be taken and summoned his closest advisers – Jesuits mostly – to his palace.

"The task," the Cardinal said, "is to obtain some sort of statement from him – preferably written – in which he at least acknowledges the existence of a Creator."

"Deism?" said an elderly prelate with a shudder and a shimmer of his silken robe. "Are we to be a party to *Deism*?"

"We can hardly expect him to ask for Last Rites," said a youngish, black-clad Father dryly, provoking discreet laughter.

"Anything," said the Cardinal, "would be better than a death-bed proclamation of Atheism. Imagine the effect."

A murmur of alarm reverberated softly through the sumptuously furnished room like a breeze through a cloister.

In attacking the State, Voltaire had employed powerful weapons: the steely logic of the rational mind, the passionate appeal of the humanist poet, the forensic skill of the lawyer. But for his assault on the Church he had reserved his deadliest fire: ridicule.

With piercing sarcasm, perfectly aimed irony and irresistible wit he had picked away at the edifice of the Christian religion until he had reduced it to a rubble of intellectual absurdities. In retaliation, the Church had banned, burned and even buried his books. To no avail. Because – as every man in the Cardinal's *grand salon* knew – ideas, being abstract, cannot ultimately be banned, burned or buried. And if borne on the wind of a few excellent jokes, they spread like cholera.

"What pressure can we bring to bear?" asked the black-clad Father.

"There are certain members of his inner circle who understand the delicacy of the position," the Cardinal replied. "They have undertaken to speak to him, persuade him to make the required gesture."

"Hmm," said the Vicar-General of the Order of the Cross Triumphant. "Thin."

"I have been given to understand," His Eminence continued, visibly nettled by the Vicar-General's intervention, "that Voltaire's dearest wish is to die in Paris. One must presume therefore that it is also his desire to be buried here. And in matters of the burial of the dead, I need hardly point out, the Church is all-powerful. Voltaire no doubt dreams of some grand ceremonial attended by vast, grieving crowds. We can ensure that the disposal of his mortal remains degenerates into a farce."

There was a hiss in his enunciation of the word "farce" and a fierce, malevolent gleam in his hooded eyes. The black-clad Father looked at him with a new respect. He had glimpsed something of the serene contempt for his fellow men that characterised the French nobility, of which the Cardinal was a scion. What a Pope he would make, he thought. A match for any damned Italian.

In those days, before Baron Haussman's ivory ruler and demolition squads separated rich from poor, fashionable society from the *demi-monde*, Paris was still a mixed bag of a city in which the town-houses of the nobility often jostled alongside teeming slums and stinking workshops.

M. de Villette's mansion on the *rue de Beaune*, for instance, with its view of the river, secluded garden, and well-bred neighbours, was only a stone's throw from a maze of dark alleys and gloomy courtyards where the poorest of the poor slept a dozen to a room, small craftsmen and artisans plied an uncertain trade, prostitutes prowled and the miseries of the daily struggle to survive were boozed away in innumerable little grog-shops.

At the heart of this wretched *quartier* stood the ancient, mouldering Church of Sainte Quitterie. The parish priest was a short, thickset man of forty-two called the Abbé Vignau.

Vignau was a rarity among the Roman Catholic clergy of the time in that he was without ambition, indifferent to money, oblivious to creature comforts, wholly and solely dedicated to the service of Christ – about whom he had what the Cardinal Archbishop would have regarded as bizarre if not downright heretical ideas. (Fortunately for the Abbé, His Eminence was barely aware of his existence.)

Vignau's Christ was not that lofty figure, the Eternal Word of John's Gospel; not the gentle healer of Luke or the enigmatic taskmaster of Mark or the mighty miracle-worker of Matthew. He was not even the ethical genius of the Sermon On The Mount. Vignau's Christ was the itinerant teacher who sat down to eat with outcasts, who touched lepers, took a prostitute as a disciple, defended an adulteress against a mob, knew hunger and thirst and danger and in His last extremity, on the Cross, made practical provision for His mother.

Vignau's Christ was also, of course, the man who had – uniquely – been raised from the dead and had afterwards grilled fish for His disciples on the shore of Lake Galilee. And for Vignau, Christ was still, metaphorically at least, grilling fish. The Abbé could not remember a time when his whole being had not been suffused, illuminated, consumed by an absolute conviction of Christ alive and at work in the world.

Every year, at the Feast of the Ascension, he preached a sermon in which he enjoined his flock to rid themselves of any received notions of the Lord's rising like some majestic bird and vanishing into the unimaginable realms of Heaven but to think of Him rather as having diffused Himself, like the smoke of the incense round the altar, into the reality of the everyday world. The Church hierarchy would have been scandalized by such notions and no doubt a member of the congregation would have denounced the Abbé had there been any among them who understood a word of what he was talking about.

"Love one another," was the beginning and the end of Vignau's ministry to the wretched denizens of the *quartier Ste Quitterie*. He taught by example. The Sunday *quête* was immediately distributed to the poorest and neediest in the parish as were all other collections – at weddings, funerals, Masses for the dead and so on. Vignau never touched a sou. The majority of his own modest stipend was given away in similar fashion.

But Vignau's idea of loving charity went far beyond the mere handing out of money. There was no disease contagious or horrific enough in its symptoms to prevent the Abbé from bringing comfort and an attempt (usually hopeless) at healing to the sufferer, no depravities vile or shocking enough to make him withhold the possibility of forgiveness from the sinner, no grief sharp enough to resist his gentle words of consolation, no sense of hopelessness so deep that he could not shine some light of hope into the abyss.

His reward was to observe, from time to time, little acts of kindness among his flock – a debt cancelled, a betrayal forgiven, a meal shared, a handshake between old enemies – which he ascribed not to his own efforts or virtues but to the wonderful working of his Master through the Divine Mystery of the Mass.

Absorbed though he was in his parish, the Abbé was not entirely inward-looking. He was only too aware of the almost complete corruption of the Roman Catholic Church in France and indeed throughout Europe; of its arrogance, lust for power, pursuit of wealth. He was aware too of the counter-forces that had inevitably arisen: Protestantism in its various guises; Science and its beguiling wonders; above all, the measured, dignified and dangerously persuasive Humanism promoted by figures like Voltaire. It seemed to him that Christianity was approaching a great crisis, a cataclysm, that it was poised on the brink of destruction.

Far from being discouraged or dismayed by this apocalyptic vision, he was excited – thrilled would not be too strong a word. Because he believed that history was flowing with the irresistible force and inevitability of a tide towards the Second Coming of Christ.

What other answer, after all, could there possibly be to the present state of the Church and the world?

Sometimes, in the small hours, when he prayed alone, the presence of his Lord seemed palpable, as if He was standing on the other side of the door, or waiting quietly on the stairs. A phrase of St. Paul's ran constantly through his mind as he picked his way through the filth-strewn alleys of his parish: *He will come as a thief in the night.*

He would find himself pausing to look at a beggar, slumped in the mud, huddled in rags, holding out a claw-like hand for alms and wonder: *Is it He?* He would stop to give a coin to some half-starved urchin and linger for a moment, searching the boy's eyes – eyes burning with that strange, lustrous fire of hunger – for some trace of the Divine. He was tormented by the idea that one day he would turn a corner and a stranger would pass – a country lad, perhaps, dazed by the savageries of the city, or a broken-down peddler, or a cripple – and it would be He and he would not recognize Him.

Towards the middle of May, one of the Abbé's parishioners, a scullion in M. de Villette's kitchens called Jean Chabret, happened to mention, after Mass, that the old blasphemer Voltaire had taken to his bed and was likely to die and go to Hell at any moment. "It's the Witch has done it," Chabret told the priest. [He was referring to Mme Denis.] "After his money, of course. The old stick [he meant Voltaire] was going on all right while Spectacles [Wagnière] was there to see to him but she's got rid of him. Packed him off back to Switzerland on some trumped-up errand. The Noses [M. and Mme de Villette] was in on it too. Took to his bed he did, the poor old bugger, and never likely to leave it again on his own feet."

The Abbé's mother, the daughter of a small country squire in the Berry and the widow of another, had always told her children never to pay *any* attention to tittle-tattle from the servants' hall, so at first the Abbé ignored Chabret's news. But the following Sunday, the scullion brought a further bulletin. Voltaire was sinking fast and a small host of doctors now made part of the crowd permanently pressing round the invalid's bedside. The Abbé began to think that he ought to do something.

M. de Villette's house lay within the boundaries of his parish and therefore, technically speaking, Voltaire was a member – if only a temporary one – of his flock. The Abbé pondered the question, prayed about it, and one Saturday night – it was 30th May – he suddenly decided that it was his duty to offer the mocker of religion the Last Rites of the Church. Voltaire would no doubt refuse and the Abbé would accept his refusal but he would at least feel that he had fulfilled the obligations of discipleship. And of course, there was always the chance that Christ himself, ever active in the world, would bring about some late transformation of the great sceptic's soul.

Soon after eleven o'clock Vignau set off for the *rue de Beaune*. As he approached M. de Villette's house he saw four or five carriages waiting outside and as he came to the door another drew up. The windows on the first floor were brightly lit and the shadows of people moving about inside the rooms made a constant play against the drawn blinds.

The Major Domo, on opening the door and casting a cold, supercilious eye over Vignau's clerical garb, refused him entry. The Abbé merely bowed and withdrew. He waited a moment behind one of the stationary carriages, then, when the Major Domo had admitted the new arrivals and had shut the street door, he slipped discreetly round the side of the house, went down the steps to the basement and knocked on the kitchen door.

It was Chabret himself who opened it – and the Abbé could not help but feel that there was a Providence at work. In a low voice, he told the scullion what his intention was. "I could lose my place," Chabret whispered. The Abbé said nothing. "Least I'd get'd be a thrashing." The Abbé made no reply. "In any case, you'd never get near him, Father." The Abbé maintained silence. "Old grab-your-arse [The Major Domo] he'd spot you in a second." The Abbé did not utter a word. "Oh, all right then," said Chabret.

Vignau followed the boy past the kitchens, where spits were turning, pots and pans were ringing like bells and a frantic *chef* was cursing his underlings in the twanging accent of the *Midi*. They came to the foot of the back stairs. In frightened whispers, Chabret told the Abbé where Voltaire's room was – on the first floor – and warned him that he would find it full of people.

On his own now, the Abbé whipped up the back stairs and slipped through the service door into the hall. A quick glance showed him the broad back of the Major Domo as he strode towards the street door in response to the peremptory knocking of yet another arrival. Breathing a prayer of thanksgiving for the continuing gifts of Providence, the Abbé swiftly crossed the hall and ran up the main stairs three at a time.

The landing was deserted. Through the half-open door of Voltaire's room he heard a low hubbub of voices. He slid into the room – and found himself immediately blocked by an impenetrable press of people, some of whom turned and stared at him. A woman, a member of the nobility to judge by her jewelled dress, her elaborate coiffure and the jagged outcrop of her nose, whispered urgently to him: "Do you come from His Eminence?"

Naturally, Vignau had no knowledge of the conference

that had been held at the Cardinal's palace, of the machinations that had ensued, of the finely judged prevarications, procrastinations and ambiguities by which Voltaire had foiled every manoeuvre of the clerical party. It flashed into his mind, however, that if he told a lie – he would not even have to speak, a slight nod would do the trick – he might be escorted to the bedside with no further trouble. But he could not lie. Instead, he hunched his powerful shoulders, lowered his head, and like a mole (an animal he somewhat resembled) burrowed his way through silks and satins and brocades, past elbows, shoulders and knees to the enormous state bedstead in which Voltaire lay, propped up against a pile of pillows and cushions.

In the course of his twenty-year ministry, Vignau had attended innumerable death-beds. He had learned to recognize the signs of approaching bodily extinction with an accuracy that no medical man of the time could have approached. As he looked at the pinched, drawn features below the night-cap, at the yellowish pallor of the skin, at the spidery fingers twitching at the bed-clothes; as he listened to the fast shallow breaths puffing out between lips that were as thin and brittle and colourless as nail-clippings, he knew that Voltaire had but minutes to live. And yet … the eyes!

The eyes were not those of a dying man. There was not a trace in them of the opaque dullness, produced by pain, or fear, or resignation, or dumb anger, or loss of mental faculties, that was, in the Abbé's experience, another inevitable mark of imminent death. Voltaire's eyes could have been those of a young man; a young man, moreover, of exceptional brilliance and energy. There was a dazzling glint in them, as of morning sunshine captured in a dewdrop. But at the same time there was another sort of light that had nothing to do with the dash and sparkle of youth. It was a deeper, steadier radiance, a sort of smiling glow (he was never quite able to describe it to his own satisfaction) that spoke of a complete knowledge of the world transformed by an invincible sense of humour into a profound and supremely tolerant understanding.

Those amazing eyes turned upon the Abbé and held him speechless. It was Voltaire who spoke first.

"Good evening, Monsieur L'Abbé," he said. "What can I do for you?"

Vignau was vaguely aware of buzz of voices behind him. "Who is he?" "What does he want here?" "Who let him in? "The effrontery!" "A creature of the Cardinal's, perhaps." "Disgraceful!" It mattered less to him than the scratching of cicadas on a summer night in the Berry. He was savouring the delicious little irony of Voltaire's remark as one tastes the subtle flavour of a herb or a spice in a well-made dish.

"Perhaps," Voltaire continued, "you think there is something you can do for *me*?"

The Abbé found his voice at last. "I am your parish priest. I have come to offer you Last Rites."

Behind him, the voices grew suddenly more strident and angry. He felt a hand pluck at his sleeve. He threw it off with a sharp movement of his elbow but he realized that at any moment he could be seized and bundled violently out of the house. He decided to take the initiative.

"François Marie Arouet, *dit* Voltaire," he said in a loud voice, "do you renounce the Devil?"

There was a collective hiss of shock. Then silence. Then Voltaire spoke again.

"My dear Abbé," he said. "You see the state I'm in. This is no time to start making enemies."

The Abbé choked.

Or at least that was how the majority of people in the room interpreted the sound. In fact the Abbé wasn't choking. He was laughing – or to be strictly accurate the choking sound was the beginning of a burst of laughter that welled up from the pit of his belly and exploded through his gullet in uncontrollable waves, as the waters of a spring, long choked by sediments and mulch, are released by a well-aimed pickaxe.

The Abbé laughed and laughed and laughed. Tears streamed down his cheeks. He clutched at the elaborately veneered bed-head.

Voltaire himself had started to chuckle. But as the Abbé's paroxysms continued he too was consumed by mirth. The strain on his lungs and his enfeebled heart was too much. He went white. He struggled for breath, failed to find it, found it and with a final effort, he gasped out: "I die laughing at my own joke. What a magnificent end! And what a judgement."

There followed a prolonged, dry rattle in his throat. Then he died.

The following day, Sunday, a few of the more percipient worshippers at the church of Ste. Quitterie noticed that their priest was strangely distracted and preoccupied. He moved to the pulpit like a sleep-walker and stumbled up the steps as if the worse for drink. His homily, delivered in a hesitant, *distrait* manner seemed to make even less sense than usual. Chabret, who would have been able to cast some light on the mystery, was not present. He had been locked up in a broom cupboard at M. de Villette's after a thrashing enthusiastically administered by the Major Domo, his role in admitting the Abbé into the house having been betrayed by a fellow servant – a contemptible, snivelling, warty little sneak called Mauvezin.

After Mass, Vignau returned to his Presbytery, locked and barred the door (something he had never been known to do before), shut himself in his bedroom and fell into deep, trance-like prayer. At about midnight he was aroused by a ferocious and persistent knocking. Leaning out of his window he saw M. Lapotère, the tallow chandler, standing in the street below. "You must come at once, Father," Lapotère shouted. "It's my wife. She's very bad." Mme Lapotère was a notorious *malade imaginaire*, but Vignau's sense of duty remained strong, in spite of the intellectual and spiritual turmoil into which the events of the previous night had plunged him.

He therefore accompanied the chandler to his little shop in the *rue des Salières* where he found Mme Lapotère sitting in an armchair by the fire, her six daughters kneeling round her, holding her hands, stroking her hair and weeping copiously.

"Ah, Father, you are come just in time," said Mme Lapotère in a feeble voice that Vignau saw through immediately.

"Have you seen a doctor, Madame?" His tone was brusque, curt, and so unlike his usual manner that Mme Lapotère was startled – and a little frightened.

"Yes, yes," Lapotère answered for her. "Dupleix was here less than an hour ago. He said her condition was grave, very grave."

"It's difficult to say who is the greater impostor," said the Abbé, picking up a bottle of medicine from a table, "your wife, who's as healthy as a puppy, or Dr Dupleix" – here he uncorked the bottle and sniffed at it – "who has sold you, no doubt for a stiff price, what I can assure you is plain water flavoured with a few bitter herbs."

Lapotère goggled at him stupidly. But his wife rose from her chair, her eyes flashing with anger.

"You villain! You slanderer! And you call yourself a man of God!"

"That's what I used to call myself," said Vignau quietly, more to himself than to her. Then he added, in a firmer tone: "In any case, I seem to have set you on the road to recovery. I wish you good night, Madame."

On leaving the shop, and starting out for home, the Abbé fell into a reverie. He walked mechanically, without any idea of his direction. Reflecting on the recent scene in the tallow chandler's shop, he was astonished at the harshness of his own behaviour – and ashamed of it. Mme Lapotère, he recalled, had been a beautiful girl. All the young men of the *quartier* had danced attendance on her. Constant child-bearing and the smoke and stench of the chandlery had quickly ruined her beauty. She conjured up these imaginary ailments simply so that she could feel, from time to time, that she was still the centre of attention. It was all harmless enough, since her husband could well afford to pay the doctor and to buy his useless potions. And Dr. Dupleix gained because he was generally known to be a charlatan and had a large family and few clients. It was a little system that suited everybody – and he had tried to destroy it. Why? He would never have acted in such a way before – before …

Another image arose in his mind, the image that had been invading it relentlessly for the past twenty-four hours. Voltaire. His eyes. The eyes of – but no, he must not allow himself even to think it. It was an abomination. Madness. But he could not escape it, the new phrase that assaulted him on all sides like a besieging army.

The eyes of Christ.

He groaned aloud. He stopped. He shook himself physically. It was no good. He said aloud: "The eyes of Christ, yes, they were the eyes of Christ."

He was standing in a courtyard, by a wall. He banged his head against the harsh stone, once, twice, then again, as if by that means he could somehow dislodge the thought from his brain as one knocks an unwanted nail from a beam.

"No, no, no," he cried hoarsely.

Above him, a shutter opened with a clatter and an old woman in a night-cap poked her head out. She peered down.

"Oh, is it you, Father?" she said. "Are you all right?"

"Quite all right, thank you," he managed to reply. "Yes, quite all right. Good night to you."

He walked quickly away. He took out a handkerchief and dabbed at the blood on his forehead. He tried for the hundredth time to calm himself, to think clearly and rationally. How could Voltaire, the avowed Enemy of Christ, be Christ? It was impossible. And yet those eyes. So full of wisdom, compassion, understanding, humour. Then the life, the work: the championship of the poor, the love of justice and freedom. Had not Voltaire too been oppressed, forced into exile, his writings excoriated by Church and State? But no. The man had denied God, had mercilessly ridiculed religion. Yet had not Christ done similarly? Had he not expelled the money-changers from the Temple, challenged the sterile orthodoxies of the Scribes and Pharisees, denounced the pettifogging regulations of the Law?

With these conflicting thoughts banging about in his head like a loose door in a gale, the Abbé stumbled blindly through the twisting streets and alleys. He emerged eventually into a wider boulevard and saw the river ahead of him.

He stopped to get his bearings. He was on the *Quai Malaquais*. There was no moon. A watchman was making his round, carrying a lantern. Behind him, a great carriage-and-six was approaching. The watchman stopped. As the carriage passed him, the bright glow from his lantern lit up the interior. Sitting inside, dressed in night-cap and dressing-gown, was Voltaire himself.

He was looking out of the window, smiling. He nodded to the watchman. Then he saw the Abbé. His smile broadened and he nodded again. And then, as the carriage rolled past, close to him, the Abbé saw the man he knew for an absolute certainty to be dead raise his right hand and make the Sign of the Cross in blessing.

The carriage trundled away and vanished into the dark. With a few tremendous strides the Abbé caught up with the watchman, who had resumed his round. "You, watchman!" he roared. The man turned, startled. "Did you see that man – in the carriage?"

The watchman stared for a moment, then: "The old gentleman? Yes?"

"Was he dead or was he alive?"

"Well, Father, he – he looked live enough to me."

"And to me," said the Abbé. "God bless and keep you. Goodnight."

The Abbé went directly to his Presbytery, sat down and wrote a letter to the Archbishop resigning his cure of souls at Ste. Quitterie. First thing in the morning, he handed the letter to the porter at the Episcopal Palace then went straight to a furniture dealer in a nearby street. By noon he had sold, for cash, the entire contents of the Presbytery – the beds and chairs and chests and tables and pictures and pewter-ware he had inherited from his mother and had, for sentimental reasons, always kept by him. He spent the afternoon going from bookseller to bookseller and by sundown he had bought all the works of Voltaire currently available – plays, dialogues, novels, poetry, essays, scientific and philosophical papers, polemics, satires, reviews. Next morning, over a hundred books and pamphlets were loaded onto a carriage and the Abbé left Paris for the Auvergne.

He rented a tiny cottage, perched on the side of an extinct volcano, with views over the most remote, savage and least populated area of France. The nearest village was five miles down a stony, serpentine track. A few passing goat-herds were his only neighbours. Subsisting on the tiny annual income derived from his share of the family estate in the Berry, he devoted every waking hour to the study, analysis and annotation of Voltaire's writings. Three times a year he made the six-day journey, on foot, to Clermont-Ferrand to renew his supplies of paper, pens and ink and to collect his money.

It took him seven years to complete the first phase of the work he believed God had called him to do. He then proceeded to the second phase: a radical reinterpretation of Scripture in the light of his Voltairean studies. Four years later, when he was within sight of finishing this task, on one of his visits to Clermont-Ferrand, he learned of the summoning of the Estates General and the start of the Revolution. It only confirmed his sense of the End of Things and the ushering in of a new order. He pressed on.

Two years passed. In his mountain fastness he was hardly aware of the events that were shaking the fabric of French society as the volcano on which he lived had once rained lava on the primeval forest. But then, on one of his visits to Clermont-Ferrand, he found the banker's house burned out and a general state of chaos in the town. Accepting the fact that he could no longer rely on the income from his patrimony, he spent his last few francs on the purchase of a small herd of goats and by careful husbandry managed to carry on. By now he was into the third and final phase of his appointed work: the formulation of a complete theology of the new Christian-Voltairian faith, with appropriate liturgies in the vernacular rather than Latin. It only remained for him to compile a lectionary – and this task was completed at the beginning of the year 1793. Concealing his books and manuscripts in a cave near his cottage, he set out, on foot, to Paris.

He arrived in the capital in mid-February, unaware that King Louis XVI had gone to the guillotine less than a month before and that the city was in the full grip of Robespierre's Terror.

He made straight for Nôtre-Dame. His idea was to proclaim the new Gospel on the steps of the Cathedral in the same way that Christ (according to St. John) had launched His saving mission in the Temple at Jerusalem. He was followed every inch of the way by agents of the Committee of Public Safety, who had been alerted to a possible danger by the way he was dressed. He was wearing what he believed would become standard clerical garb in the reformed Faith: a night-cap and a dressing-gown.

Nôtre-Dame had recently been re-dedicated as a Temple of the Cult of Pure Reason, but the Abbé was only vaguely aware of this as he prepared himself to address a small crowd that had been attracted by his bizarre appearance. Before he could utter a word he was arrested.

He was taken to the local office of the Committee and after a couple of hours in a cell was brought before a panel of citizen-judges. The chairman was a young man in his mid-twenties, wearing the revolutionary cockade – and the Abbé felt immediately that his face was familiar. Jean Chabret recognized his former parish priest instantly.

"Father Vignau!" he was about to exclaim – but stopped himself just in time. The Abbé sensed his hesitation, interpreted it correctly and gave no sign of recognition. The panel listened to a report of the arrest, then Chabret, after a brief discussion with his colleagues, announced that he would interrogate the prisoner personally.

Three hours later, Chabret had learned every detail of how the Abbé had spent the past fifteen years. He ordered the gaoler to bring "Citizen Vignau" a good dinner, and warning the Abbé to reveal nothing of his past to anybody, went away to wrestle with his conscience.

He paced the streets of Paris till dawn. Then he returned to the Abbé's cell.

Having made absolutely sure that he could not be overheard, he sat down, took the Abbé's hand and spoke as follows:

"What I am about to tell you, dear Father, is the truth. It will be painful to you – and I have been debating with myself all night whether or not I should reveal it to you. I have decided that I have no alternative. A few hours after Voltaire died I was given a thrashing and locked in a broom-cupboard. There was so much going on in the house that they forgot about me, so though I could see nothing, I could hear everything. The Marquis and his wife had learned of a plot by the Archbishop to deny Voltaire burial. They were determined to foil it. Early in the morning, they called in Levasseur – yes – the embalmer.

By nightfall, he had prepared the body. They clothed it a night-cap and dressing-gown, carried it out into the yard and placed it in Voltaire's own carriage-and-six. One of the other servants – a little wretch called Mauvezin – accompanied the corpse. His job was to move the head and agitate the limbs so as to give the appearance of life. That was what you saw. The body was taken to an abbey near Troyes, in Champagne, where a cousin of the old man's was Abbot. They said Mass and buried him the next day. Of course, the Bishop of Troyes wrote to forbid it but the letter arrived too late. A couple of years ago they dug him up, brought him to Paris and put him in the Pantheon. I was there. The carriage was drawn by twelve white horses – and you should have heard 'em cheer."

For a moment that seemed like an age to Chabret, the Abbé remained silent and motionless. Then his whole body – much leaner now, almost emaciated, in fact, after the privations of the last few years – trembled and shook as if he was in the grip of a fatal seizure. A gargling sound bubbled in his throat and then laughter, hysterical laughter beyond anything in his power to control, utterly consumed him. In the confined space of the stone cell, the sound was doubled and re-doubled. It was as if the full peal of the bells of Nôtre-Dame was ringing out between those narrow walls. Chabret put his hands to his ears. The laughter went on and on and on. Then suddenly it ceased. The Abbé slipped sideways off his chair and fell dead to the floor.

Some years later, happening to be in the Auvergne, Chabret decided to make a pilgrimage to the Abbé Vignau's cottage. A goat-herd led him up the track, reminiscing, in an almost incomprehensible *patois*, about the strange hermit who had appeared and disappeared so mysteriously before the Revolution. When Chabret asked whether he knew of a cave nearby, the man became suddenly reticent. Chabret paid him off, telling him that he would find his own way back to the village, waited a little, then set out to look for the cave. It did not take him long to find it or to confirm what he already suspected, that it had long since been pillaged.

That night, by spending money freely in the village inn, he learned that the Abbé's books had been sold to a travelling dealer and his manuscripts used for tapers and fire-lighters. However, knowing the frugal habits of the villagers, next morning he went from house to house offering to pay handsomely for any surviving scraps of the hermit's writings. In a tumbledown cottage on the edge of the village, a very old woman produced one fragment that Chabret, from a faint memory of the Abbé's hand-writing, judged to be genuine. (The ten or twelve other specimens that were presented to him later in the day were obvious forgeries.)

On the yellowing slip of paper he bought from the old woman were the following words:

"[t]he hidden purpose of the Divine Creation can thus be [rev]ealed as [*three words indecipherable*]."

*

Editor's note: It is a matter of historical fact that Voltaire's body was embalmed and smuggled out of Paris the night after his death exactly as described in the narrative and for the reasons stated.

The story was found, in the form of a typescript (which can be dated to the 1930's), among the papers of the late Comtesse de Castelnau, who was a direct descendent of Jean de Chabret, Baron D'Arcueil (1768-1856), a quartermaster in Napoleon's army who made an immense fortune during the First Empire, was ennobled in 1813 and under the Restoration became well-known as a patron of the Roman Catholic Church, endowing numerous schools. He was particularly associated with the Jesuits.

Biographical material on de Chabret is scanty, but an

obituary in *Le Nouveau Journal de Paris* (October, 1856) states that in his youth he had been "in the service of a nobleman of enlightened views."

There is no record of a church in Paris dedicated to Sainte Quitterie, a Visigothic Princess martyred in the 5th century, whose cult is largely confined to South West France. No trace can be found of any family called Vignau owning estates in the Berry region.

One other fact is worth mentioning. The archives of the Paris police contain a record of a duel fought in 1828 in which a man called Pierre Etienne Mauvezin was killed by a single shot to the chest. The report describes Mauvezin as "former confidential secretary to the late Marquis de Villette." An attached memorandum states that his suspected assailant was Jean de Chabret, Baron D'Arcueil, but that in the absence of any direct proof, there could be no prosecution.

Twelve Curious Deaths in France

CAESAR

When I first came to Danville, over twenty years ago, the railway ended at Vernier-le-Chateau and one travelled the last few miles to the coast in a lumbering *calèche*, drawn by two stout horses, through gently undulating countryside dotted with small farms and orchards.

Today, I changed trains at Vernier and took the branch line that runs along the littoral. With an increasing sense of outrage, I passed by places I had once known as charming fishing villages. I found that they had been turned into pert, vulgar resorts, with rows of cheap hotels staring insolently at the sea. Worse was to come. As the train steamed into the new station at Danville, I discovered to my horror that the town had been re-baptized into an alien faith and was now called Danville-sur-Mer!

Declining the services of porters and cabmen, I walked, portmanteau in hand, through brash boulevards lined with horrible villas, stupefied not so much by the heat – though it was tremendous – but by the changes that had overwhelmed this once decent, sleepy Norman port.

It was with a feeling of some relief, therefore, that upon entering the principal street that twists down to the harbour, I found myself once again in familiar territory, sure of my way, passing shops and houses that I remembered. And there was some shade! Approaching the harbour itself, I was in high hopes that the *Pension Crique*, where I first met and talked with Godiveau, might have survived the rape of Danville – I beg its pardon – Danville-sur-Mer.

It was gone.

In its place stood a blinding white building like an

upended wedding-cake that proclaimed itself to be the *Grand Hotel Atlantic*. I entered this pretentious establishment, asked if they had a room available and was told by the clerk at the desk – a young man to whom I took an immediate dislike – that they were full. The only accommodation they could offer was the Royal Suite on the first floor. I engaged it immediately. Why not? What does anything matter any more?

On being shown to my rooms – I beg their pardon, the *Royal Suite* – I took Godiveau's sacred manuscript out of my portmanteau, placed it in the drawer of a fake Empire desk (alas poor Napoleon!), locked the drawer and tucked the key into my waistcoat pocket. Putting a pair of scissors into another pocket, I set out – with what trepidation may be imagined – to see if my Aunt's house in the *rue Jean-Baptiste* had fared better than the poor *Pension Crique*.

It was still there.

Indeed, I could detect very few alterations. The entrance gates had certainly been re-painted – but in a perfectly acceptable grey-green. For a moment I considered ringing the bell (it was the same bell, only needing a little polish) but the house, with its closed shutters, and the gardens, in which nothing stirred, not even a leaf, had such an air of stillness that I decided that the owners, whoever they were now, must be away. In any case, if I encountered someone, I had my story ready.

Having already noticed that the gates were unlocked (this would never have been allowed in my Aunt's day), I pushed them open and stepped boldly onto the flagstone path. I looked to my left and there, beyond the lily pond, were the laurel bushes, exactly as they had been all those years ago.

Moving more quickly now, conscious that my next action would certainly puzzle and possibly even alarm anyone who might be watching, I skirted the pond and made directly for the laurels. I took the scissors out of my pocket and quickly snipped off half a dozen branches.

Concealing the glossy leaves beneath my jacket as best I could, I made my way swiftly back into the street and closing the gates carefully behind me walked to the nearest grocer's shop where I bought a bottle of their best red wine – a Bordeaux – and a flask of olive oil. I then returned to my hotel – which brings me to the present moment.

I am sitting at this detestable desk, looking out through tall windows (which I have opened) at the harbour and the sands beyond. I note that yachts and other pleasure boats now outnumber the fishing vessels and that the beach, where sturdy ponies used to pull the bathing machines in and out of the water, has now been colonized by women in absurd hats that have the appearance of *mille-feuilles* cakes. They swelter under their parasols while their half-naked brats disport themselves in the waves like elvers.

But my business is not to describe Danville as it is today (*sur Mer!*) but to recall, as accurately as I can, the crucial scenes that took place here so long ago.

I was twenty-three years old, living with my parents and sister in the substantial house my father had built at Neuilly-sur-Seine. Every working day I took the omnibus into Paris, where I had a promising position in the editorial department of *Junod et Frères*, the leading publishing house of that era.

My father, who owned a large printing works, gave me a generous allowance to supplement the somewhat meagre salary M. Junod, *aîné*, saw fit to pay to the younger members of his staff. I was engaged to be married to Mademoiselle Irène Griffonet, a girl of surpassing beauty [*two words indecipherable*] and brilliance whose collection of poetry ("*Particularités*") my father had recently had the honour of printing and which had achieved a great success among her circle, which included the popular novelist Isidore Patpapier and other leading intellectuals.

Irène's family, who had a virtual monopoly in the manufacture of water-closets, was in a position to give her a handsome dowry and my father had undertaken to match it. Everything seemed set fair for me. In my professional life I felt certain of swift advancement, my financial future was assured, and I was devoutly in love with the enchanting creature who had accepted my hand. Then suddenly my health broke down.

To this day we do not know the precise nature of the malady that afflicted me. The symptoms were, *inter alia*, a chronic lassitude and inability to concentrate, loss of appetite, and certain (minor) mental aberrations such as a fixed idea that our cook was attempting to poison me. Our family doctor, the famous Professor Decoin, did mention the possibility of a slight brain fever but this so upset my mother that the worthy man re-examined me and confessed himself to have been mistaken. He recommended a period of complete rest in some quiet coastal spot. Regular sea-bathing, he believed, would greatly speed my recovery.

My mother immediately thought of a distant relation of hers, a Mme Pingret, who had resided since the death of her husband, a stockbroker, at Danville on the coast of Normandy. She wrote to this lady and received a reply by return in which Mme Pingret stated that she would be delighted to receive me and offer me what hospitality she could until the end of September, when she would be departing to take her annual cure at Baden-Baden. She hinted tactfully that she was in somewhat straitened circumstances and that any contribution towards the expenses of my visit would be welcome.

"But old Pingret was as rich as a Nabob, wasn't he?" said my father. "And Baden-Baden don't come cheap. Still, the last thing we want is to be beholden to the old trout. Here, my boy–" he took out some large banknotes "– this should see you through."

"Dear Adeline was always considered a trifle eccentric," said my mother. Then, to me, with a slight wink towards my father: "Be sure to make a good impression, Zézé darling. She has no children and no relations nearer than ourselves that I can recollect."

"*You will call me Aunt.*"

These were the first words spoken to me by Mme Pingret when the maid showed me into the *salon*. The thing that instantly struck me about my relative was her extreme tallness and boniness. Even sitting, as she was, in a high-backed armchair, she gave an impression of great height. With her full black skirt spreading to the floor, her narrow waist and charcoal-thin arms encased in black silk, her slender neck encircled by a choker of shiny jet beads, she looked like nothing so much as that new tower they have built for the Paris Exhibition – I forget its name. She wore a close-fitting wig of tight, glossy black curls and a black silk cap. Her eyes, behind the iron frames of her spectacles, were also black – and very penetrating, shrewd eyes they were.

The second strong impression I received was of the room itself. Every article of furniture – and there were many – was dust-sheeted. The only objects on view, apart from my Aunt's chair, were portraits of Napoleon III and the Empress Eugenie. Other pictures hung on the walls but they too were dust-sheeted.

"To calculate the exact degree of consanguinity that exists between us would be a wearisome task," my Aunt continued, "and though I like – indeed demand – a strict precision in all things, in the present case we will have to resort to a generality. You will call me Aunt and I will call you Nephew." Aunt and Nephew we became from that moment. And – I insist on adding – the very best of friends.

My Aunt possessed something that one very rarely encounters in this deluded world: a completely rational mind. The dust-sheets, for instance (all the furniture and pictures in the principal rooms were dust-sheeted), which might have been considered an oddity, were in fact completely logical. M. Pingret had been a great collector of antique furniture, pictures and *objets d'art*. Every one of them reminded my Aunt so powerfully of her late husband that she could not bear to look at them. At the same time, since they were of great (and increasing) value it made perfect sense to protect them from the ravages of dirt, scuffs and direct sunlight. The dust-sheets therefore served a dual purpose.

Mme Pingret applied this same principle of duality to every domestic arrangement. Her maid doubled up as cook, her gardener as butler. A meal was served at eleven o'clock in the morning, thus neatly combining breakfast and luncheon. A second repast, at six o'clock in the evening, married afternoon tea with dinner along similar lines. She kept absolutely regular hours. She rose at seven o'clock precisely and spent the morning reading an astonishing number and variety of journals and newspapers. This was not out of any vulgar interest in politics or Society gossip but as a means of protecting and enhancing her investments.

"Information is everything," she would say. "And it is always to be found between the lines." In the afternoon she dealt with her correspondence, which was voluminous, since she employed numerous brokers, bankers and financial agents. ("Plenty of baskets means plenty of eggs!" I quote her again!) After the evening meal she would sit for half an hour in the *salon* in reverent contemplation of the Emperor and Empress, under whose glorious rule M. Pingret had made his fortune. At seven o'clock, on the dot, she retired.

This unvarying routine was, of course, admirably suited to an invalid. My health rapidly began to improve. In time, I developed a little system of my own that chimed in perfectly with my Aunt's habits. In the morning I would take a walk along the coast. In the afternoon I would bathe in the sea.

Ah, the sea, the sea!

I had learned to swim in the small lake we had on our

country property in the Solange but I had never before dipped so much as a toe into the briny. At first, I confess, I was a trifle intimidated by the waves. Rearing, roaring, crashing, they seemed to me like an endless artillery barrage being unleashed from the unseen shores of Perfidious Albion. Yet the immovable rock and subtly shifting sands of France never failed to deal with them, exploding them into fragments of flying spume or sucking out their force and sending them, hangdog and limping, back whence they came.

This sense of an invincible *patrie* encouraged me, after a few days of paddling in the shallows, to venture out of my depth. What joys were then mine! I discovered a new world peopled – yes, I say peopled – by a wonderful variety of characters.

These were none other than the waves themselves! When the breeze was light they were cheerful playmates, splashing one's face, dancing around one, glittering in the sunlight, seeming to laugh out loud. When there was a swell they would rock one gently in a warm embrace and carry one off on long, lazy journeys across the surface of the ocean. But when the wind was blowing hard they turned into formidable foes, great curving, foam-topped combers lifting one off the sea-bed, turning one upside down and hurling one gasping and choking towards the shore. Yet slowly, as my skill and confidence grew, I learned to master these monsters. I discovered that I could swim up their shiny flanks then dive below the boiling crests, and having outwitted the beasts, watch them spend their force uselessly in hissing surf. I shall never forget the day that I dared to ride one. I lay atop it, perfectly balanced, and it became my chariot and I raced towards the sands as if at the head of an all-conquering army. Ah, the exhilaration!

After a few weeks, my Aunt, with her refined and exquisite tact, hinted that the extra mouth to feed at the evening meal was upsetting the delicate balance of her daily budget. She mentioned that at the *Pension Crique* one could get a wholesome and substantial supper for a price so reasonable that one evening, several years ago, she had herself considered dining there. She was prevented from doing so only by the (perfectly correct) thought that any habit of expense, when once acquired, is difficult to shake off.

That inaugural supper at the *Pension Crique* is another imperishable memory. I can still taste the savour of the plump beefsteak Mme Crique served me, with its rich sauce of cream, black pepper and *cèpes*. (I realize that I am ravenously hungry, having not eaten since yesterday morning. But that is all to the good!) As for the *tarte tatin* that followed – ah, an apple was an apple in those days, especially in Normandy. Even when cooked (and with a touch of Calvados) the fruit retained the subtle scents of the blossom from which it sprang. But I digress most culpably, wasting time and ink on gastronomic trivia when I should have proceeded directly to the momentous event that changed my life: my first sight of the immortal genius Alphonse Godiveau.

He was dining alone, at a small table in a far corner of the room, a slight, elderly gentleman with long, greying hair, pointed beard and curled moustachios, dressed in a much-patched and mended frock coat. He wore iron-rimmed spectacles, rather like my Aunt's, but with much thicker lenses, through which (when I first noticed him) he was peering down at his soup rather in the manner of someone who has just thrown a pebble into a well to test its depth.

There was something about this person that immediately aroused my interest but of course I did not attempt to introduce myself. This was partly out of a certain shyness that runs in my family (my sister Henriette, for example, could hardly ever bring herself to address even my parents and is now a Sister in an Enclosed Order) but mostly because of the aura of splendid isolation with which he surrounded himself. No man is an island, so the saying goes. How utterly wrong – at least in the case of Godiveau. He was a man who had, through long, painful and heroic struggle, achieved a complete detachment from everything but the great work upon which (I was eventually to learn) he was engaged.

Over the next few evenings, I continued to observe him as closely as good manners permitted. I noticed that his fingers – which were as thin and fine as a violinist's – were stained with ink. He ate nothing but a bowl of soup and the *plat du jour* and I never saw a bottle of wine on his table. Though it was clear that he was a resident, he never spoke to anyone, not even to the waiter.

Mme Crique was a friendly, gossipy sort of woman and I had made up my mind to ask her about her mysterious lodger. But as it turned out, it was Godiveau himself who crossed the Rubicon. It was a Saturday night and the dining-room was crowded. Having finished my dinner, I decided to take my coffee, Calvados and cigar outside, to escape the racket in the dining-room and to enjoy the sunset.

It was a magical evening. The great orb of the sun, sinking in crimson splendour, was reflected in the glassy sea, so that it seemed as if there were two fiery spheres approaching and melting into one another. I was deep in contemplation of this wonder when a voice spoke behind me.

"The Ancients, of course, were perfectly aware of the rotation of the Earth and its orbit around the sun. It is almost impossible to imagine the impenetrable quality of the darkness that fell upon the European mind after the fall of Rome. Has the light yet fully dawned again? I wonder."

I turned. Godiveau himself was standing behind me. Fiery reflections of the sunset were captured in the thick lenses of his spectacles.

"I once met a member of the Flat Earth Society in the waiting-room of a railway station," he went on. "A few lines from Seneca, quoting Anaxagoras, were enough to demolish all his arguments." His voice, while cultivated and mellifluous, contained just a hint of the hard, flat accent of the North. "Good Madame Crique, who knows everything and understands nothing, informs me that you are a publisher. I am a writer. Permit me to introduce myself. Alphonse Godiveau."

He bowed and offered his hand. I rose, bowed in return and we shook hands. I had placed my cigar on the edge of the table and he caught a whiff of it. "Ah! A Havana! It must be, what, twenty years since I last had the pleasure of smoking a Havana."

I hastened to take out my cigar-case and offer it to him. "You are too kind," he said, carefully selecting a cigar and sitting down at my table. As he cut and lit the Havana (it was a Monte Cristo) I asked if he would do me the honour of joining me in a cup of coffee and a Calvados.

"Thank you," he replied, "but I must confess to a slight preference for Cognac."

I called for a coffee and two Cognacs. Godiveau's cigar was lit now and pulling well. "I hope you don't object to this unceremonious approach," he said, through fragrant clouds of smoke. Before I could answer he went on to ask me about my family and my circumstances in the most sympathetic way, expressing his commiseration at my recent loss of health and congratulating me with the sincerity of an old friend on its recovery.

I called for more Cognac and we each smoked another cigar. The conversation became general and I found that Godiveau's ideas on almost every subject coincided exactly with my own. It was only when we began to discuss the Modern Novel that I found myself – well – how can I put it? I was startled half out of my wits! I do not exaggerate!

All my literary gods, according to this extraordinary person, had feet of clay. Balzac was a fraud, Victor Hugo a pompous bore; Georges Sand was novelettish, Feuillet superficial; Stendhal was over-rated and even Flaubert's reputation was largely undeserved.

"People go into palpitations over the fact he took seven years to write *Bovary*. Seven years is nothing, my dear sir. Nothing at all. And what proof do we have that he spent that time exclusively, as we have been led to believe, in polishing his so-called masterpiece? How many hours were in reality frittered away at the dining-table or in dalliance with women? A great many, I suspect. And is not the scene in the carriage simply pornographic?"

I went back to my Aunt's that night, my mind reeling with Godiveau's ideas – so utterly revolutionary and yet so strangely attractive. It was only when I snuffed out my candle, before going to sleep, that it occurred to me that he had told me absolutely nothing about himself.

Next evening I was at the *Pension Crique* earlier than usual. I had noticed that Godiveau was invariably at his table before me and I hoped to precede him and thus be in a position to invite him to join me. My little stratagem proved successful. He was not there when I arrived. I ordered an aperitif and waited. After ten or fifteen minutes, I overheard Mme Crique remark to the waiter that Monsieur Godiveau was late. Indeed, it was a further ten minutes or so before he appeared. To my delight, he made straight for my table, the invitation was offered and gracefully accepted.

My goodness, how he ate! As course after course was devoured I began to realize that he was half starved. His conversation was as enthralling as ever – but still not a word about himself. Then at last (over a plum tart) he gave me an opening. He had reverted to the subject of *Madame Bovary*. "It is unquestionably an immoral work," he said. "I would never permit my daughters to read it."

"You are a married man, then, M. Godiveau?" I said, seizing the opportunity.

"Yes, yes," was the reply. "Married – with seven daughters."

And suddenly the floodgates of personal biography were opened and over the next few hours I learned everything about him.

He had been for many years an official in the Post Office at Lille. The work was, of course, uncongenial to him but as the head of a large family he had unavoidable responsibilities. His consolation was literature. He read voraciously and incessantly. The years passed. Six of his seven daughters were married He was approaching the time when he would be able to retire upon pension. Then – but let him tell the story in his own words. (I remember them with perfect clarity.)

"I was in Roubaix, on official business, waiting for the train that would take me back to Lille, reading a translation of Shakespeare's *Hamlet*, when it came to me in a flash that this play, so vastly admired, so promiscuously quoted, was nothing but twaddle! An over-written, pseudo-poetical melodrama of complete absurdity! My train arrived. I meditated further upon this revelation. By the time I reached home I had come to the conclusion that every word of every book I had ever read was utter tripe. I awoke next morning knowing exactly what I must do with the years remaining to me. I must devote every waking moment to the composition of a novel that would be truly worthy both of the infinite complexity of human character and of the noble measures of the French language."

He could not, of course, proceed with this plan immediately. Practical necessities made it imperative to wait until his retirement. This occurred two years later. The interim had not been wasted. Every moment of leisure had been devoted to research for the great work. His pension secured, his research complete, he began to write. But he found it impossible to concentrate at home. "The din from the kitchen, the constant interruptions from my wife and daughter, the barking of the dog next door – these things drove me mad."

He came to an arrangement with his wife. He would

find a cheap *pension* in some out-of-the-way spot and stay there, living as economically as possible, until his novel was finished. His wife and daughter would remain in Lille. Two thirds of his pension would be remitted to them; he would subsist on the remaining third. A chance recommendation had led him to Danville and the *Pension Crique*, where he had been resident for the last fifteen years. Recently, his wife's health had begun to fail and the consequent medical expenses had obliged him to reduce his share of the family income quite drastically. He confessed, with the most disarming candour, that he was desperately short of money. I immediately offered him a loan – which he declined in the most dignified manner imaginable.

Next day, in lieu of my morning walk, I went to the market and lingered among the stalls until I caught sight of Madame Crique. My plan was to "bump into" her – seemingly by chance – then to accompany her on her walk home and by subtle questioning learn the full facts of Godiveau's financial position. But she instantly spotted me and forging her way through the crowds of shoppers, wielding her basket like a legionary's shield, she came up to me.

"Ah, Monsieur," she said. "What a happy chance that we should meet this morning. I was going to take the liberty of calling on you at Mme Pingret's. I think you have been sent by Providence to save poor, dear M. Godiveau." As we strolled together through the streets, she told me all. Godiveau owed her six months' board and lodging.

"What can I do, Monsieur? I don't know which way to turn. I have been as patient as I can with him but I'm not made of money and prices never seem to fall but always to rise. And he is ill, you know. He says nothing, but I can detect the signs. He works day and night. He never quits his room. If I ask him to leave, where will he go? He will die, Monsieur, and I will go to my own grave feeling that his blood is on my hands." Whereupon she burst into a flood of tears.

By the time we reached the *Pension*, my mind was made up. In the privacy of Madame Crique's sanctum, behind the dining-room, I paid up Godiveau's arrears and advanced a sum sufficient to see him through to the end of the year.

That evening, Godiveau approached my table with tears in his eyes. "What can I say? How can I thank you?" His voice quivered like a harp-string. I begged him to speak no more of the matter, indeed never to mention it again.

"Impossible, dear sir, impossible," he replied. "It must be regarded as a loan – a temporary loan – which I shall repay out of the large advance I expect to receive when my novel is finished. I can tell you – in the strictest confidence – that I am within sight of the end. A few weeks more and it will be done." Here the soup was served (a *velouté* of fresh vegetables, perfectly delicious) and I made so bold as to ask him a question that had been burning on my lips since our first meeting, but which my respect for him had prevented me from putting: namely, the subject or theme of his great work.

"That," he said, "is something I have never divulged to another living soul – not even to my wife."

He ate three or four spoonfuls of soup and I decided that to press this singular genius on the point would be an egregious lapse of taste. A moment passed, he wiped his moutachios with a napkin and said:

"However, in view of the extraordinary generosity you have shown towards me and of the nature of your character, with which I have had the honour of acquainting myself these past few days, and which I judge to be completely honest, upright and sincere, I will tell you that the subject of my novel – and it's title – is nothing less than –

THE DEATH OF CAESAR."

I have written these words in large capital letters in an attempt – feeble enough I admit – to reproduce not only the sonorous tone in which Godiveau spoke them (it had something of the swelling majesty of a Cathedral organ) but also to convey a sense of my own feelings upon first hearing them. I was completely overwhelmed.

"But that, that–" I stammered, "is – immense. Superb. Extraordinary."

Once again, the floodgates of Godiveau's eloquence were opened and in the next four or five hours, during which he paused only to eat, drink and smoke, it was my privilege to hear, from the lips of the author himself, the intimate conception of a masterpiece. I wish I could reproduce here the complete flow of Godiveau's discourse. But night is falling. Time presses. I cannot refrain, however, from quoting the following:

"There are three scenes only: Caesar's final farewell to Cleopatra; the walk to the Senate; the assassination itself. But into these scenes I have compressed a life, an Empire, a world!"

Over the next two weeks we dined together every night. We talked of nothing but his novel. It was enthralling. One memory (the final one, alas) stands out as clear as the street lamp opposite this window. There was a full moon. It seemed to light up Godiveau as an actor upon a stage.

"Caesar knew of the plot against him, knew every detail of it," he declaimed. "Of course he did. Nothing happened in Rome without his knowledge. Why then did he go to the Senate that morning? Why? Because he had achieved everything that a mortal man can achieve. He had won glorious victories, conquered nations, amassed incalculable wealth and power – my God he had even mastered time by instituting a new calendar. *There was nothing left for him to do!* Except one thing. To die in such a manner as would echo down through the centuries and thus ensure that the name of Caesar would never perish!" He lifted his balloon glass as if in a toast to Diana,

Goddess of the Moon.

In the early hours of the following morning, an incessant ringing of the bell brought me out of slumber, bed and bedroom to find my Aunt, in her night-clothes, advancing along the passage, wielding a brace of duelling-pistols.

"Revolution!" she cried. "I've been expecting it! There was an article about the Syndicalists in the *Revue Politique* last week!"

I volunteered to go to the gate myself (an act my Aunt considered heroic) but found only Madame Crique, in a state of extreme agitation, though not tearful.

"He is gone!" she cried. "Poor Monsieur Godiveau is gone!"

As we hastened to the *Pension*, she described how, less than half an hour earlier, a great thump on the floor of the room above her own (Godiveau's) had woken her. The thump was followed by a sound like the drumming of feet. She had risen quickly and rushed upstairs. On getting no reply to her knock, she had opened the door with her pass-key and found Godiveau lying stone dead on the floor.

As I entered Godiveau's room, the first object that caught my eye (I confess it here) was not the body of my poor friend, still lying on the floor, covered with a sheet, but the vast pile of manuscript stacked neatly on the small table in the corner. *The Death of Caesar!* By a supreme effort of will-power I wrenched my eyes away from that magnetic sight and managed to attend to the immediate business of sending for a doctor, informing the proper authorities, and calming the chamber-maid, who was inclined to hysterics.

More than three hours passed (during which the doctor confirmed that Godiveau had been carried off by an embolism and the body was removed to the Mortuary) before Madame Crique and I had the following conversation.

"A sad, sad business, Monsieur."

"Indeed, indeed. An immediate question arises, Madame, namely, who is to take charge of his manuscript?"

"Ah, but that's not the only question, Monsieur. Who's to pay for his funeral? I'm sure I can't afford to."

"Naturally, I will pay for it."

"There'll be other expenses, too."

"I will attend to them."

"And who's to write to his wife?"

"I will undertake that melancholy task. On the matter of the manuscript—"

"Does it have any value, do you think?"

"Until a publisher agrees to buy it, none at all."

"You are a publisher, of course."

"In any case, the rights in the work belong to his heirs – his wife and daughters."

"Yes. That's a point. Why don't you look after it, Monsieur?"

"If you have no objection."

"No, no. None at all." And there and then she gave me the loan of a basket to carry the prize home to my Aunt's.

I went straight to my room. My first action was to turn to the last page and there I found written –

FINIS

So Godiveau had lived to complete his novel! With a trembling hand I then turned to the first page. I began to read. I read through the whole of that afternoon. As dusk fell, I lit a candle and continued to read. I read all night. As dawn broke I was still reading. By noon, I had finished. I had read the whole of it!

Dizzied by the overwhelming power and beauty of Godiveau's work, I walked to the beach and swam in the sea. Still in a state of rapture, I returned to the *rue Jean-Baptiste*, where to my astonishment I found my Aunt sitting in the hall (a chair had been un-sheeted for the purpose) waiting for me. I quickly learned the cause of this unprecedented break in her routine. She had discovered, via the maid, that I had consumed a whole candle in a single night. It took me some time, first, to persuade her that I had not gone mad and, second, that I could well afford to defray the expense of the candle. This went some way towards soothing her disordered nerves.

That afternoon I wrote to Mme Godiveau, informing her of the tragic loss of her husband, of the date, time, and place of the funeral and offering to act as her agent in the sale of *The Death of Caesar*. Two days later I received a reply from the daughter informing me that Mme Godiveau was far too ill to travel, that she herself would be prevented from attending her father's obsequies by her duties towards her mother and agreeing that I should attempt to find a publisher for the novel.

A few days later, after poor Godiveau's funeral, which was attended by myself, Mme Crique, the waiter and the chamber-maid (in paroxysms of grief) I bade my Aunt farewell and returned to Paris.

My marriage, which had been postponed by my illness, now took place and was celebrated in a style and manner suitable to the fortune of the Griffonet family. No less than four hundred people sat down to the dinner. M. Patapier made an eloquent speech which was received (most suitably) in the silence of awe.

It was not until I returned from my honeymoon, which was spent in the Solange, and to my professional duties, that I had time to consider the matter of Godiveau's masterpiece. It seemed obvious that *Junod et Frères* should publish it and to that end I gave the manuscript to my colleague, Alain Perçoux. Some days later, he entered my office, Godiveau's manuscript in his hand, tears still fresh upon his cheeks.

"Ah," I said, "the tragic power of the ending has affected you as it affected me."

"Tragic power?" the wretch exclaimed. "My dear

fellow, it is the most ridiculous, prolix, preposterous farrago of nonsense I ever read! I mean to say–" here he spluttered with an almost hysterical sort of laughter "– Caesar's last speech to Brutus. It – it – it goes on for over fifty pages when the whole world knows that all he said was '*Et tu Brute!*'" Fresh laughter overwhelmed the creature. I began to be incensed. "His descriptions," Perçoux continued. "One loses count of the adjectives. There are whole dictionaries of them! His dialogue, with its 'thou's' and 'thee's' and other absurd archaisms! Unreadable! As to the story itself – three scenes with over five hundred pages apportioned to each? It's ludicrous."

By this time I was in the grip of an ungovernable rage. The word "ludicrous" was the final spur to my fury. I snatched up a paper-knife, rushed at Perçoux and stabbed him to the heart.

My father told me later that had the swine not been wearing a particularly thick waistcoat, I might have inflicted a serious injury. "And then, my boy, it would have cost me a pretty penny to hush it all up. As it is, young Perçoux has agreed to forget the matter for a small consideration and my old friend Junod has very decently agreed to accept your resignation instead of dismissing you on the spot, as he intended. Nothing will appear in the papers. I've seen to that. I reckon the time has come for you to join me at the Works and learn the printing business."

I think it more than probable that I would have accepted my father's offer and returned Godiveau's manuscript to his widow and daughter had it not been for my beloved wife. She had [*three words indecipherable*] decided to read *The Death of Caesar* herself. A little time after the events described above, as we were sitting down to dinner in the apartment we had taken near my parents' house, she confessed this to me, adding, with a vibrancy I find it hard to describe, that the book was unquestionably a great work of literature.

"But of course," she said, "in these days of crass commercialism, you'll never find a publisher willing to take it. Look at what happened to *Particularités*. Universally rejected. Why? Because it breaks the mould, assails new barriers, scales new heights. No, if *The Death of Caesar* is to reach the reading public – and it *must* – we have no alternative but to publish it ourselves."

So was born the famous publishing house of *Fougard et Griffonet*.

The practicalities of launching this enterprise presented few difficulties. The financial settlements that had been made upon our marriage provided us with a sufficient capital, the whole of which we were prepared to sink into the business. There was, happily, no question of starting a family. My dear wife had a complete horror of children. Even the sight of a nursemaid wheeling a perambulator in the Luxembourg gardens made her feel quite faint and ill.

I wrote to Mme Godiveau, offering a generous advance and a handsome scale of royalties. I received a reply from her legal man saying that his client, having consulted widely among her family, preferred an outright sale of the copyright. The price asked was pretty stiff but Irène and I were in perfect agreement that to haggle over it would be to dishonour ourselves and the memory of poor Godiveau.

Three years later, as all the world knows, *The Death of Caesar* was published in two handsome duodecimo volumes, with coloured illustrations by the famous artist Barbouillet, an intimate friend of M. Patpapier. And, as the world also knows, it fell victim to a monstrous conspiracy by a cabal of reviewers led by that unconscionable viper A. Perçoux. Only M. Patpapier himself, writing in *Les Ruelles Litéraires*, gave the novel the accolade it deserved, hailing it (I quote) as "beyond the powers of your reviewer to describe." But even this encomium failed to generate any sales and we were forced to withdraw almost the whole edition.

I fully admit that this debacle shattered my spirits. My

wife, however, was cut from finer cloth. "There can be no doubt," she declared, "about the greatness of the work itself. Reviewers and so-called literary journalists are nothing but a set of self-serving liars and slanderers. Remember what they wrote about *Particularités*. Yet we must face the fact that the general public has been entirely indifferent to the book, in spite of the fortune we have spent in advertisements. Why? Because they know almost nothing of Roman history. It isn't the fashion. People regard it as obscure, difficult and irrelevant. We must change that. We must create the climate in which *The Death of Caesar* will be able to flourish."

"But how?" I remember exclaiming.

"We will commission the leading academics in the subject to produce a complete history of Rome from Romulus and Remus to, let us say, the Reformation. I estimate that it would run to twenty volumes."

I was aghast at the boldness and brilliance of this plan – but somewhat perplexed as to how it was to be financed, since our losses on *The Death of Caesar* had been heavy and we had been forced to reduce our household to six living-in servants. I decided to apply to my father. I was about to approach him when tragedy struck our family.

My mother, who had been greatly upset by the hostile reception afforded to *The Death of Caesar*, came to me in a state of extreme agitation and distress and revealed to me that my father was having an affair with the cook – the same cook I had once suspected of trying to poison me. "We all thought you had imagined it," my mother said, with heartrending sobs. "But I now see that you were right all along."

I immediately confronted my father.

"My dear boy," he said, with a bellow of laughter, "look at her. Legs like a Charentais bullock and a pimple on her nose that would stop a stag in the rutting season. And in any case, I have dismissed her."

I was somewhat reassured by this and persuaded my

mother to return to the family home, intending to broach the subject of a loan with my father when the domestic waters were in a calmer state. But only a week later my mother, having found out the place of the cook's new employment, attempted to attack her with her sewing scissors. Fortunately, the assault was prevented by other servants. Professor Decoin was consulted and advised that my mother should spend a few weeks of rest and retirement at our country house, accompanied by some specialist nurses.

What happened next remains a profound mystery. My own theory is that my dear mother, through some slight misunderstanding of Professor Decoin's recommendations, was under the impression that regular bathing would speed her recovery as it had once aided my own. In any case, early one morning, before dawn, she went down to the lake, broke up the ice with an axe (it was mid-winter) and entered the water. A few hours later she was found [*two lines indecipherable*].

It was not until well after the funeral that I felt I could discuss the matter of the loan with my father. Imagine my horror, therefore, when, less than two months after that melancholy event, he announced his engagement to a Vaudeville actress called Natalie Plairage, a woman thirty years his junior. It was too great an outrage against the memory of my beloved mother to be forgiven or forgotten. All communication between us ceased.

My dear wife and I now faced a very uncertain financial future – but faced it, I think I may confidently say, with courage. We reduced our household further – to a mere three living-in servants – and set about devising further economies. Then the same Providence that had led me to the discovery of Godiveau's masterpiece intervened a second time. A great-uncle of my wife's, a M. de Marlièvre, a bachelor who had, owing to ill-health, resided in an Institution in Switzerland for many years, suddenly died. Irène's share of his estate was enough not only to restore our domestic situation to a reasonable degree of comfort but to enable us to commission our Roman history. The expenses of this were formidable but we never wavered in our determination to carry out our grand design – and in the back of my mind there always lingered the possibility that Mme Pingret might mention me in her Will.

My dear Aunt did eventually die and she did remember me! She bequeathed me the portraits of Napoleon III and the Empress Eugénie. The residue of her estate (some twenty-three million francs) was left in Trust, the income to be added to the capital, until the return of the Bonaparte dynasty, whereupon the accumulated funds would become the property of the restored Emperor.

The publication of the Will caused a sensation and provoked this vile Republican government of ours into contesting it. My Aunt's Trustees approached me and invited me – as the only other legatee – to join with them in a counter-suit, assuring me that if we were successful, as they had no doubt we would be, I would be entitled to a half share in – but I hear the clock of the *Mairie* strike four. I must hurry. Briefly, then, the litigation over my Aunt's Will dragged on year after year. Confident of a successful outcome, I borrowed heavily to complete the Roman History, now running to some thirty volumes. A warehouse was rented to store the books as they were delivered from the binder because we were convinced (I remain convinced) that to publish piecemeal would be to dilute the effect upon the public. Then, three days ago, the case was finally settled. The Republicans were utterly defeated. The Trustees and I triumphed. But it was a Pyrrhic victory. Almost the whole fortune amassed by M. Pingret during his lifetime, and doubled by my shrewd old Aunt after his decease, had been swallowed up in the expenses of the case. There was nothing left. We were ruined.

I now come to the most painful part of this narration.

The night before last my beloved wife [*five lines indecipherable*] and so perished in the conflagration.

Enough. The clock strikes the half hour. Soon it will be dawn.

A little later. I have placed Godiveau's divine manuscript in the empty grate. The match waits only to be lit. I have robed myself in the toga. The laurel wreath is about my head. The bottle of Bordeaux is uncorked, the olive oil is to hand. When the deed has been done I will have accomplished everything. There will be nothing more for me to do in this life. I will go, like my namesake, to where my friends and my enemies await me, to that great Senate called the sea.

[Signed] César Fougard, the Ides of July (his month.)

*

Editor's note: César Fougard's manuscript was discovered by a chambermaid in the Royal Suite of the *Grand Hotel Atlantic* in Danville-sur-Mer on the morning of 15th July, 1889. By the evening of the same day it became clear that M. Fougard had gone missing. The police were called. They made a careful examination of the suite. In the fireplace they found traces of a mixture of ashes, wine and olive oil. Two days later, a body was washed up on the coast three miles south of Danville. It was naked except for a purple-coloured Roman-style toga. A day later, children playing on the beach at Danville discovered a wreath made of laurel leaves entwined in a piece of wire. The body was later identified by M. Paul Fougard as that of his son, César.

M. Paul Fougard was able to inform the authorities that on the night of 13th July, 1889, M. César Fougard's wife, Irène (neé Griffonet), had perished in a fire at a warehouse in Paris. An investigation into the tragedy was still under way but it was already clear that Mme Fougard had started the fire deliberately, using methylated spirits, and had immolated herself in the flames. The warehouse had contained over one hundred thousand copies of a thirty-volume history of Rome that was about to be published.

An autopsy was performed on César Fougard's body. The stomach was found to contain a mass of undigested paste consisting of ashes, red wine and olive oil.

Certain parts of M. Fougard's narrative (published here for the first time) were rendered indecipherable by the author's tears. The passages are indicated by square brackets.

During the preparation of this collection, my collaborator, Michel Walrangis, came across a copy of Godiveau's *The Death of Caesar* in a second-hand bookshop in Paris. He bought it for €10 and e-mailed me as follows: "I think it must be a review copy and judging from its condition (pristine) has never been read. I HAVE read it (though not quite as fast as Fougard!) and I think it's rather marvellous. I've sent a photocopy to an old friend who teaches 19th century French Literature at the Sorbonne."

About two months later Michel forwarded me his friend's response: "I agree. The novel is amazing. Godiveau was at least half a century ahead of his time. That was obviously the problem. This is the James Joyce of *Ulysses* and *Finnegan's Wake* – only better. I passed the photocopy on to my colleague, as discussed. I attach his response."

The attachment read: "Better than Joyce? Certainly. But who, in his right mind, could be bothered to wade through Joyce?"

The hunt is now on for a copy of Irène Griffonet's *Particularités*.

STOP PRESS! Six months ago, a friend of mine was browsing in a bookshop in Hay-on-Wye when she came

across a battered volume of the late 19th century called
The Divine Afflatus in France by Rev. Humphrey
Masham-Gore. Aware of the project I was working on, she
plucked the book from the shelf and turned to the index.
There, to her astonishment and delight, she found the
entry: GRIFFONET, Irène. She rang me immediately on
her mobile phone and read out the poem reproduced below
and Rev. Masham-Gore's translation. Two days later the
book itself was in my hands. And a very strange book it is.
Privately published in 1897, it is basically an anthology of
French poetry, from the *troubadours* to the late 19th
century, with translations by the author, interspersed with
short essays – called "Musings" – on subjects as diverse
and peculiar as the drinking habits of Francois Villon and
the Siege of Perpignan, during which the 16th century
poetess Louise Labé apparently dressed up as a man and
rode into battle in the Dauphin's army. Rev. Masham-
Gore's selections can best be described as quaint. Among
the troubadours, for instance, there is far too little of
Bernart, far too much of Cercamon and nothing at all of
Marcabru. In the section devoted to the Renaissance
Pléiade we get acres of Pontus de Tyard but only a small
patch of Ronsard. The translations are idiosyncratic to say
the least. Here is the Rev's rendering of perhaps the best
known and loved lines in all French poetry, the opening
stanza of *Sonnets Pour Helene Book II: XLIII* by Ronsard.

Quand vous serez bien vielle, au soir, à la chandelle,

Assise aupres du feu, devidant et filant,

Direz, chantant mes vers, en vous esmerveillant:

Ronsard me celebroit du temps que j'estois belle.

When you are full of years and spin and twine

Your wool at eventide, by candle-light, beside the
chimney's flame,

With wonder, as my verses you recite, breathe out my
name

And say: 'Twas Ronsard sang me then, when beauty still
was mine.

When it comes to Irène Griffonet's poem, *Quatre-Temps*,
the Rev. really lets himself go, in effect fleshing out a
whole new poem on the admittedly very bare bones of the
original. One wonders whether "reading between the
lines" has ever been taken further. In spite of his heroic
efforts the poem remains more or less incomprehensible.
Maddeningly, he is silent about where and how he
discovered the poem and tells us nothing about its author.

IRÈNE GRIFFONET

1847-1889

Quatre-Temps	*Ember Days*
Ô Quatre-Temps! Ô usurpation!	Ember days usurp the throne of life
Ô ébranlement! Ô lacération!	Unhinging reason, cutting like a knife!
Ô larmes! Ô écœurement!	Tears fall, the heart near breaks
Ô pénitence!	Until the soul repentance takes
Ô recueillement!	In contemplation.
Ô entonner! Ô transvaser!	Then joyous song strike up, pour wine,
Ô endurer! Ô nuancer!	Endure: sweet Nature's subtle shades are thine!

Ô transcender! Ô inverser!	Upon the high clouds ride, turn back the tide!
Ô oasis!	Water and date palm in a waste of sand
Ô nudité!	Is all the nakedness of this thy land!

I cannot resist adding a note about Rev. Masham-Gore himself. Born in 1863, the son of a Hampshire squire, educated at Winchester and Oxford, he was ordained in the Church of England in 1888, served as curate at St. Barnabus, Wiching-under-Blean, 1889-1894, and became Vicar of St. Anne's, South Hoxton in 1895. An extreme Anglo-Catholic and one of the early promoters, with Lord Halifax and Revd. H.J. Fynes-Clinton, of the Anglican Papalism movement, Masham-Gore hit the headlines in 1913 when he held an outdoor procession of the Blessed Sacrament through his parish, with young girls strewing the streets with flowers. Low Church outrage forced the Bishop of London to place St. Anne's under episcopal ban. In 1919, Masham-Gore "swam the Tiber" and became a Roman Catholic. He died in Biarritz in 1937, though in what circumstances, curious or otherwise, I have, alas, been unable to discover.

ALPHONSE ALLAIS

OBITUARY

It was with great sorrow and a sense of irretrievable loss that the public learned of the sudden decease of the celebrated humorist, M. Alphonse Allais, which melancholy event occurred on 28th October, in Paris. M. Allais was fifty-one years old. Born on 20th October 1854, at Honfleur, the son of a pharmacist, M. Allais ... but no, sorry Mr Editor, I cannot go on in this pompous style. I'll have Allais himself turning in his grave, or at least writhing in sardonic laughter and regular readers of this publication storming the bookstalls and demanding their cash back. It is, of course, an honour (well, there's no money in it) to write this tribute to an old and dear friend but I must do it in my own way and in a manner appropriate to its subject. Besides, as one of the last of his circle to see Allais alive and certainly the first to learn of his death, I am in a position to reveal certain details about his passing that by no stretch of the imagination (except perhaps that of Allais himself) could be included in a conventional obituary notice but which, I trust, will intrigue and even amuse devotees of the great man's unique brand of wit and fancy and go some way towards consoling them in their distress at his premature departure from the scene. Plus there is a surprise bonus at the end (absolutely free of charge).

Unfortunately the Editor has insisted that the usual biographical information should be included and since I, my wife, my numerous children and various mistresses are

almost entirely dependant on commissions from him, I
have no alternative but to comply. I know, I know, the
temptation to skip this bit and make a beeline for the
delights that await you over the page is overwhelming, but
I am relying on your natural honesty and good taste, Dear
Reader(s), to fortify you in resisting it.

Well then, it was always said of Allais (for date of birth
etc. see above) that he did not speak one word until he was
three years old, leading his parents to assume that he was
dumb. I once asked him about this. He said it was perfectly
true and explained that he had simply been biding his time
until he had something amusing to say. "Since children
generally have to wait until they're at least eight to
develop a sense of humour," he added, "you will
appreciate that I was extraordinarily precocious." When I
inquired if he could remember the joke that initiated a
lifetime of loquaciousness and comic fantasy, he replied
that the consumption of alcohol over many years had
drawn a veil (green) over the distant past but that he had a
vague recollection that it had to do with catfish.

Allais's father (a pharmacist in case you have already
forgotten) was keen that his son should follow him in his
profession and sent him to study in Paris. There, the young
Allais immediately and without hesitation fell joyous prey
to the allurements of the big city, abandoned his studies
and gravitated to the famous Montmartre cabaret *Le Chat
Noir*, of hallowed memory, where he wrote monologues
and performed his own sketches. But it was when the late
M. Rodolphe Salis, proprietor of *Le Chat Noir*, launched
the humorous paper of the same name, that Allais found
his true, if precarious, path in life, contributing the
hilarious pieces that rapidly established him as the
foremost comic writer of his day. When *Le Chat Noir* ran
out of lives and vanished from the stalls, Allais went on to
write for *Le Journal, Le Sourire* (of which he improbably
became chief editor) and many other magazines, including
this one. It would be tedious to list the number and variety

of his works (some 1680 stories, many collected into single volumes, verse plays, poetry, novels – you see I told you it would be tedious so let's stop.)

But Allais's fame does not rest solely on his journalism. He was an inventor. Among the ingenious contrivances to emerge from his fertile brain readers (congratulations on staying the course, by the way) may recall the frosted glass aquarium for shy fish; the necromobile, a vehicle designed to cremate the dear departed en route to the funeral, the engine being powered by the heat from the fire; and an inspired means of collecting blackmail money by homing pigeon.

He was also a painter of note, one of the first to exhibit in the *Salon Des Incohérents*, of which he was a leading light. If I may be permitted to jog your memories again – thank you – the *Salon* was founded in 1882 by the late M. Jules Lévy (everybody in this obituary seems to be dead) in response to complaints by the leading art critics that modern painters like Manet (dead), Gauguin (dead) and Monet (alive! hurrah!) no longer knew how to paint. Anybody was entitled to submit works to the Salon on condition that they could prove beyond a shadow of doubt that they had received no training in art whatsoever and that they avoided any subject that could be remotely conceived of as serious. In the first year, Allais exhibited a ground-breaking composition, a large, rectangular canvas painted entirely black and entitled *Negroes Fighting In A Cave At Night*. In later years he followed up this triumph with, among others, a completely red canvas, *Apoplectic Cardinals Harvesting Tomatoes By The Red Sea* and another, wholly white, *Anaemic Young Girls Going to First Communion Through A Blizzard*.

And I would remind those solemn literary gentlemen who are inclined to dismiss Allais's *oeuvre* as too ephemeral and light-hearted to earn him a place among the immortals of French literature, that he was in the vanguard of an important development in poetry, namely the holorhyme, a form of verse in which all the words in one line rhyme with all the words in the following line. I cannot refrain from quoting one of his couplets, in fact make that a couple of couplets:

> *Par les bois du djinn où s'entasse de l'effroi,*
>
> *Parle et bois du gin ou cent tasses de lait froid.*

And the even more sublime:

> *Alphonse Allais de l'âme erre et se f--- à l'eau.*
>
> *Ah ! l'fond salé de la mer ! Hé ! Ce fou ! Hallo.*

We now come to the events surrounding Allais's death. He had spent the summer, as usual, in his native Normandy, at Honfleur, with his wife and daughter. In early October he returned, alone, to Paris to consult his doctor, while his family proceeded to a resort in Belgium, where he was to join them.

Rumours had been circulating for some time about the poor state of Allais's health but it was not a subject he ever cared to discuss among his friends and certainly not one that any of his friends would have cared to broach with him. He had once famously declared that the only occasion on which it was permissible to mention the subject of health was in the act of raising a glass. On his return to Paris, however, word got out that he was staying at the Britannia Hotel, in the rue d'Amsterdam, opposite the *gare St. Lazaire*, confined to bed on doctor's orders and unable to receive visitors.

I must confess that many of us, myself included, thought that this was probably one of his elaborate jokes because it is well known that Britannia (England) was one of his favourite targets for satire. You must remember the article in which he first revealed that the English, having mined so much coal and other minerals in their lust for wealth, had rendered their island so light that it had actually begun to float and was drifting towards America. In a further scoop, he informed the French public of the dastardly means by which the English had sought to rectify the situation: persuading other nations to invest in undersea telegraph cables whose true purpose was not, as perfidiously claimed, to improve communications between Continents but in fact to serve as mooring ropes. In a final burst of patriotism he warned the authorities that in the event of war the English would be able simply to 'slip their cables' and using their powerful Navy as tugs, tow the island to safety. When the French invasion fleet arrived it would find itself floundering helplessly in the maelstrom thus created.

The idea that it was all a joke seemed to be confirmed when, on Friday night, 27th October (but I forget the exact time) Allais appeared in the *bistrot*, where a whole crowd of us was gathered as usual, smoking, drinking and debating such profundities as the minimum amount required to buy a concierge's silence and the maximum amount per line to be extracted from editors. Allais looked perfectly well, or at least as well as he ever looked, which was not particularly well, and launched almost immediately into an account of the latest exploits of his friend Captain Cap, the Canadian seafarer. The civil war currently raging in the South American republic of Santo Pecado, was not, he told us, a struggle between Right and Left as was being widely and falsely reported in the press. The whole thing had been fomented by Captain Cap. It seems that on a brief visit to the capital, Ciudad Muladar, the Captain had been arrested and fined two pesos for spitting in the street. Outraged by what he considered a gross miscarriage of justice, he had appealed to the High Court and on losing the case decided that the appeasement of his wounded pride and restoration of his honour required nothing less than the fall of the Government. As to whether the Government in question was of the Right or the Left, Allais confessed that he was hazy, excusing himself on the eminently rational grounds that in politics it is almost impossible to tell your left from your right (and vice versa) and that the left hand never knows what the right hand is doing (and versa vice.) In any case, the Captain had proceeded to the docks where, with fiery speeches and the free distribution of even fierier rum, he had succeeded in stirring up a Naval mutiny. This had escalated into a general uprising during which, from the balcony of a first class hotel, the Captain had watched the rebels burn the Palace of Justice, raising his glass at each burst of leaping flame.

With an elevation of his own glass, Allais retired to the small table in the corner where he scribbled away industriously at his latest story. This was so much part of his routine that, in spite of the absence of the usual printer's devil waiting anxiously to rush the completed work to the presses, we concluded that the rumours of ill-health were indeed part of one of the elaborate hoaxes for which he was celebrated. So much so that when he returned to our table one of the bolder spirits taxed him with it directly. Allais shook his head.

"Tomorrow," he said, "I will be dead." There was a roar of laughter. "You laugh," he said, with another shake of his head, "but I'm not laughing. Tomorrow I will be dead." This only provoked further hilarity. For some reason, perhaps because I was laughing the loudest, he turned to me and said: "Come to the Hotel Britannia tomorrow morning and I bet you ten francs that you'll find me dead."

"Done!" I replied.

Allais bowed and without another word quit the *bistrot*, leaving us to discuss what wonderful twist to the tale would be revealed on the morrow.

The following day, Saturday, I rose at crack of dawn, in other words at about eleven o'clock and proceeded to the Hotel Britannia. I hope you won't mind if I insert a few dashes here as I need a moment to gather myself before carrying on – – – – – thank you, I feel so much better. Where was I? Oh yes. The Hotel Britannia. I ascended to the first floor and was approaching Allais's room when the door opened and four undertakers' assistants emerged, carrying a coffin. They were followed by the hotel manager who informed me that M. Allais was dead. At this point I was still convinced that this whole scene had been arranged as part of the hoax. It was only when I entered the room itself, expecting Allais to burst out of a cupboard, perhaps, or from under the bed, but instead discovering that most eminent of medical men, Dr Belin, actually making out the death certificate, that I was forced to the tragic conclusion that Allais had indeed died – of a pulmonary embolism, Dr Belin informed me. He went on to confide in me that Allais had recently consulted him, that he had diagnosed phlebitis [*une phlébite*] and ordered bed-rest and strict abstinence from alcohol [*le repos absolu au lit et le regime sec.*] Then, with a sigh, followed by a little laugh, he handed me some sheets of paper covered in Allais's flowing hand. I recognized the pages as those Allais had scribbled on, the night before, in the *bistrot*. I was holding in my hands the last story he ever wrote and its reproduction here is the surprise bonus promised earlier. I will take another breather and let you enjoy it.

THE WAGES OF SIN

A lady recently wrote to me complaining that I have done little or nothing in my career to raise the moral tone of the French Nation. In order to forestall any more presumptuous accusations of this sort, I offer a cautionary tale.

In a life dedicated to venality of every kind my old friend X. (no, Madame, I am not attempting to conceal the wretch's true name, it was Xavier) committed all seven of the Cardinal sins with a regularity unparalleled since the exploits of those Princes of the Church, in the Renaissance period, after which they were named.

His family, who were extremely pious, constantly predicted that his sins would be the death of him. Whenever, by means of some shady business deal, he added another million or so to his already enormous fortune they predicted that Avarice would be his downfall and that he'd end up bankrupt or in prison or preferably both. But he just got richer and richer.

He was eaten up with Envy. The sight of some man he considered better-dressed, better-looking or better-heeled than himself would drive him into a frenzy and the family circle consoled itself with the thought that if his financial malpractices didn't do for him he would certainly die of an apoplexy brought on by jealous rage. But nothing of the sort happened.

Never mind, they thought, if Avarice and Envy have let the side down, Wrath will surely do the trick. X. had the most ferocious temper. He made my friend Captain Cap look like a mystic in a nunnery. He spent half his life bellowing at cabmen, berating waiters, hurling furniture at servants and grossly insulting complete strangers in public. This led to innumerable duels, brawls, fisticuffs and riots, in one of which, the family reasoned, he would inevitably be killed. He never received a scratch.

Avarice, Envy and Wrath having all fallen at the first, they put their money on Lust. Surely, they argued, such a notorious adulterer and womaniser would fall victim either to an outraged husband or to an unmentionable disease. Well, it is true that a certain Count D'Ucoc, on learning that his Countess had spent a week with X. at Biarritz, emptied both barrels of his shotgun at him, but he missed completely, succeeding only in blasting off the head of a priceless sculpture of Athena that had been in his family for over six hundred years. It is also true that at one point X. did contract a disease that is certainly not mentionable in a respectable magazine like this. He was cured.

In increasing desperation the family pinned all their hopes on Gluttony. X. was certainly a glutton. He would often accept four or five invitations to dinners on the same night, eat them all, then look into a restaurant for a spot of supper before bed. Such monstrous over-indulgence would surely carry him off, they thought. Not a bit of it. He had the digestive system of a mastiff and the figure of a greyhound. I never once heard him so much as burp.

So far, they had not considered the sin of Sloth. Among the other runners, it seemed to be a complete outsider. The fact that X. never rose before noon, kept a servant whose sole duty was to put the sugar in his coffee and stir it and another to hold up his opera glasses when he went to the theatre was certainly scandalous but hardly posed a threat to his life or liberty. An idea that one day he would simply be too idle to go on breathing circulated briefly but was dismissed as fanciful.

The last hope thus rested on Vanity and indeed, outside politics and the stage, I never met a vainer man than X. There were more mirrors in his bedroom than in the Palace of Versailles. Wardrobes full of his clothes occupied a whole wing of his mansion in Paris. He had his teeth professionally polished and his moustache waxed at least three times a day. When his hair began to recede he spent a small fortune on restorative treatments, and when these all failed, employed a wig-maker full-time. When his eyesight weakened and he was prescribed spectacles he refused to wear them in public, with the result that he was constantly bumping into objects and people.

The final blow to his vanity came when he became hard-of-hearing and his doctors advised the use of an ear-trumpet. X. commissioned a trumpet from Fabergé but even though it was an object of rare beauty, encrusted with precious stones, he would use it only in conditions of the strictest privacy, among his most intimate friends and advisers. It was this that finally fulfilled the hopeful prophesies of his family.

He had spent the summer at his chateau on the Loire. The trumpet had accompanied him but, by some oversight, had been left for several weeks in one of the numerous summer-houses dotted about his estate. Wasps made a nest inside it and then buzzed off, leaving a body of wax in the interior. On his return to Paris, X., feeling unwell, made an appointment to see his doctor. He took the trumpet with him, unaware that the wax inside had rendered it useless. The doctor examined him and told him that he was suffering from phlebitis [*une phlébite.*] X. was somewhat puzzled that the doctor had felt it necessary to conduct a plébiscite in order to arrive at a diagnosis but the thought tickled his ever-active vanity. And he was delighted with the treatment prescribed: complete bed-rest and total abstinence from alcohol [*le repos absolu au lit et le regime sec,*] which he heard as *le pot d'absinthe à l'Ile de Ré et le sexe*. He departed immediately for the Ile de Ré where he engaged rooms – and a pretty little widow – in the best hotel and ordered a dozen bottles of absinthe. The ensuing exertions and potations killed him.

Phew! What a splendid story – Allais on top form – a prime example of how he would turn incidents in his life (or in this case his loss of it) into the stuff of his delightful fictions and the first and last posthumous work by the author of *Les Oeuvres Anthumes*!

I hope I may be forgiven for ending this obituary on a personal note. I owe Allais everything (plus ten francs.) When I first met him I was a penniless, unpublished author. Now, thanks largely to his efforts on my behalf, I am a published author – though still penniless, of course. "You certainly have talent, but talent doesn't necessarily lead to talents," he said to me on giving me my first commission.

What a shame it is that no manufacturer has been bold

enough to take up his idea of the necromobile. It would have been the perfect vehicle to convey that good-hearted master of comedy on his final journey.

WATER DIVINER

*

Editor's note: This obituary appeared in the November, 1905, edition of *Le Fou Rire*, a short-lived monthly humorous magazine, published in Paris, that folded a year later. It is clear from the December edition that many readers assumed that Allais had written it himself and readers of this collection could be forgiven for thinking that Alphonse Allais is a fictional character. In fact, he really existed and did indeed die in the Hotel Britannia of a pulmonary embolism in October, 1905, having predicted his own death in precisely the way described by his obituarist. The details of his doctor's diagnosis and prescription are also precise and it seems that Allais followed his advice scrupulously for about ten days until – one can only speculate – sheer boredom drove him from the Hotel Britannia to the company of his cronies in the *bistrot*. At the time there were persistent rumours that he had committed suicide and perhaps, in a sense, he did.

The details of his life and career are also strictly accurate. There was a *Salon Des Incohérents*, to which Allais contributed the paintings mentioned; he *did* invent the necromobile; the two couplets in holorhyme are from his pen.

The identity of "Water Diviner" remains a mystery. He was clearly a member of Allais's circle and his soubriquet, "*Sourcier*" in French, suggests that he was part of the hard-drinking group that called themselves, with deliberate irony, *Les Hydropathes*, meaning something like "the friends of water." It is fair to deduce, on the same principle, that "Water Diviner" was in the habit of cadging drinks.

Signing articles with a nickname was a fashion in the magazines of *fin-de-siècle* France but it means that the identities of the authors have mostly been forgotten. Allais himself has been almost wholly forgotten, which is astonishing given the fame he enjoyed during his lifetime and the supreme quality of his work. To some this will be proof of the old *canard*, promoted largely by the British, that the French have no sense of humour. They certainly had one during the *belle époque*, when Allais flourished, but his subsequent oblivion does perhaps support the idea that they must have carelessly mislaid it some time during the early 20th century.

"Water Diviner" consciously apes Allais's style, with asides to the reader, puns, and deliberate irrelevancies, even going so far as to adapt one of his mentor's most celebrated literary jokes: 'Do you mind if I open a bracket? It's getting rather stuffy in here.' The mention of *Les Ouevres Anthumes* may have had readers reaching for their dictionaries. "*Anthume*" is one of Allais's many neologisms, difficult to render into English, but meaning something along the lines of Ante-Posthumous, or indeed Anthumous, a reference to the still prevalent penchant of publishers to issue posthumous collections of an author's works. Allais published many collections, one of which was devoted to the adventures of his most famous protagonist, Captain Cap (allegedly a Canadian sea-captain called Albert Capron) to which he gave the title: *Captain Cap: His Life, His Ideas and His Cocktail Recipes*.

Recently, interest in Allais has revived in France (elsewhere he remains virtually unknown) with various websites devoted to him. One of the best is *Assocation des Amis D'Alphonse Allais*. Google him.

IGNACE MORDEUX

My predecessor as Bishop is generally regarded (in contrast, I imagine, to me) as having been pious, unworldly, even saintly. Only those who knew him intimately came to see that as well an authentic spirituality, centred on what I always thought was an excessive veneration of The Blessed Virgin, at times almost amounting to Collyridianism, he had a firm grasp of worldly affairs and a penetrating insight into human character. In some respects he did have the qualities of a Saint but then Saints have been some of the shrewdest, most determined, even ruthless servants of the Church, as is evident if one reads between the lines of the Lives. St. Teresa of Avila springs to mind, to say nothing of Loyola or Joan of Arc, so recently canonized by the late Pope, God rest his gentle soul. *Blessed are the peacemakers.*

A piece of advice the Bishop was wont to offer to his priests was never, if it could be avoided, to revisit parishes in which they had formerly served. No good could come of it, he said. If the place was in a more flourishing condition than heretofore, feelings of envy and self-doubt would arise. If, on the contrary, things had declined, there was the risk of what Schopenhauer calls *schadenfreude*. (In fact, the Bishop never used this useful word himself – I doubt if he knew it – but would quote the old proverb: *le malheur des uns fait le bonheur des autres*.) In either case, he cautioned, much spiritual damage could be caused and furthermore memories would inevitably be revived which, if pleasant, might engender an unhealthy nostalgia and if the opposite, a revival of thoughts and emotions best left in the shadow of the past.

Yesterday, I learned for myself the wisdom of that advice. In my own defence I must stress that I did not choose to return to Caubet. Circumstances conspired to give me no alternative.

The priest there, Father Malroix, had been my chaplain and his mother is one of my great friends as well as a generous friend to the Church. Upon hearing the sad but not entirely unexpected news of her son's death, I hastened to her house to offer her what consolation I could. I found her in a state of terrible distress. Amid her tears and barely coherent lamentations, two things impressed themselves on me: first, that she blamed herself – and to some extent me – for allowing her son to take up the cure of souls in Caubet – "That dungheap of a village," as she described it – and second, that she expected me to preside at the Exequial High Mass and interment. Assuming that poor Malroix would be laid to rest in the family vault and that therefore the Mass would be said in the Cathedral, I readily agreed. It would be an honour, I declared, and in an attempt to calm her and relieve her of the immediate agony of her grief, I turned the conversation towards practical matters. The Cathedral organist, I reminded her, was absent on a Retreat, but was due to return in a few days and in the meantime one could discuss what music – but there she stopped me. "No, no," she cried, "he's to be buried in Caubet." Evidently, I failed to conceal my dismay because she went on: "I know, I know, it's horrible but it's what he wanted. The last time I saw him he talked about it. It's in his Will."

So it was that yesterday I found myself being driven by my chaplain over abominable country roads to the remote village where I began my ministry over forty years ago. As the motor rattled and juddered and the suitcase, containing my vestments, jumped about on the back seat, I tried to concentrate my thoughts on what I would say about Vincent Malroix in my address.

The truth was that with his intelligence, education and

family background he could have looked forward to a distinguished career in the Church. He had the makings of a considerable theologian. But his faith was of that passionate, tormented kind that seems bent on some sort of self-immolation. As a boy, he had been consumptive and in his early twenties he was obliged to interrupt his studies in Rome and spend two years in a Swiss sanatorium. The parlous state of his health pointed towards academic study, centrally-heated houses and ready access to the best medical advice: he was clearly unsuited for the rough-and-tumble of parish life. For that reason I made him my chaplain. He performed his duties admirably but I was always aware of an underlying restlessness. Even so, I was amazed that when the parish of Caubet fell vacant he begged me for the appointment. I tried to reason with him but he insisted that God was calling him to this type of ministry – "*aux friches*" as he put it – and he spoke with a fervour that I recognized, having encountered it, without ever understanding it, in others during my steady rise through the hierarchy.

His zeal baffled me – but how could I raise up my own spiritual inadequacies as a barrier to his Christian journey? It would have been a crime against The Holy Ghost. I therefore agreed to send him to Caubet and then, with some relief I admit, departed to Rome, for the *Visitatio*, leaving my auxiliary to make the practical arrangements. In that way I was able to deal with his mother's protests and pleadings by correspondence rather than face-to-face. She is a formidable woman.

That was the truth. But how much of it could I tell? Not much, I decided. And after all, *Pilate saith unto him, What is truth?*

Caubet lies on a high ridge about one hundred kilometres north of the mountains. In summer, the heat masks the ragged line of peaks from view and when the air occasionally clears, and they appear, it is a sign that in two or three days rain will fall, depending on how close they seem to loom. In the autumn and winter months they are more frequently visible and provide a less accurate forecast of the weather. On a clear night in winter, when the moon is full and shines on the snow-clad pinnacles, the sight is so beautiful that people living in the plain toil up to the ridge to gaze at it.

Since it is October, and yesterday was clear and fine, we had caught glimpses of the range during the journey. But it was only when we turned off the main road and took the winding lane (still innocent of tarmacadam) up to Caubet that the mountains appeared in their full majesty, a glistening curtain of natural spires, crests and battlements stretched across the horizon. As we approached the village, I looked about me for signs of change. Apart from a stark stone memorial to the sons of Caubet lost in the Great War, there were none that I could see. A *paysan* was tilling his field with an ox-drawn plough. A young blacksmith was at work in the door of the forge. The tiny shop, in my day kept by Madame Maupas, was open and an ancient woman, who might have been Madame Maupas herself, was sitting on a stool outside, warming her bones in the brilliant sunshine. The houses, jostling along the single street, looked more patched-up and unkempt than ever, especially, I noted, the presbytery.

The little church stands at the far end of the village, almost on the edge of the escarpment. Opposite is the schoolhouse, built only ten years before I came to the village and, as I remembered it, fresh, clean and modern. Now it looked dilapidated and weather-stained, a grim testament, in flaking paint, cracked tiles and bulging stucco, to the creeping poverty and decay of rural France.

Madame Malroix's great, black Panhard was parked near the churchyard gate, along with three or four other motors belonging, I presumed, to members of the family. The gate itself, hanging askew, its iron bare and rusting in patches, emitted the same well-remembered squeak when my chaplain swung it open for me. We walked along the path that runs below the south wall of the church. To our left was the churchyard, its jumble of crosses, stones and monuments enclosed by low walls and beyond it, the immense vista across vineyards, plains, forests and rolling hills to the mountains. My chaplain stopped for a moment – as everybody does – to take it in. "What a view," he said. "The blessed dead must rest easily here." If only you knew, I thought, and had a sudden urge to go straight to the schoolmaster's grave and then to Ignace Mordeux's nearby. I resisted it. It would have looked very odd and in any case I would find an opportunity later.

As a young priest, I used to prepare my homilies meticulously, writing them out and often learning them by heart. All this changed, in '05, as a result of the infamous *Law of Separation of the Churches* and the State and the disorders that followed. I happened to be in Beaupréau, in the Mauges, when the Government sent troops in to enforce the expulsion of the seminarists. *They shall lay their hands on you, and persecute you.* In the circumstances I had no time to prepare a sermon and preached extempore. *Settle it therefore in your hearts, not to meditate before what ye shall answer: For I will give you a mouth and wisdom, which all your adversaries shall not be able to gainsay nor resist.* And in effect I found that the words came naturally to me and that my mind was able to formulate the flow of ideas into an orderly structure without conscious effort. My sermon that day was widely reported in the Catholic press – notably in *Le Corrrespondant, Le Sillon, L'Univers* and *La Croix* – and was, I later learned, discussed in the highest circles in Rome. The fact that no written text was available to be picked over by the authorities, civil or indeed ecclesiastical, was an advantage I was quick to appreciate and from that moment I entirely abandoned the practice of preparing my sermons, thus saving myself a good deal of time, trouble and effort. Of course, I look at the lectionary in advance and run over in my mind various appropriate themes but essentially I rely on the inspiration of the moment.

In the case of Victor Malroix's Mass it was that pause before entering the church and my chaplain's remark about the view that gave me my cue. I took my text from Isaiah, 52: *How beautiful upon the mountains are the feet of him that bringeth good tidings, that publisheth peace.* I proposed the mountains, clearly visible through the wide-open doors of the church, as a symbol of Christian faith, for most of us too often obscured by heat or storm, but in Malroix's case never veiled, perpetually in sight. After I had spoken, and as the Mass continued, I had an opportunity to assess how successfully he had been able to translate that faith into a revival of religious life in Caubet during the three and a half years of his ministry. The evidence was not encouraging. It was a thin congregation, mostly the elderly, very few young people, hardly the overflowing pews one would expect on such an occasion. Significantly, only two priests from neighbouring parishes were in attendance, in spite of the presence of the Bishop. (At the small reception afterwards in the presbytery, I gathered that Malroix's relations with his fellow clerics in the area had been dreadful.)

The fabric of the building itself showed signs of neglect – patches of damp on the walls, mildew on the canvas above the altar. The thurifer, a gangling youth, one of the Ricau tribe, had no idea what he was doing, constantly fumbled and had to be prompted to cense the congregation. The tide of secularism had clearly engulfed little Caubet and Malroix had been powerless to turn it aside. My mind drifted back to the events of '05 and '06 and the speech the dreadful Viviani made in the Chamber of Deputies. *We have bound ourselves to a work of anticlericalism, to a work of irreligion. We have extinguished in the firmament lights which shall not be rekindled. We have shown the toilers that heaven contained only chimeras.* There, in that forgotten corner of

France, Viviani, it seemed, had been the victor and Victor Malroix, the vanquished.

During the interment I had to summon up all my powers of concentration to perform the rite properly, so vividly did the mound of thick clay-earth beside the open grave remind me of former occasions.

All through the reception I was chafing to return to the churchyard and remember almost nothing of it apart from the dank, cheerless condition of the presbytery, the conversation with the two priests and the way Mme Malroix shuddered faintly and turned her head slightly away each time a member of the lower classes presumed to shake her gloved hand.

But at last the black Panhard rolled away and I was able to tell my chaplain that I wanted a moment of quiet reflection alone. The sexton had finished his work and departed during the reception, poor Malroix's grave was filled, and I had the churchyard to myself. I forced myself to walk slowly and by an indirect route to the simple headstone that marks the final resting-place of the schoolmaster. Time, wind and weather had somewhat eroded the cheap sandstone and the incised lettering was clogged with yellowish-grey lichen but still legible: ROMAIN BEZIAN 1856-1882. DIRECTEUR DE L'ECOLE DE CAUBET. The plot had not been tended for many years and weeds obscured the base of the stone. I squatted down and cleared them away and there it was, the inscription I had ordered the mason to add all those years ago: ET CXXI.

I rose and strolled to Mordeux's grave. It was in an even more neglected state than the other, the stone leaning and the lower part of it encrusted in ivy. A vertical crack ran through the name and dates: IGNACE MORDEUX 1815-1882.

I moved away and stood for a time by the wall. The *vendage* was over. The vineyards on the nearer slopes had already taken on their Autumnal hues of crimson, purple, brown and gold. In the hazy, fading light of late afternoon they looked like vast stained-glass windows. Beyond, I fancied I could make out the roof of old Mordeux's house. I felt a resolution forming in my mind, unbidden and beyond my ability to control, as a cloud materializing in a clear sky: I would look out the schoolmaster's journal and read it again.

As we drove away from Caubet, I wondered if this impulse would fade, but it didn't and as soon possible after the visit I felt obliged to make to Mme Malroix, I went to my private safe and took out Romain Bézian's dog-eared *cahier*. This, in spite of the fact that the palace and indeed Mme Malroix's dinner-table had been abuzz with the news of the march on Rome by the *fascisti*. Where my thoughts should all have been about the consequences of Mussolini's *coup* for the Holy See they were entirely taken up with the *cahier*. It lies on my desk as I write.

Why am I writing? Why do I feel compelled to tell a story which, if it were ever discovered, would gravely damage my reputation? My old Bishop was right, it is dangerous to revisit, I mean physically revisit, scenes of the past. Sights, sounds, smells are powerful keys in unlocking the casket of memory, which seems to be a sort of Pandora's box, once opened impossible to close. I hardly slept last night. No kind of mental effort could stop me from re-living those days and even when I drifted into a shallow doze, Bézian and old Mordeux invaded my dreams and became part of a ceaselessly flowing stream of uneasy retrospection. Am I attempting to exorcise their ghosts by writing? Or is it something else? Are these pages a form of Confessional? Is that what I need? I make my confession regularly to the Abbot but it is a calculated business, cleverly enough contrived to pass muster even with that wily old Father, but spiritually valueless. Is it my age? I am sixty-six, in excellent health, but the death, in January, of Pope Benedict, almost my exact contemporary, is a reminder that Judgement may not be not so far away.

And there must be some significance – but what? – in the fact that I have somehow slipped naturally into a way of telling the tale, with personal reminiscences, descriptions of character and place that would not be strictly germane to a bare account of the events but would certainly add essential colour and texture to a composition intended for publication. Yet I can never publish it.

In spite of this I still feel constrained to continue in the same style, and therefore, before inviting my imaginary and never-to-be public to read Romain Bézian's Journal, to provide certain introductory information.

First then, Bézian himself. He took up his post a year after I arrived in Caubet. We were about the same age, he attended Mass regularly, he lived alone in the schoolhouse as did I in the presbytery and it would have been natural if we had become friends. We never did. We saw each other frequently and our relations were cordial enough but there was never any real intimacy. He was supposed by many to be a young man of exceptional gifts but I failed to see it. His ambition was to be a writer and he would sometimes talk to me of his ideas. They seemed to me to be devoid of any originality. He was addicted to the poetry of Baudelaire, seduced by its polished outer surface, its mysticism, melancholy and cult of decadence but apparently oblivious to the terrifying nihilism that lies beneath or indeed to the conflicting religious sensibilities from which it springs. He claimed to be writing a novel in the style of *La Fanfarlo* (a very bad idea) and when he spoke of it I could tell that it would be shallow, derivative stuff. So far as I am aware he never actually penned a word of it. He saw himself as an intellectual but knew nothing of philosophy, which is my own passionate interest, though one I am forced to pursue very discreetly, since the works of virtually all the great philosophers – Kant, Locke, Spinoza, Nietzsche – are on the Index.

In appearance Bézian was unremarkable, of middling height, with sandy hair, worn quite short and in his dress he was thoroughly conventional. In other words there was nothing about him to suggest the Baudelairean – no flowing locks, fancy waist-coats, extravagant cravats. He came from the Charente, Barbézieux if memory serves, where his father kept a stationer's shop.

Within a few months of his arrival he met a girl called Louise Dulac, the daughter of the *notaire* in Charmeuil, the market town in the plain, and fancied himself to be in love with her. I once happened to encounter him in the lane near Mordeux's house, where he had been drinking *absinthe*, and he confided in me that he thought the affair was hopeless, owing to the father's implacable opposition. In Bézian's mind Maître Dulac was a tyrannical *paterfamilias*, uncultivated, coldly ambitious, interested only in money and position – in other words a character out of a cheap novel. In reality, Dulac, whom I knew quite well, was a very ordinary man, pleasant, friendly, unreflecting, with modest abilities and no greater ambition than to earn a comfortable living. As the Journal shows, Bézian was often invited to the Dulacs' spacious and agreeable house in the main square of Charmeuil so it is difficult to see where the schoolmaster got the idea that his beloved's father was such an immovable impediment to the course of true love. The truth is, perhaps, that Bézian was compelled to over-dramatize his own life in an attempt to turn its essentially prosaic quality into some sort of poetry.

This was also, I thought, the explanation for his friendship with Ignace Mordeux because once, when I asked him why he spent so many of his evenings with the old man, he replied: "But he's straight out of Baudelaire!" At the time I regarded this as nonsense but, as will become evident, I have been forced to revise that opinion.

Ignace Mordeux, a bachelor, lived in a large farmhouse to the south of the village, about a five-minute walk. He had been a horse-dealer, and was reputed to have made an enormous fortune from supplying the great cavalry depots of Tarbes, but by the time I knew him he had retired from that trade and taken to money-lending. As a result, he was universally detested, so much so that when he occasionally attended Mass several of my flock would ostentatiously refuse to come to the altar rail. That only made old Mordeux smile, with a sort of grim satisfaction. I think he was a natural misanthrope and actually enjoyed the way his neighbours shunned him. He lived alone except for a female servant – Jeanne – who was naturally assumed to be his mistress, though she was neither young nor beautiful. In fact she was extremely ugly as was Mordeux himself.

He was a short, thickset fellow, bald except for a line of grey fluff that ran from ear to ear round the back of his head. For a man of his age and breeding – he was well past sixty and of *paysan* stock – his teeth were surprisingly good, white and even, but with a Meerschaum pipe almost permanently clenched between them. His eyes were dark brown and deep-set and glittered with a mixture of scorn and cynical amusement. He said little – at least to me – but when he did speak, in the nasal accent of the region, it was invariably to make some disagreeable remark. Of Mme Maupas, at the shop, for instance, he once said: "She's a real prestidigitator with that scale of hers, adds a little bit of magic to every kilo!" – a reference to that lady's alleged skill in pressing on the scale when weighing goods. Or of Alban Ricau, a local farmer, known for his extravagance: "He's the type that pisses before he makes his water."

Extravagance was a fault of which nobody could accuse Mordeux himself. He dressed in shabby old clothes, drove himself about in an antiquated gig pulled by a raw-boned pony, spent little, except on tobacco and *absinthe*, gave nothing – in short, he was the complete miser. As to family, his parents were long dead, he had no brothers or sisters, but there were numerous cousins, with whom he would have nothing to do and whose expectations of a large inheritance were tempered by the thought that their horrible relation would doubtless devise some means of cheating them out of it.

There you have the two principal actors in the drama, Bézian and Mordeux, but before the narrative shifts to the former's Journal I should explain that in those days the practice of medicine in rural France was in a state of the most abysmal ignorance and incompetence. An event of the type about to be related was not uncommon in that era. In fact examples were so frequent that as a matter of course breathing-holes were drilled in the sides of coffins. I must add that the local doctor, Bouchard, whose practice was in Charmeuil, was notorious for his wrong diagnoses and misconceived treatments.

Journal of Romain Bézian – 13th – 18th October 1882

<u>Friday, 13th October, 11.30 pm</u>. Most extraordinary, unimaginable, grotesque, phantasmagorical day of my life. Nothing like it to be found in any fiction, not in Maupassant, not even in Poe. Must note details – plot of novel that will make my name. Learned of Ignace M's death (!!!) during mid-morning break, news brought by Maupas boy, delivering bread and stew. IM found by Jeanne drowned in pond, Dr. B summoned, IM pronounced dead. Immediate thought, must have been drunk – M boy thought same – then – strange end for such a unique character, so little understood by these thick-headed peasants. M boy speculating on size of inheritance for cousins – typical brute cupidity. Overheard two lads – IM's relations – discussing same, cuffed them both – little barbarians. After school to the curé who confirmed all, said undertaker from Charmeuil summoned by IM's cousin (Paul G), funeral arranged for tomorrow. I said – indecent haste. Curé said Paul G in charge of all arrangements. Decided to finish correcting before going to IM's to pay last respects. 7 pm walked to IM's. Stopped by pond, thought again how strange. Dipped hand in water –

cold, cold, cold. Light showing in kitchen window, knocked on door, no answer. All very still, silent, strange. Opened door. Jeanne in chair by fire, dead drunk, snoring. Absinthe. Took candle, went upstairs – first time ever in that house – saw candle-light in bedroom. Coffin on trestles by bed with candles at head and foot and saw to surprise and anger that coffin already closed. Put candle down on table, fumbled it, in attempt to catch knocked decanter and glass off table. Decanter smashed. Then heard sound – like muffled voice – and hair literally rose on nape of neck – and saw coffin shifting slightly as if body inside agitating it. Felt physical sickness. First thought, My God he's still alive. Went to coffin, rapped with knuckles on top. Voice from within unmistakable but could not make out words. Overwhelmed with panic – open coffin – but how? – screwed down tight. Screwdriver – Jeanne. Rapped on coffin again, shouted: It's Bézian! I'll fetch a screwdriver! Ran out of bedroom. Tripped on stairs – pitch dark – into kitchen. Shook Jeanne, shouted at her, useless, dead drunk. Rushed to side-board, opened drawer after drawer, nothing, kitchen utensils, knives, forks, thought of outhouse but no time and search in dark fruitless. Took table knife and back upstairs. Rapped on coffin again then attacked screws with rounded end of knife. It served, but horribly slow, difficult business and no sound from within coffin. At last done – twelve screws in all – lifted away lid, IM threw aside linen shroud, sat up. Face grey, running with sweat, eyes wild like lunatic madman. His first words: Bézian, Bézian, my God, my God. My first words: I couldn't find a screwdriver, Jeanne's drunk, I couldn't wake her. Then IM said: That murderer, Bouchard, that assassin. Then – she's drunk, you say, she doesn't know anything about it. I dazed, appalled, shaken, trembling from horror of it all. As in dream gave arm to IM, helped him out. He fully clothed. Best suit. Helped him to bed. He sat on it. He too shaking. Water, he said, get me water. Went down to kitchen.

Jeanne still snoring. Carafe of water by absinthe bottle. Took it back upstairs. Found IM on hands and knees using hairbrush to sweep up fragments of broken decanter. Amazed by this. Too tired, can write no more. Tomorrow.

<u>Saturday, 14th October, 10 pm</u>. Another utterly astonishing day. Is this all a fantastic dream? Can it really be happening? My first, essential task must be relate what took place last night in as much detail and with as much clarity as I can while all is still fresh in my memory – though I am exhausted and hardly able to comprehend the extraordinary, unprecedented circumstances I find myself in. No matter. This is surely a gift from Destiny herself. The wheel of fortune has turned at last and is showering gifts upon me. I must drive my pen forward like a knightly steed, my words must flow with a river's smooth swiftness, I must capture in ink the scenes and dialogues that I will later transform into a work of literature that will astonish the world. Taking up the story, then, from the point at which, last night, I abandoned it through utter exhaustion, both physical and mental, I return to the moment that I re-entered IM's bedroom with the carafe of water and found him kneeling on the floor, sweeping up the broken glass. Before I could ask him what he was about, he rose abruptly. "Is she still asleep?" he demanded and upon receiving my affirmative reply he gripped my arm. "Listen to me," he said. "Do you want money? I mean a fortune." Without waiting for a reply, he seized the carafe and gulped down the water like some desert-traveller coming suddenly upon an oasis in the trackless wastes of sand. "You know I'm rich," he continued, having slaked his raging thirst. "What you don't know, what nobody knows, is how rich. There's a million francs in cash and kind in this house and half of it's yours if you do as I say. I'm dead and dead I mean to stay if you'll help me." These were not, perhaps, his exact words – indeed at the moment of their utterance I was barely capable of

taking in their meaning – but I must eventually improve on what was actually said, for the sake of good literary style, and I may as well start the business now. "Let them believe I'm dead," he went on, "let them bury me and then let them ransack my house for the money and find nothing!" There he laughed, that guttural, wheezing, harsh, deep laugh of his. "Gang of thieves! Carrion crows! They'll get nothing but a few sticks of furniture, a house that's falling down and a bit of land not worth a spit." He gripped me again, thrusting his face close to mine. "But it all depends on you, my friend, my only friend." He then proceeded to pour out his plan in a few swift, half-whispered, breathless sentences. We would conceal all evidence of his revival, weight the coffin and let it be buried on the morrow. He would come to the schoolhouse, conceal himself during the day and remain under my roof until it was safe for him to go. "But where will you go?" I asked him, still utterly bewildered both by the turn and the precipitate pace of these events. "I don't know," he replied, "far away – but will you do it?" I hesitated. It seemed a mad plan, utterly mad, conceived in the disordered mind of one who had suffered the inconceivable horror of being taken for dead and of then returning to consciousness to find himself immured in a coffin! I stammered out these objections but again he gripped me, vice-like. "No, no, no," he expostulated, "it's easy, easily done. Come with me. Hurry." He picked up the candle and I followed him along the passage and up a short ladder into an attic. It was heaped with rubbish, broken furniture, dusty crockery and a great pile of old bedding – mattresses, bolsters and blankets, all damp and rotting and giving off a highly unpleasant and pervasive odour of decay. He rummaged in this noisome mass and pulled out a bolster. In the flickering light of the candle, he laid the disgusting object, like an enormous, bloated, hideous slug, on the floor. "Stinks, don't it?" he said with a gravelly, deep-throated chuckle. "Those vultures would

have burned it along with the rest. All up in smoke! That's
what I was counting on. But it could have gone wrong.
They could have nosed it out like the pigs they are. Well,
nothing can go wrong now – if you're with me in this, my
only friend." While speaking thus, always in a half-
whisper, he ripped open the outer covering of the bolster,
plunged a hand into the repellent mess of putrid cotton and
drew out a bag. It was somewhat in the shape of the
bolster, though shorter and thinner, and was made of oiled
silk. He opened it and took out a handful of banknotes. "A
million," he said. "Half of it yours. Think! Money buys
time. Time's what you need to write your books. Money
buys respect," he went on – but I was barely listening.
That line from Baudelaire was ringing in my head like a
bell, yes, like a bell sounding across misty, morning fields,
calling me to my Destiny: L'Art est long et le temps est
court. "That damned lawyer in Charmeuil will put his arms
round you," IM was saying. "That girl's yours if you want
her. You might do better." Did I hesitate a moment longer?
I think I did. But only for a moment. As Baudelaire writes:
C'est le diable qui tient les fils qui nous remuent! "I'll do
it," I said. "What a friend you are," he exclaimed, "but we
must hurry." Hurry we certainly did. First, IM searched
about until he found a decanter to replace the one I had
broken. While he cleaned it with a scrap of rag, he told me
to take the weights and pendulum of an old clock lying on
its side under the eaves. We returned to the bedroom. IM
carried his money-bag and the decanter while I took the
weights, pendulum and an old stone mortar, minus its
pestle. On IM's whispered instructions, I placed these
objects in the coffin and IM added the fragments of the
broken decanter. "More weight, more weight," he
muttered. "I have an idea. Come, quick, quick." We
returned to the attic. We shifted the old clock to reveal the
topmost stones of the outer wall of the house. Water had
evidently been seeping through the roof for many years,
the mortar was soft and rotten and it was an easy matter to

prise up a stone and lift it away. Four heavy stones were removed in this manner and placed in the coffin, then we returned for the last time to the attic and took up blankets with which we packed out the coffin so that none of its contents could shift. We then replaced the lid and screwed it back down. Throughout these efforts I was continually amazed at IM's vigour, which was astonishing not only in one of his advanced age but in one moreover who had almost drowned and had then been nearly suffocated! Nothing like single-minded purpose to lend strength to a man's arm! When all was done to IM's satisfaction and the room was restored to the condition in which I had found it upon first entering, we descended the stair, with the candle I had brought up, and entered the kitchen to find Jeanne still safely slumbering. While I put the candle back on the kitchen table, IM stepped to a cupboard, opened it and took out one of a dozen or more bottles of absinthe stored therein. Outside, he whispered to me to return to the schoolhouse by the lane. He himself would come by the fields. Less than a quarter of an hour later we were sitting together in my little salon, with the shutters tightly closed, the money-bag reposing on a chair, IM mixing two glasses of the "Green Fairy" and complaining that my domestic arrangements did not extend to the possession of an absinthe spoon! I decided to apprise him immediately of a serious objection to his scheme that had occurred to me during the short walk up the lane to my abode, namely, how I could possibly explain my sudden acquisition of a sum as vast as half a million francs? "Easiest thing in the world, my dear young friend," was the reply. "Invent an Aunt!" I was flummoxed. "Or a great-Aunt," he went on, "or a distant cousin – what does it matter? A relation of yours has died, somewhere abroad perhaps, America for instance, and has left you a fortune. *L'oncle d'Amérique!* You're a writer. You can think up a story. You've no family hereabouts to give you the lie." I made the obvious objection, that though I had no family nearby, I nevertheless did have a family. How would I explain my sudden wealth to them? "Dear me, you're not much of a writer if you can't think of a way round that," was the somewhat less than polite rejoinder. "During your time here you made the acquaintance of some rich old person who left you money. That wouldn't be so far from the truth! Or you won a lottery. Or you've speculated successfully in gold-mining shares. Whatever you think they'll believe. They won't question you too closely, I'll be bound!" Cogitating upon a story likely to convince my parents and brothers, I heated up the stew, off which IM and I supped. As we ate we discussed the arrangements to be made during his sojourn. It was agreed that his nights should be spent on my sofa and that during the day he would lie concealed in the cellar, the door of which would be locked against any unauthorized invasion by one of my pupils. I ventured to press him a little on the question of how long he anticipated remaining in hiding, to which he replied that the moment to depart would suggest itself naturally. I had to be content with that.

This morning. I spent a wretched night. In spite of my fatigue I slept very badly, waking frequently and then finding it almost impossible to resume my slumbers owing to the extreme agitation of my spirits and a terror of awaking too late to hide IM away before school. In the event, finding myself wide awake at six o'clock, I went downstairs to find IM sound asleep on the sofa. It was with some difficulty that I aroused him and he expressed some considerable annoyance at being awoken at such an hour. When I took him down to the cellar he complained bitterly about its cold, damp condition. With exceedingly bad grace, he accepted a couple of blankets, two candles, a bottle of water and some cold meats to see him through the morning, then demanded a bucket to enable him to answer calls of nature.

This afternoon. School ended at noon and having locked

all the doors I descended to the cellar to find IM seated in a corner, hugging his money-bag, in a state of extreme irritation. He complained bitterly about the cold and damp of the cellar, saying that it would be the death of him (!) to remain there another hour and demanding that we should devise another plan. During the course of the morning he had made use of the bucket which I had to take outside to empty in the privy – an excessively disagreeable task. When I returned I discovered that IM had made a tour of my little domain and had discovered the box-room next to my bedroom. He declared that it would be a much more comfortable place of concealment than the cellar and was inclined to blame me for not having thought of it earlier. His main reproach, however, was towards himself for having forgotten to bring his pipe and a supply of tobacco. I pointed out that the odour of tobacco smoke in the school would occasion remark as I, myself, was not a smoker. At this he only grumbled the more.

Later this afternoon. I attended the funeral. There were no more than twenty or thirty people present – almost all of them IM's relations. As the coffin was carried into the church I was beside myself with anxiety lest something should go amiss and the deception should be detected. During the service I was troubled by the thought that these solemn rites were being enacted in the presence of a coffin full of stones and old blankets and that prayers were being offered for the repose of a soul still inhabiting a living body and that these were terrible blasphemies. I had to fight hard to remind myself that all these rituals are mere flimflams and that true religion resides in the mystical communion of man's feeble spark of spirit with the omnipotent, eternal, inextinguishable flame of the Godhead, which is all Spirit. I asked myself what Baudelaire would have made of the occasion and decided that he would have laughed heartily and then made of poem of it – something I must attempt myself. When we went outside for the interment I was utterly horrified when happening to glance across the grave-yard towards the school, I saw IM's face in my bedroom window. I was appalled and incensed by his reckless folly in so exposing himself and kept my eyes on the ground, fearing that if I looked towards the school again somebody might follow the direction of my gaze and observe him. When I returned home I upbraided him in no uncertain terms for this mad act and was further infuriated when he merely laughed and declared that no man could be blamed for failing to resist the temptation to watch his own funeral. I retorted that if he was so careless of public exposure he could empty his own bucket. At this, he showed some signs of remorse and apologised for the shock he had caused me. He then questioned me closely about the funeral, demanding precise details about who had been there, what had been said and so forth. Then, with a swift return of his previous ill humour, he chided me bitterly for being unable to supply this information, owing to my distracted state during the proceedings. His temper did not much improve during the remainder of the day and it was with no inconsiderable relief that I bade him good night and am now able to find some consolation in confiding these matters to my journal. Have I made a terrible mistake? Well, it's too late now.

Sunday 15th October, 10 pm. IM is asleep in the box-room next door. We quarrelled again this morning. It started at breakfast when he complained of not having enough to eat. I explained that my food is provided by Madame Maupas, at the shop, who cooks me three hot meals during the week as well as sending other provisions regularly by her boy. It would inevitably cause comment if I suddenly increased my order. Another domestic difficulty then occurred to me, namely Bernadette Ricau who comes on Tuesdays and Fridays to sweep and clean the schoolrooms and my own quarters. IM would have to hide in the cellar during her visits. I then told him that I was engaged to lunch with the Dulacs and asked him to hand over my share of the money so that I could buy flowers for Madame Dulac and a present for Louise. This he adamantly refused to do. "I can't have you splashing out all of a sudden," he said. "You've got to prepare the ground." Luncheon with the Dulacs, he thought, would provide an ideal opportunity for this endeavour. He suggested that I should drop a hint or two about this mythical American relation, recently deceased, and the prospect of an inheritance. I said that an advance of a few hundred francs could hardly be the cause of a catastrophe. "You've never had money," was the rejoinder. "You don't know what it is. The fatter your wallet the greater your urge to spend. Where money's concerned, I mean great sums, it's all or nothing. Either you spend it, and spend too much, or you keep it and spend too little. There's no half way." There was no time to argue further and it was with feelings of no small resentment that, after Mass, I walked to Charmeuil. The air of slight indifference with which my dearest Louise greeted me upon my arrival at her father's house, a subterfuge I know she is forced to practice but which never ceases to pain me, reminded me of what enormous changes would come about as a result of my acquisition of IM's money and expunged certain regrets about my arrangement with him that had been arising in my mind. I determined to follow his advice and during luncheon subtly turned the conversation towards the recent death, in America, of a near relation of my mother's. That mercenary creature, Dulac, immediately pricked up his ears and on learning of the possibility of an inheritance offered his services in any legal difficulties that might ensue. I could not refrain from glancing across the table at my dearest Louise – an exquisite Sevres vase amidst the coarse earthenware of her family – to see how she was taking this and found that she was looking at me directly – a thing she would not normally dare to do – and with widened eyes, blue as sapphires. How enchanting, how desirable was she then. Fruits purs de tout outrage et vierges de gerçures, dont la chair lisse et ferme appelait les morsures! Ah, Louise, Louise, my Louise.

<u>Monday 16th October, 10.30 pm</u>. Alban Ricau's barns burned to the ground last night (BR's uncle.) News brought by Maupas boy. Seems that only sudden shift in wind saved house from being consumed by flames. Cause unknown. Discussed with IM over supper. He said, Where will Ricau get the money to rebuild barns now that I'm not there to lend it to him. Laughed. Horrible. Dog tired from work and strain of IM's presence. More quarrels. Absinthe bottle nearly empty. Wanted me to go to shop for another. Said I'd never bought a. – would look strange. He said impossible to hide in cellar tomorrow, risk of BR finding him in box-room slight. I said, very great. Insisted on cellar.

<u>Tuesday 17th October, 11 pm</u>. A storm is raging outside. It burst upon us an hour ago with violent thunder, lightning bolts and torrential rain. But it is nothing to the storm that rages within me. It has been a terrible, terrible day. There was another fire last night, this time at Paul Galliax's farm. The conflagration started in a barn and spread rapidly to the house. The family barely escaped with their lives. All this I learned at the shop where I went after school to buy absinthe, IM having persuaded me that it would be safe to do so. Mme M told me that the gendarmes from Charmeuil had been called to the scene because arson is suspected. They are now investigating the previous fire at the Ricau farm. Mme M is convinced that there is an arsonist on the loose, some deranged madman. As I returned to the schoolhouse a terrible thought struck me – that IM could have been responsible for the fires. I remembered hearing that he had once taken AR to law over an unpaid debt and that there was bad blood between them. Paul G is IM's cousin and nearest relation and I know for a fact that IM

hates him. BR was still at work when I got back. She too is convinced that the fires are the work of an arsonist. While waiting for her to finish, before letting IM out of the cellar, I was in a state of extreme agitation, unable to decide what to tell him. If I said nothing and later IM let something slip about the second fire, that would be proof positive of his guilt. On the other hand, if he was indeed the guilty party he is also far too shrewd, canny and circumspect to give himself away and the fact that I had said nothing would instantly alert him to my suspicions. The best way, I concluded, would be to tell him all and observe his reaction to the news very closely and with the greatest attention. This is what I did once we were in the better light of the kitchen. "Well, well, well," he said. "So they think it's arson, do they? Why do they think that?" I replied that, having received the information at second hand, I had no precise idea as to what evidence the gendarmes had uncovered. While saying this I was observing IM keenly until, suddenly meeting his eye, I was obliged to turn away and attend to the preparation of our meal. Though there has been nothing in IM's manner or conversation overtly to suggest his guilt, I am now convinced of it. That two of his sworn enemies should have been afflicted with disaster in the space of two days is too great a coincidence – and of course the fact that he is believed to be dead provides him with a perfect opportunity to commit these heinous crimes of vengeance without any fear that the finger of suspicion could be pointed at him, which, if he were alive, would most certainly have been the case. For the last two nights I have slept like a log. IM could very easily have crept out in the small hours. The Ricau farm is a twenty minute walk away, the Galliax farm even nearer. I have been cursing myself for not thinking of this earlier and so failing to discover if there are traces of mud on his boots. Tomorrow I will do precisely that. If indeed I find such to be the case, so that any doubt about his guilt is banished, what then? I am in a desperate quandary. Should I denounce him to the gendarmes? That would mean forgoing the money – and an end to the dreams I have been weaving round it. Have I myself already committed a crime in concealing the fact that he is alive and in harbouring him here? If so, I would be arrested and that would be the end of everything – my reputation ruined, my professional career over, my hopes for Louise Dulac forever blasted. Another hideous thought strikes me. What if he intends to commit further acts of arson or even worse, a murder? He does not lack for enemies and he is capable of anything! How could I ever have been his friend? I was blind. But I see now. I see what he is. Heartless, vengeful creature. I know I won't sleep tonight. My mind is in too great a turmoil. I will stay awake and if I hear that villain in the next room stir, I will follow him and if I find that he is bent on some evil design I will confront him, demand that he hand over my share of the money and immediately quit my house, now, tonight.

Romain Bézian's journal ends here, some time after eleven o'clock on the night of October 17th, 1882. The following morning his body was found in the lane about a kilometre south of the school, not far from Ignace Mordeux's house. He had been struck by a violent blow on the head by a branch ripped from a tree in the storm. The roads round about were strewn with such detritus. The cause of death was clear. There was no suspicion of foul play. The only mystery was why he had been out walking during such a tremendous storm. The most widespread theory was that he had been returning from some tryst with a woman. My own view, at the time, was that in his pursuit of the "poetical" he had decided to "commune with nature" – something he often talked about. The body was taken to the undertaker in Charmeuil, the Mayor informed Bézian's parents, by wire, and it was agreed that the funeral should take place, in Caubet, on Thursday – the 19th.

Soon after dawn on that day, I left my presbytery and walked to the church in order to say the morning Office and to make certain preparations for the Exequial Mass, which was to be said at eleven o'clock. The air was clear and the rising sun was flushing the mountain tops a delicate pink. It was a beautiful sight and I stopped for a moment to contemplate it. In the foreground was the mound of earth by Bézian's grave. If I had not stopped to admire the view I doubt if I would have noticed the object lying at the foot of the grave. It looked like some sort of note-book. I walked over to investigate and in stooping down to pick it up – it was Bézian's journal – looked down into the grave and saw a body lying face down at the bottom. I recognized it instantly from the semi-circle of grey hair at the base of the head. It was Ignace Mordeux.

In fiction and sometimes in autobiography, when the writer comes to some great turning-point in his story, where a crucial decision is made or a critical truth is revealed or perceived, he almost inevitably plunges into a long description of the thoughts running through the mind of his character or of himself. Perhaps, for the sake of clarity, this is technically necessary but in real life, when such moments occur, even if the brain is actually functioning in this way, one is not consciously aware of it. Thought becomes action, instantly, without any perception of the process by which one leads to the other. It is only in retrospect, therefore, and by the use of logic rather than memory, that I can analyze, or attempt to analyze, the thoughts in my own mind upon discovering Mordeux's body. The first must have been that whatever had been in the coffin I had buried a week before it was certainly not Mordeux's cadaver and that there was a mystery here; the second, that this mystery was in some way connected to Romain Bézian; the third, that nobody must know anything about it until I had investigated further.

I went directly to the church, into the vestry, where the spare key to the sexton's outhouse was kept. I went to the outhouse and found the sexton's ladder. I carried the ladder into the churchyard, conscious that by now the village would be stirring and that there was a real possibility of detection. However, there was nobody in the lane and I let the ladder down into the grave and descended. The first thing was to confirm that Mordeux was in fact dead. In the circumstances, anything seemed possible! He was indeed dead and *rigor mortis* had set in. Something odd about the way he was lying struck me. His arms were folded beneath his torso, as if he was hugging something. In the narrow confines of the grave it was difficult to turn him on his side but I managed to do it. Clutched tight against his chest was the oiled-silk money-bag described in Bézian's journal.

With some effort I extricated the money-bag from the dead man's embrace, not knowing for certain what it contained but having a shrewd idea. Then I climbed back up the ladder and hurried into the church, hardly daring to look towards the lane to see if anyone was passing. I could smell wood-smoke. It wouldn't be long before people were out and about, which made the next part of the plan that was unfolding in my mind the most dangerous. I placed money-bag and journal in the vestment chest and locked it. I strode as swiftly as I could, without actually running, to the outhouse and took a spade. I returned to the grave. I descended and shifted the body so that it lay face down again then climbed back up. In terror now that someone would see me, I shovelled earth from the top of the pile into the grave until I judged that there was enough to cover the body. I went back down the ladder, spread the earth evenly and tamped it with the flat of the spade. I climbed up and surveyed my handiwork. It was by no means perfect but mourners don't generally peer into open graves and by the time the sexton returned to his work Bézian's coffin would be in place and nothing underneath would be visible. I stepped back to the pile of earth. It was the one weak point in my plan. If the sexton noticed that it had been disturbed or that the level was lower he would come to me – and then what would I do? It was useless to think about it at that point. The immediate problem was how to get the money-bag to the presbytery undetected.

I decided to trust to the luck that had so far held so wonderfully and do it immediately. I returned the spade and ladder to the outhouse, then went back into the church. My soutane was stained with mud but there was nothing I could do about that and in fact it gave me an idea. I took out some vestments, picked up the money-bag and the journal then draped the vestments over them. In that way I carried my prizes back to the presbytery and did not encounter a soul on the way.

I went straight to my study. The shutters were closed and I lit a lamp. I opened the money-bag. It contained banknotes, mostly of a high denomination, and bearer bonds. I did not make a tally at that point. I wanted to read the journal. I devoured it. Obviously, it explained a great deal, but by no means all. What had happened between Bézian's last entry on Tuesday night and my discovery of Ignace Mordeux's body on Thursday morning? Surely it would be possible by studying the journal and applying simple logic to form an idea of the intervening events. Yes. But I was in no state to do so. My anxiety about what the sexton might observe after the funeral was too great.

The Mass and the interment passed without incident. The attendance was large, which I think went some way towards consoling poor Bézian's parents and brothers, who were naturally in great distress. Afterwards, at the Mayor's house, the mother took me to one side and asked me innumerable questions about her son. I pretended to a friendship deeper than had actually existed between us and exaggerated my regard for his talents while trying to keep my mind from wandering in the direction of the churchyard where the sexton would already be at work. At the time I felt ashamed of this behaviour. Today, I look back on it with horror. Mme Bézian's face, taut and anguished, rises in front of me. I see her desolation and her courage. Her eyes, red-rimmed and swollen, stare at me with an accusation against which I have no defence. Enough. I will be judged.

Before returning to the presbytery, I went to the churchyard. The grave was filled and the sexton was in the outhouse. Summoning all my courage, I approached him and made some commonplace remark. He replied in the same style. Clearly he had noticed nothing amiss. I was safe. For the first time that day I felt a sense of excitement. So long as I was circumspect, my life could be transformed.

The first thing I did when I got back to the presbytery was to count the money. Mordeux had lied. There wasn't a million. There was a million and a half. He had intended to cheat Bézian. Or, I now began to wonder, had he ever really meant to share the money? Had he planned to kill the schoolmaster from the first? There was no doubt in my mind that Mordeux <u>had</u> killed him. It was not difficult to reconstruct the crime. Mordeux left the schoolhouse on the night of the storm. True to the resolve recorded in his journal, Bézian followed him. He probably did this clumsily and gave away his presence, though in any case a type like Mordeux would soon be aware that somebody was following him, unless that person was an expert. Mordeux rounded a bend in the lane and there on the ground was a branch torn from a tree by the wind. He picked it up, stepped into the shadows and waited. When Bézian appeared, Mordeux stepped forward, swinging the branch, and killed the schoolmaster with one tremendous blow.

Even if murder had not, in fact, been Mordeux's initial intention, I thought that Bézian was in any case doomed. The clue was in that last entry in the journal. *While saying this I was observing IM keenly until, suddenly meeting his eye, I was obliged to turn away and attend to the preparation of our meal.* There could be little doubt that a man as shrewd and worldly as Mordeux would easily have read the suspicion in Bézian's eyes. In that instant, the young schoolmaster's fate was sealed. Whether Mordeux deliberately left the schoolhouse that night, either to lure Bézian outside in order to kill him, or to test him, or whether he was in fact bent on another act of arson and seized the opportunity to commit a murder on which he had already decided, was a question that could never be answered.

But there were further questions. Why, having killed Bézian, did Mordeux not leave the area immediately? Why was he still in Caubet two days later? Again, it was possible to reconstruct the events. Mordeux returned to the schoolhouse for the money-bag. He discovered the journal, read it and saw immediately that he must destroy it. The obvious way would be to burn it. Why didn't he? My suspicion was that by this time it was too late. Dawn was breaking and smoke from the chimney of the schoolhouse could be noticed. Or he might simply have fallen asleep. He was an elderly man, after all, and had been exerting himself to an uncommon degree. In either case, once the sun was up, he was trapped. He could neither burn the journal nor leave the schoolhouse. There, he was comparatively safe. He could count on the school's being closed for several days, as in fact it was. Why then did he not leave on the Wednesday night, taking the journal with him to be destroyed later? Again, I found the answer in the journal itself. *When we went outside for the interment I was utterly horrified when happening to glance across the grave-yard towards the school, I saw IM's face in my bedroom window.* Mordeux had been keeping watch from that same bedroom window and had seen the sexton digging Bézian's grave. It occurred to him immediately that the safest place in which to get rid of the compromising document was in the grave of its author, where it would be buried for eternity. He waited until the small hours, then stole out of the schoolhouse, carrying the money-bag and the journal, and crossed the lane to the churchyard.

What happened next? How did he die? It was not perhaps such a riddle as at first appeared. I cast my mind back to the previous week when he had been found apparently drowned in his pond. How had he fallen in? What if he had not been drunk, as everybody supposed? What if he had been suffering from some ailment that caused him to lose consciousness but also had the potential to bring about his death? The more I thought about it the more convinced I became that this was the explanation. He came to the grave. His intention was to throw in the journal, then cover it with a few handfuls of earth. But before he could carry out his plan, the malady – of the heart perhaps – struck again, fatally this time. Dropping the journal, but still holding fast to his money, he toppled head-first into the grave and lay there until I found him. *He hath graven and digged up a pit: and is fallen himself into the destruction that he made for the other.*

Only one question remained. Where would Mordeux have gone and what would he have done with his money had he lived? It was of no particular relevance but nonetheless it intrigued me. I turned again to the journal. It was evident that between the moment of his release from the coffin and the return of Bézian with the water, Mordeux had taken a crucial decision, namely to conceal, if he could, the fact that he was still alive. Why? It was not, I thought, simply a matter of ensuring that his legal heirs got as little as possible, though that was part of it. I imagined him in that coffin, knowing that help was at hand and realizing not only that he had been given a second chance at life but also that this new life could and should be completely different. I believe that, with or without sharing his fortune with Bézian (the latter seems much more likely) he meant to go to some part of the country where he was not known and perhaps under a false name – an easier matter to contrive then than it would be now –

spend the money to the acquisition of which he had devoted his former existence. At one blow he would achieve two objects: rob his heirs and change his world. Instead, by a chain of astonishing events, he had changed my world.

Forty years later, still living in that transformed world, I think back and try to remember my state of mind in those first days after Bézian's funeral. I felt no guilt at all about the money, or the way I had come by it, or even about the fact that in keeping it I was suppressing the truth of no less a crime than murder. But what of my conscience as a priest? Yes, there I was troubled. But curiously what troubled me was not, as I have said, the deception I had practiced, or indeed the further deceptions I would be forced to practice in devising a plausible story to cover my sudden affluence, but the thought of Ignace Mordeux's empty grave and of the other grave in which two men lay, the one the murderer of the other. What did that matter, you might ask? I don't know. I can only say that it mattered to me and that was why I went to Charmeuil, to the stone-mason, and ordered him to add the inscription mentioned earlier, ET CXXI, to Bézian's headstone. The grave-plots in the churchyard at Caubet, as in most churchyards, are numbered. The numbers are listed in a book and against each one is the name of the occupant of that plot. Ignace Mordeux's stone-filled coffin had been buried in plot 121.

There was one other matter that disturbed me: Bézian's journal. I simply could not bring myself to destroy it, though that was the obvious thing to do. I had not been his friend; I certainly did not admire the style in which he had written the less hectic and more obviously studied entries in his journal: yet that document was the sole legacy of a young man, naïve perhaps and with an inflated idea of his own abilities, who had dreamed of being a writer. No. I could not destroy what he had written even though it was unlikely that anyone would ever read it.

The following summer, when my annual holiday came round, I went on a walking-tour in the Swiss Alps. Ignace Mordeux's money went with me and was deposited in a bank in Geneva. In the interim I had devoted much thought to the problem of explaining my new-found wealth to my superiors in the Church. The difficulty was that, unlike Romain Bézian, I had no family. I could not "invent an Aunt." My father died when I was five and a year later I lost my mother. There were no relations on either side near enough, or indeed willing, to take charge of me so I was sent to the orphanage of the Brothers Of The Little Friends Of Christ. The Church became my family and remains so to this day. I have known no other and wanted no other.

In the end I decided to follow Mordeux's advice to Bézian and invented an uncle of my father's who had emigrated to America and made his fortune there. *L'oncle d'Amérique!* This fairy-tale has never been challenged.

I had always been ambitious and I now had the means to advance my career in the Church. First, I applied for permission to read for a doctorate in theology, at my own expense. Permission was granted and during my period of study the income from the capital, invested safely and profitably over the Swiss border, enabled me to entertain men of distinction and influence in the Church. Nothing like a successful dinner party to improve one's prospects! On the recommendation of these new friends I was appointed to a position in the Curia and went to Rome for that "bath in *romanita*" essential to anyone with an eye on a Bishopric.

I have been Bishop here for seven years now. There is talk of a Cardinal's hat. I think it unlikely. The death of Pope Benedict, whom I knew well and admired whole-heartedly, has robbed me of what little chance I had: my acquaintance with his successor is slight. In any case, I suspect that even Benedict would have hesitated. He had that sort of highly developed, deeply experienced sense of the spiritual that enables its possessor to detect a false or shallow spirituality in others. My old Bishop, with whom I began this narrative and with whom I conclude it, and who might well have become a Prince of the Church if he had lived, had the same gift. We were once having a practical discussion about the provision of wafers in the Cathedral when he suddenly said: "We don't consume the host. The host consumes us." Interpreting my blank look correctly, he added: "Ah. You don't understand." Then he shook his head and sighed. More disturbing was a later occasion, when I had become his auxiliary. I gave a dinner for him – rather a grand one. He took a sip of wine and having savoured it appreciatively he said, quietly and as if making a general observation: "You know what Balzac says? Behind every great fortune lies one great crime."

*

Editor's note: The *vide grenier* – literally meaning the emptying or clearing out of an attic – has become a popular and widespread phenomenon in rural France in recent years. A cross between a car boot sale, but with rickety tables substituting for boots, and an open-air antiques market, it especially attracts owners of second homes, particularly the British, who are to be found swarming round the stalls, going into ecstasies over dilapidated *chevets*, worm-eaten cartwheels and chipped art deco crockery. Originally, these gatherings may well have been organized by local people who really were clearing out their attics but today they are dominated by dealers – and for a good reason. It's a tax dodge. Goods sold at a *vide grenier* are not subject to the dreaded TVA (VAT).

An interior decorator, a friend of my collaborator, Michel Walrangis, had been commissioned to do up a restaurant in the commercial district of Lyon. At a *vide grenier* he found an old safe, dating from early part of the last century, that he thought would be perfect for his scheme. The safe was open, empty, and the key had long since been lost – none of which mattered to Michel's friend, who bought it for fifty euros. How he got it home is a story in itself but not one to tell here. Before putting it in the restaurant he had to clean it thoroughly – not just the exterior but the interior as well, and in doing so discovered that it had a false bottom. There was a tiny indentation, previously hidden by rust, which enabled one to insert a screwdriver and lever up the floor-plate. Underneath was a shallow cavity and in the cavity was Romain Bezian's journal and the accompanying narrative in the Bishop's neat hand-writing. Just as he had felt compelled to preserve the young schoolmaster's writing, it seems that the Bishop had felt unable to destroy his own.

While approving my use of the King James Bible for the passages of scripture quoted by the Bishop, Michel questions why the translation retains some French here and there. Some words, *paysan* for instance, don't have a completely accurate equivalent in English. "Peasant" doesn't give the sense of a small farmer, probably owning his own bit of land. "Yeoman" doesn't quite work either. Neither does "countryman." "American uncle" doesn't convey the proverb-like flavour of *l'oncle d'Amérique*. For some reason Baudelaire defies a really good translation into English (even Yeats nods), rather in the way that Shakespeare doesn't read well in French. Besides, retaining a dash of the original may impart a whiff of France, like the smell of *caporal* tobacco and freshly-baked croissants in a café.

"Mammie, Mammie."

"What – what? Oh. It's you. I was dozing."

"You were fast asleep! I wouldn't have woken you but–"

"What's that you've got there?"

"A plant. An orchid."

"Orchid! You must be making money."

"Flowers are no good. They never last. Where d'you want me to put it? On the table over there, by the television, where you can see it? It needs looking after rather carefully. The instructions are on the label."

"They're short-staffed."

"This is so much better. Your own bathroom. A little terrace all to yourself."

"And what's it costing?"

"You know you don't have to worry about that."

"I'm not touching my savings, if that's what you're thinking."

"What a view! Is that the spire of Ste Marie de Peyroux? It must be! You can almost see the farm! This must be one of the best rooms."

"I didn't ask to be moved. I don't remember complaining."

"But this is so much better."

"What difference does it make? I can't get out of bed without help. They're short-staffed. You have to wait an age for everything."

"Elie sends her love. And Pierre and the twins. Oh yes! Raffy came second in Maths. He wanted me to make sure I told you."

"What time is it?"

"Half past two. I was going to tell you, I can't stay long, I've got some clients arriving. That English couple again. Did I tell you about them? The ones who are looking for a house?"

"Foreigners are buying everything. They'll own France one of these days. So things are going well are they?"

"I'm booked up till the end of September."

"Quite the businesswoman."

"Not exactly! But – it's something to do. Something to think about. It makes one feel less lonely."

"First a new room. Then an orchid. Now tears."

"Don't, Mammie."

"Pff. I know what you're after."

"Why are you like this?"

"My part of the house is mine. I have the right of occupation for my life. That's the law."

"There's never been any argument about that. We're not going to let your part. That's never been the intention. Try to understand. All we want to do is renovate the back bedroom so we can let it. But the regulations–"

"Pff! Regulations!"

"If you want to be officially registered with the Chambres D'Hôtes you have to abide by the regulations. That's why I only do bed-and-breakfast. If I wanted to provide an evening meal we'd have to spend a fortune on the kitchen – just to comply with the regulations. You're only allowed to let a certain proportion of the house. They won't allow us to include the back bedroom unless we can show that your rooms are unoccupied. All you have to do is sign a bit of paper. It doesn't mean anything, it doesn't change anything–"

"I'm not signing any paper."

"I don't understand why you're being so stubborn about it. Nor does Elie. After everything I've done for you, why can't you do this one little thing for me? Why?"

"More tears."

"You've always hated me, haven't you? You never thought I was good enough for Robert. But of course nobody would have been good enough."

"What do you think it feels like to outlive your only son? Eh? What do you think that feels like?"

"What do you think it feels like to lose your husband?"

"I lost my Georges."

"And had a son to take over. To work the farm, look after you, do everything for you, run around after you like a puppy."

"Robert was a good son."

"You think I wasn't a good wife to him? But of course! I didn't give him a son. What a failure! What a crime! Only a daughter. D'you hate Elie too – because she's a girl not a boy?"

"Don't be ridiculous, Babette."

"I've obviously made a mistake. We're not living in the twenty-first century after all."

"You certainly are."

"Well, there's no point in discussing it any further. You've always tried to make my life as difficult as possible. It was idiotic to expect anything to change. I'll just have to wait."

"Ah, yes. When I'm dead, you won't need any paper."

"Exactly."

"On the other hand, I may live many years more. My father lived to be ninety-three."

"You don't have to remind me."

"I remember when you and Robert were engaged he said that you'd make him an excellent wife. I thought so too. But then –"

"Go on."

"What's the point?"

"Go on."

"It was the tractor."

"The tractor?"

"After your honeymoon, when you came to live at the

farm – but how can I tell you? It's too humiliating."

"What are you talking about, Mammie?"

"I'm not senile. Not yet, anyway. All right. Why not? It was a few days after you moved in. There were some bales of hay in one of the lower fields that Robert was going to move but he had to go into Montaillon – I don't remember why. So you did it. I was in the milking-shed. I remember watching you as you jumped onto the tractor and drove it out of the yard. I'd never seen you drive a tractor. I don't think I'd ever seen any woman drive one. You did it so easily, with such skill and confidence. My God, the envy I felt. I wanted to be you, on that tractor. Georges would never have let me drive his. It would never have occurred to him to teach me how to drive it – or to me to ask him. Then, half an hour later perhaps, you drove back into the yard, with the bales on the trailer, neatly stacked and tied. I went to Confession that Thursday to try to get rid of the envy burning inside me. It was no good. Day after day, year after year, I saw you and Robert working side-by-side. There was nothing he could do that you couldn't do. I used to lie awake at night thinking, what have I ever done? Women's work, that's all. Cooking, washing, ironing, milking, looking after the *potager*, embroidering the coats we put on the oxen. Pff."

"Why didn't you ever say anything, Mammie? I could have shown you how to drive the tractor."

"Sometimes I think you have no intelligence at all, Babette. It would have been utterly beyond me, of course. I was born into a different world. I hardly spoke a word of French till I went to school – only the *patois*. We worked the land with oxen until well after the war. It was too late. It was all too late. Now I'm crying. You've never seen me cry before, have you? Not even at Robert's funeral. I've never found any relief in tears. It's not my nature. I'm stubborn – you were right there – and I'm hard. I wonder how many times you've wanted to accuse me of that!"

"Many times!"

"Listen to me, Babette. I don't want to stay here. No, no, I don't mean I want to come home. It's impossible. I've accepted that. I mean I want *l'adieu d'oie*. Don't look so shocked. I did it for my father. Robert did it for his."

"What are you talking about?"

"He didn't tell you. I know that. We discussed it. "

"I don't believe it."

"I would have done it for Robert but it was impossible, with the hospital, the doctors. And of course, you hardly ever left his side."

"You're mad."

"They helped me to the bathroom at half past one. Nobody will come near me till four thirty at the earliest. As I said, they're short-staffed. The doctor's told them that my heart is very weak. It's true up to a point. It is weak – but not as weak as they think. I know my own body. I could go on for years, lying here, watching that hideous orchid drop its petals and grow new flowers, being heaved in and out of the bathroom like a sack of potatoes, with nothing to hope for and only regrets and bad memories for company."

"I don't believe Robert did – that."

"Of course he did. He was a good son – and a sensible man. If he was still here, he'd do it for me – out of love. I know you don't love me, Babette. God knows I've never given you cause to love me. I admit it. Everything you've done for me – and it's true, you've been good to me, very good – you did it all for Robert's sake. For his sake, I ask you to do this one last thing."

"No. No – I can't."

"There's no danger to you. I've heard them talk. 'The old Magnon woman could go at any moment.' They expect me to die. Nobody will ask any questions. Nobody will suspect anything. Look, here, my old pillow, that I made you bring me, my good goose-feather pillow that I had on my wedding day. Feel how soft it is. There won't be trace. Nothing. It's completely safe."

"It's a crime."

"No, it's not a crime. Robert never thought it was. No sensible person does. It's a mercy. I'm not afraid to meet God. I know he'll be merciful to me and I'll see Robert again – and that old devil of a husband of mine – and you too one day – and I'll thank you. And Robert will thank you. Please, please, Babette, do this for me."

"I – I don't know if I could. I don't think I'd have the courage."

"Of course you have the courage. You're a strong woman. Like me. Look at the way you've coped since Robert died. Letting the farm, selling the stock and machinery for a good price. Going into business. It's astonishing."

"I've had Elie and Pierre to help me."

"But you're the strong one. You'll make a big success. There's only one obstacle in your way. Well, you can remove it. All you have to do is take the pillow – here – take it – that's right. You don't have to look. I didn't look when I did it for Papa. I turned my–"

*

Editor's note: It was at this point that the tape ran out in the recorder hidden under the duvet of the late Marie-Louise Magnon's bed. The staff of the *Maison de Retraite* found her dead at about five o'clock in the afternoon. The machine was discovered a little later when her body was removed to the mortuary. The autopsy revealed that she had died of asphyxiation.

Her daughter-in-law, Elizabeth Magnon, was arrested and charged with her murder. After a sensational trial, which gripped the French media for weeks, she was found guilty. The evidence of the tape-recording proved fatal to her case.

HELENE RAGET

I was in Wales, running a positional analysis on my third marriage, when the Berlin Wall came down. To be strictly accurate – because, of course, the wall did not fall, Jericho style, in a single crash – I was in Wales, running a positional analysis on my third marriage, on the day – November 9th, 1989 – when the first mass invasions of the crossing-points were made by East German citizens, presaging the eventual demolition of the wall.

I remember with perfect clarity sitting in my in-laws' rebarbative living-room watching the news coverage on TV. The camera lingered for a moment on a young border-guard. Thousands of people were surging around him and past him and he was standing there, clutching his gun, with a look on his face that is difficult to capture in words. It was a mixture of bewilderment and anger, tinged with fear. His world was turning upside down. Nobody was afraid of him any more, nobody was intimidated by his uniform or his weapon, nobody in fact was paying any attention to him at all. And there was nothing he could do. Without orders he could not shoot – one burst over the heads of the crowd might have been enough – and he had received no such orders. Everything he had planned for his future, everything to which he had already committed himself, was being washed away on a tide of laughing, cheering, exultant humanity to whom he had become not only invisible but irrelevant.

The next day, Friday, my wife and I went for a soggy walk before lunch. I told her how the image of the border-guard, brief though it had been, still haunted me. "You had the same sort of look on *your* face," she said. "You're more or less fucked, aren't you?" We were trudging up the lane towards the hideous bungalow her parents had built for what my father-in-law would irritatingly describe as "the evening of our days" and I felt a sudden rush of anger.

"God knows how they ever got planning permission," I said. The bungalow was in full view, a banal construction of plate glass and weather-boarding, with attendant double-garage, plonked in the middle of an Elgarian landscape of fields and woods and dry-stone walls. "Christ, it's ghastly," I added. To which my wife replied:

"Oh dear, now what have I said?"

And there you have the Anna of 1989 – perceiving instantly that I was displacing my anger into an attack on her parents' taste while at the same time knowing precisely what had provoked me in the first place: her statement of the plain truth. The whole problem of our relationship was encapsulated in that moment, rather as the essence of the sea-change in German, European and indeed global politics had been caught in that glimpse of the young border-guard.

Nobody understood my failings better than Anna – the remoteness, the inability to engage whole-heartedly either in relationships or career, the tendency to retreat from reality into books and music – and nobody was as relentless in confronting me with them. It was what had first attracted me to her: her willingness to face up to things, bring them out into the open, deal with them and then to prod, tease and challenge others into doing the same. In the first years of our marriage I felt that I was breathing new air, ascending to some sunlit upland after fruitless wanderings in a shadowy plain. But the ozone of Anna's moral and spiritual high ground proved too rarefied for my corroded lungs. Opposites do attract and ideally the result is a fusion in which contrasting qualities are mutually enhanced and developed in productive ways. But in our case there had been a gradual fission, a process in which the differences between us had become so entrenched that our relationship had descended into exchanges of sniper fire across an emotional no-man's-land.

If the wall had fallen even five years earlier, the exchange between us would have been very different. It might have gone something like this:

Anna: You looked a bit shell-shocked yourself. Something huge is happening, isn't it?

Self: Well, theoretically, an East German border-guard and a British Cold War warrior, even a back-room boy like me, are mutually dependent. If the wall comes down we could both be out of a job.

Anna: D'you really think so?

Self: I have a feeling that my masters are already measuring me up for my de-mob suit.

Instead, what did we get? An attacking "You're more or less fucked," provoking an indirect counter-attack via a satellite state, in turn producing a polished if somewhat childish piece of snide mockery: "Oh dear, now what have I said?"

If that last speech was unworthy of the true Anna, what had triggered it was certainly unworthy of the true me. When conflict between husband and wife is conducted in this way, it is time to part. We had reached a point where we were starting to diminish each other. But all this was a later rationalisation. As we returned to the bungalow, I was still seething and Anna had a tight little, bright little smile on her face.

My father-in-law, in a Viyella shirt, baggy brown corduroys and tartan bedroom slippers, was opening a bottle of champagne – it was his wife's birthday. He was holding the bottle vertically while twisting the cork. The cork popped and champagne gushed and fizzed all over his hands and the Formica coffee table.

"Bugger," he said, while his wife rushed forward with a "For God's sake, Jack" and a fistful of paper handkerchiefs. As she mopped up, with a maximum amount of fuss, I said something like: "The trick is to hold it almost horizontally. I know it sounds counter-intuitive but in fact the science is impeccable. If you hold it upright – " I made a small circle with the thumb and index finger of my right hand " – the ratio of the surface of the liquid to the air is constricted, whereas if you tip the bottle, the ratio increases." I joined the thumbs and index fingers of both hands to form an oval rather larger than the circle.

"You'd better make a note of that, Dad," said Anna.

"Of course, we only have champagne on special occasions," said her mother.

"Well, let's get stuck in anyway," said Jack.

He was a retired chiropodist. He had spent his professional life hacking away at verrucas and his leisure hours mowing his lawn or attending to his "collection." He collected beer mats. His wife, Mary, had been a medical receptionist. I once saw her at work. While maintaining an outward air of kindly concern she subtly terrorized the ill and anxious people ringing in for appointments, revelling in her power as the group practice's gate-keeper. Her favourite word, both at work and at home, was "Sorry," delivered with a slightly exaggerated, syrupy inflection that conveyed the opposite meaning. She was odious.

I behaved appallingly over lunch, knowing that I was doing so, despising myself for it, but unable to stop. I suppose what I was trying to do was to provoke a row with Anna, but lacking the capacity – the courage, Anna would say – to set off the required explosion, I continued to conduct the conflict in the manner of the Cold War itself, by proxy, the hapless Jack and increasingly edgy Mary becoming so many Vietnams, Angolas, Afghanistans and so on.

I feel justified in recounting all this, first because it relates to the subject of this piece, namely the destructive forces that can be unleashed within a family (the "nuclear family" is well named) and second, because when I stood up, after the cheese, and headed towards the door, saying that I was going for a walk, I was literally taking the first steps along the path that would lead me to France.

There have been one of two moments in my life that might described as dramatic – a flurry or two in Germany in the '60's when I was working in the field, another time, many years later, when I happened to solve a murder case – but nothing really compares with the afternoon of November 10th, 1989.

I didn't go back.

I walked to the village Post Office, rang for a taxi, took the next available train to London and called Anna to tell her that as far as I was concerned our marriage was over.

A few weeks later, I was in West Berlin, dining in a dismal restaurant full of fake beams and pottery beer steins, with a dear old soak, let's call him Harry, who had been a CIA spook before being rewarded with a sinecure in the Security Department of the Senate, the somewhat toothless entity that officially ran the city at that time and in which, for purely cosmetic political reasons, the Americans, British and French participated.

By that time the wall was being demolished in earnest, not as yet by bulldozers but by hundreds of thousands of souvenir-hunters hacking chunks out of it. They had been dubbed *Mauerspechte*, wall-woodpeckers, Harry told me. We discussed the symbolism of this – no doubt as a way of avoiding more painful subjects. But as kummel followed kummel we found we could no longer evade the question uppermost in both our minds: the implications of all this for us personally. Harry was clear that the reunification of Germany was now inevitable and that his job would cease to exist. He regretted this because although he was over sixty he had no desire to retire, still less to live in America. I reminded him that during our last conversation, just under a year ago, he had told me that the situation with the wall was worse than it had been for some time, four people having recently been shot while attempting to escape to the West. He had predicted that the wall, and the East German regime, would remain firmly in place for the foreseeable future.

"That was all true," Harry said. "People were still trying to escape and they were still getting their asses shot. What I didn't figure was that this was the last thrashing of the snake before it dies. The whole damned system's falling apart. Gorbachev can't hold the line and he knows it. I was saying to my Mom the other day – she's ninety years old – you saw the Soviet Union come and you're seeing it go within your own lifetime. Fucking amazing."

We discussed my own situation. Harry was sanguine. He thought my Service would always need experienced Intelligence analysts. I said, "Well you got it wrong last time and I suspect you've got it wrong this time."

"Yeah, well, maybe I was just being polite," he replied, with a laugh. "But hey, look on the bright side. We won didn't we?" Then he suggested another round of kummels. It seemed like an excellent idea.

In the following months Germany headed rapidly towards reunification and conversations in the office began to revolve round the early retirement packages on offer. I had just turned fifty-five and was eligible. By this time I was commuting from Oxfordshire, where I had a cottage, having handed over the London flat to Anna. The divorce was going through amicably enough and it was becoming clear that my masters – in the nicest possible way, of course – wanted me out.

Then one Tuesday, when I was lunching at my club, I found myself entertaining an angel unawares in the form of Sir Robert Pennycuick who had been at our Bonn embassy when I'd been stationed there in the Sixties. He had gone on to be our Ambassador in various not terribly important countries and was now retired and living in South West France.

As he described his life there I began to detect the glimmer of a possible future for myself. What with two divorces already under my belt and a third going through, I was looking at what my father used to call "straitened circumstances" in spite of the not ungenerous pension on offer and the remnants of my mother's family money. Bob waxed lyrical about the peace and beauty of Gascony, the agreeable weather, the low cost of living and the fact that one could still buy a handsome property for a fraction of the price one would have to pay in England. "Life moves at the pace of a bicycle," he said. "It's like the England of the 1950's." He gave me his address and telephone number.

In early September of the same year, 1990, towards the end of the day, I found myself taking Exit 7 off the A62 autoroute and heading along the D 931 towards Condom. (It has nothing to do with the condom.) The road curled and rose and fell through a magical world of vineyards, meadows, woods, ancient unspoiled villages, crumbling farms and half-hidden *manoirs* and small *chateaux* so beautiful as to be almost absurd. I could hardly believe that such a rustic idyll still existed in a France that I had found, to my dismay, widely disfigured by indiscriminately sited *lotissements* and EU-dictated agribusiness.

It was a countryside that evoked two seminal landscapes of my past: the rural England of the wartime years, during which I had been at a Prep School in the remotest corner of Shropshire and the France of the immediate post-war period – sleepy, tumbledown and in my memory at least perpetually sunny – where, every summer until the early 1950's, my father would take us on long, whimsical motoring holidays full of mechanical crises, map-reading fracas and stupefying meals. (Where is the *Menu Gastronomique* today? Almost vanished.)

As I proceeded south, further wonders were revealed. Beyond Eauze (once the capital of the region, now a modest but very beautiful market town) I emerged onto the D 924 and found myself on a high plateau with massive views, over expanses of exquisitely shaped, richly wooded hills, towards the Pyrenees. In the early evening light, the mountains seemed like some hazy, fantastical backdrop painted onto the sky.

I had pencilled a route to Bob Pennycuick's house which from this point on avoided, wherever possible, even the yellow D roads and stuck resolutely to white-coloured country lanes. The landscape became even more sumptuously lovely. Villages and farms were sparser, adding to the impression of remoteness, of one's having strayed, like Augustin Meaulnes, into a world apart, a hidden, secret world, not quite real.

The map told me that I would all too soon be heading down into the valley of the river Adour and its tributary, the Arros, and I anticipated less exciting prospects. I was wrong. Once across the D 946, I entered a network of straight, narrow roads that ran, like tunnels, through towering fields of maize. On every side, irrigators were pumping plumes of water into the air. It was as if a myriad fountains were playing, catching the light of the sinking sun and fragmenting it into evanescent rainbows and elliptical cascades of precious stones. Such, by now, was my enchantment (or egoism) that I felt it was all some wonderful display put on to welcome me home.

Somebody (Graham Greene?) has written that one can never quite escape the landscape of one's early childhood: that, for good or ill, it haunts one for the rest of one's life – to such an extent that, in some cases, people find themselves trying endlessly and usually hopelessly to recapture it. Well, my early childhood was spent in Africa, first in Kenya and Tanganyika, later in what was then the British Protectorate of Bechuanaland (now the Republic of Botswana.) What, you may ask, has South West France got to do with Africa? Well, that was the final marvel of that day of marvels.

Somewhere between St Aunix and Belloc I took a wrong turn and was soon well and truly lost. The roads weren't signposted and it became obvious that many of them simply weren't marked on the map. After ten minutes or more of aimless to-ing and fro-ing through the maize fields, I spotted a church spire and swung left onto a farm track that seemed to be heading in its direction. A few moments later I emerged onto a better-looking road, a few hundred yards from the little church. I stopped. I was about to pick up the map when I saw, directly opposite me, on the far side of the road, a pair of sagging, rusty entrance gates hung between two leaning stone piers. Attached to the gates by twist of old wire was a small, battered wooden board, once white, now a flaking yellow, on which was the spidery, hand-written legend "AV". The right-hand down-stroke of the A was combined with the left-hand upstroke of the V. Below was scrawled a barely decipherable telephone number.

AV. A Vendre. For Sale.

I parked the car on the verge beyond the gates and walked back. I peered through the ornate iron-work. A roughly gravelled track, overgrown with weeds, disappeared into a riot of banana trees. Beyond, I thought I could make out the tops of palm trees. It all seemed improbably exotic. I examined the gates. The For Sale sign was masking a handle, half eaten by rust, and the ruins of a lock. I pushed gently. There was almost no resistance. The gates swung inwards with a rasping groan. I looked up and down the road. I couldn't see another house, let alone another person. I stepped through the gates and followed the track. Beyond the belt of banana trees was what had once been a farm-yard. It was bounded on three sides by buildings in a state of near collapse and on the fourth by the palm trees I had glimpsed from the road. And beyond the palm trees I thought I could detect the glint of water.

With a bare glance at the buildings – taking in no more than an impression of a long, single-storey farmhouse, a jumble of barns and some sort of *pigeonnier* – I pushed through the thick undergrowth at the base of the palms, through the dank shadows cast by out-of-control alders and other scrub, to the bank of a river that, judging by its width, had to be the Adour itself. A few yards from where I was standing a spit of land stretched out like a half-curled hand, creating a natural bathing pool. In spite of dense spirals of midges, I stripped off immediately, stepped into the water, which was clear and blood-warm and swam out into the lazily flowing stream. As I kicked back towards the pool I was already imagining the scrub and alders cleared away, meadow grass sloping down to the water, the whole bank opened up to the light and the air and the midges migrating to some suitably foetid spot further upstream or downstream.

It was only when I was tramping damply back to the farmyard that I finally made the African connexion and then it was sounds rather than sights that did it. Somewhere nearby hundreds of frogs suddenly started up a raucous yet mellifluous chorus while in the background throbbed the scratching percussion of cicadas. I said, out loud: "My God, it's Africa." It wasn't just the frogs and cicadas or the palms or bananas: in the half light, the buildings themselves, especially the long, low farmhouse, could have been part of a lodge at the foot of Mount Meru and the little circular *pigeonnier* with its conical roof, a rondavel. And as, a little later, and having got my bearings, I drove on, the roads were transformed in my imagination into the watercourses of the Okavango Delta and the maize fields became the reed-beds and papyrus through which they flowed.

I could tell at once that Bob Pennycuick was rather nettled by my lyrical account of all this and that his wife, Betty, was positively cross. They had gone to some considerable trouble on my behalf, visiting half a dozen local Estate Agents and collecting quite a stack of particulars of properties they thought might suit me. I dutifully leafed through them and soon realized that what they had in mind for me was a humbler version of their own house, a very beautiful early 19th century *Maison de Maître*, in a commanding position, with views towards the

Madiran wine country and the Pyrenees. Over dinner, Betty remarked, in tones that suggested that I was in danger of breaking some taboo or committing a grave solecism, that in this particular region of France it seemed madness not to go for a house with a view of the mountains and that none of their friends had ever thought of buying down in the plains.

Betty, I realized (I had not known her well before) was one of those women who like to manage other peoples' lives. I felt that this was as much due to the life she had led with Bob as to her innate character. She had spent years in out-of-the-way corners of the world looking after junior Embassy staff, making sure they lived in the right part of town, met the right sort of people, hired honest servants, never overpaid in markets, married suitably and avoided the sort of scrapes that might give rise to a diplomatic incident. In short, she was used to taking people under her wing – and I had already made a sort of dash for freedom. And I had committed a further misdemeanour. This part of France was *her* patch, *her* area of expertise. The fact that I had independently discovered what even she had to admit sounded like an exciting property, in a hamlet – just down the road – that was unknown to her, was a sort of affront.

Of course this did not stop her coming with Bob and me first thing next morning to view the property. I had wondered whether, in the cold light of day, it would seem quite so magical. Initially, I had to admit, there were some disappointments. For a start, I had somehow got the impression that it was isolated. In fact, I now saw, it was sandwiched between two other properties. To the left, mostly hidden behind a high wall, was a large, rather ugly mid-19th century *maison bourgeoise* and to the right, a scarecrow of a farm, surrounded by rusting agricultural implements and abandoned cars. Opposite this was another farm, almost as dishevelled. To the right of the church was what had been the presbytery. It was clear that it had been recently done up – and not in the very best of taste. On the other side of the road was one of those stark, stuccoed modern villas which the French have spread like a blight over their beautiful country.

"Oh dear," said Betty, eyeing it. "How hideous. It ruins what would otherwise be a very picturesque hamlet." She added: "I suppose the church is closed. They all are. I don't imagine there's been a Mass said there for years. So sad."

When we pushed through the banana trees and saw the house and its outbuildings, she said: "Blimey." And indeed, in the bright morning sunshine, I could see that the property was in a state of near-dereliction. "But wait," I said – and led them through the palms to the river bank. Betty was not impressed. "God knows what sort of flooding you'll get in winter," she said.

"But it would mean that one wouldn't have to bother with a swimming pool," I countered.

"What about Weil's disease?"

"What about it?"

"It can actually be fatal, you know."

"The real danger in river bathing is pike. They can go for your bits. Nasty business."

Which produced a guffaw (there is no other word) from Bob and a beady look from Betty.

We returned to the buildings. "I wouldn't know where to begin," said Betty.

"Well, the roofs, I suppose," I said.

"You're not going to–?"

"I am."

"But you haven't even looked at anything else."

"I don't need to."

And the truth was that I didn't. In spite of the proximity of other houses – and it remains a mystery to me how I could have overlooked them the day before – and the state of the buildings, I knew that I had to have the place, that I would be happy there and might even be able to share that happiness with others.

I was writing down the telephone number on the "For Sale" board when a man emerged through a gate in the high wall of the big house next door. He wore a beret and those overalls apparently unique to France called *bleus*. All he needed, I said later, to complete the picture of the stereotypical Frenchman was a baguette and an accordion. ("Or a string of onions and an old bicycle," said Bob. "Even a Frenchman can hardly play the accordion with a baguette under his arm," said Betty.)

Apart from the beret and the *bleus*, the man was nondescript – medium height, medium build, in his late fifties, I judged. His manner was nervous. He didn't look at any of us directly. I opened the conversation by asking how long it had been since anybody had lived in the house. He said he didn't know exactly but certainly not since the war. He spoke with a strong regional accent. Some instinct then made me say that I was thinking of buying the place. (This earned me a ticking off from Betty when we were back in the car. "Never reveal your hand to these people. They're as cunning as lynxes.")

"Ah," the man said. "I see you've taken down the number. That was old Quintan's number. He's no longer with us. You'd have to contact the Notary in Charmeuil, Maître Dulac." He spelt the name out for me and made sure that I had written it down correctly. "A lot of English are buying here," he said. "Too many, perhaps," I replied. "No, no," he said, with a faint smile. "The French don't care about old houses. They let them fall down. The English restore them, restore the *patrimoine*. It's to be encouraged, I think." Then he smiled again, a much broader smile this time and added: "Good luck with Maître Dulac. *Bon courage*."

"And what exactly did he mean by *that*?" said Betty once the man was safely out of earshot and had vanished back through the gate in the wall.

I found out that very afternoon in Maître Dulac's well-appointed office. The property, which was called

Palanouard, had belonged to an old bachelor who had died five years ago without making a Will. In such circumstances, Dulac explained, the State was entitled to sixty per cent of the estate, the remainder to be divided equally among deceased's cousins, nieces, nephews and their descendants. "There are thirty five of them!" said Maître Dulac with ill-concealed relish. The most senior, he went on, had been a man called Quintan. It had been agreed that he should handle the sale of the various properties and liaise with the notary. But since his own death, it seemed that *les trente-cinq* – as I was already beginning to think of them – had been unable to agree on anything at all and the whole process of winding up the estate had ground to a halt.

"Now I understand why the gardener wished me luck."

"The gardener?"

"From the big house next door."

I described what had happened. Maître Dulac shook his well-coiffed head. "That wasn't the gardener. That was your neighbour – well he will be your neighbour if you buy the property – Pierre-Jean Raget. It's actually his wife who owns the house. It's called Castilloux."

Dulac, an extremely elegant man in every sense of the word, who invariably wore a dark blue blazer with brass buttons and a striped tie, was a mine of further information. The scarecrow farm to the right of Palanouard belonged to an old woman called Dupeyron, the one opposite, to a *jeune agriculteur* called Cassagnau. The former presbytery was the week-end retreat of a *Juge D'Instruction* in Auch called Ducasse and the new house opposite had been recently built by the man who ran the *Maison de la Presse* in Charmeuil. His name was Olivier Barbat. Dulac had acted for all of them at various times. I later learned that he was the fourth generation of his family to practise as a *notaire* in the area.

I solved the problem of *les trente-cinq* in the simplest way: by making an offer way over the asking price. Betty was naturally appalled and even Bob blinked a bit – but from my point of view it didn't matter. Anna had agreed to settle for the London flat and a modest lump sum, leaving me free to sell the Oxfordshire cottage, which I did, very quickly, for a hell of a price.

Ask me the type of book I least like to read, indeed that I most detest and despise, and I can tell you without hesitation that it is any sort of memoir about buying and restoring a house in France. These allegedly autobiographical works are in fact largely fiction since their authors feel impelled to create a cast of characters – eccentric plumbers, gnomic plasterers, mad roofers and so on, all reeking of garlic and with no idea of time – that have no basis in reality whatsoever and serve only to feed atavistic Anglo-Saxon fantasies about the French. The fact is that French artisans and tradesmen are generally the sort of efficient, matter-of-fact, hard-working, skilful people who actually manage to survive and prosper in the building trade and most of them are in any case, at least in the South West, of Arab, Italian or Spanish origin!

About the restoration of Palanouard, its transformation into a comfortable house, with six bedrooms, a vast living room, separate quarters, with a library and study, for me and river bathing at the end of a gently sloping lawn, I will say only that it took nearly two years and cost three times the original estimate. But at the end of it all I had what Bob described – somewhat to his wife's irritation – as a *petit paradis*. And to complete poor Betty's chagrin, when the air to the South was clear, one could even see the peaks of the Pyrenees!

While the works were going on at the house, I rented a *gîte* in the former stables of a small *château*, called Harlat, on the northern side of the valley, belonging to an exiled English peer called Anthony Eames – the 16th Baron and 6th Viscount Eames of Luddenhall, to give him his full title. But since I visited the site almost every day, I got to know my neighbours pretty well even though I wasn't yet living among them. Old Mme. Dupeyron (she was in fact only in her early seventies but somehow one thought of her as old) gave me fresh vegetables from her astonishing *potager* – tomatoes so richly flavoured and finely textured that they seemed like meat – and young Cassagnau and his wife (they were in their early thirties but one thought of them as young) were friendly and helpful. I didn't see a great deal of the Judge – Ducasse – mainly because he was rarely there in winter and in summer was surrounded by family and although I regularly dropped into M. Barbet's shop in Charmeuil to pick up my day-late copy of *The Times* I did not at that stage get to know him particularly well.

I was about to write that the person I got to know best was Pierre-Jean Raget; it would more accurate to say that the person *I saw most of* was Pierre-Jean Raget. He pottered round from next door most days and we would frequently chat for an hour or more. But these conversations were so general – the weather, the vagaries of restoring old houses and so forth – and so impersonal that I learned very little about him. Although his manner was perfectly pleasant, friendly and open he managed to put up an invisible aura that was somehow impossible to penetrate with a personal question. As to his wife, Hélène, she was an enigma. Very occasionally, in summer, I would get a glimpse, through the gate in the high wall, of a slim, grey-haired woman in a blue-grey dressing-gown, watering the geraniums on the terrace in front of the house, and I assumed this was Mme. Raget. I didn't actually know.

In one of her stories, Colette notes that the French provinces are rich in fantastic figures and that every little village prides itself on possessing a mystery. She was, of course, writing about late 19th century France – but I think it's fair to say that not much has changed. I asked Mme. Dupeyron about the Ragets but all she could tell me was that they had been married for about ten years – a second marriage for her – that the house had been in Mme. Raget's family, that Mme. Raget was (she thought) from Paris and had money of her own. Mme. Dupeyron herself was from a different country (her word) – the Béarn – and therefore her knowledge was incomplete. The Cassagnau couple had only recently bought their farm and knew almost nothing. M. Barbet was equally uninformative, whether through ignorance or natural reticence it was impossible, at that stage of our relationship, to tell.

Curiously, it was my landlord, Anthony Eames, who was able, to some extent, to fill in the gaps in my knowledge of the mysterious Ragets. "Ah, la belle Hélène," he said one evening, a few weeks after I had moved into the *gîte* and was beginning to be enfolded into his inner circle. "One used to see a lot of her but since she remarried…"

According to Anthony – but, wait. He has been dead since the summer of 1999 but I hear his voice in my head. "My dear boy," he is saying in his clipped-but-languid upper-class drawl, "you haven't given me an *entrance*. I'm slipping into your story by the tradesmen's door. *Not* appropriate."

How to give a picture of Anthony? Perhaps in his own words. Of his physical appearance, he would say: "Of course, we all know I look like a cross between Lord Byron and Shylock." Of his father, the fifth Viscount: "He shot things. Grouse, pheasant, partridge and stags in time of peace and in time of war Germans, Japs and Eyeties. In the end, he shot himself." Of his mother, the Dowager Viscountess: "Double, double toil and trouble; fire burn and cauldron bubble." Of his American boyfriend, Joe, who hailed from a small town in Oklahoma called Dustin: "From Dustin thou art and unto Dustin thou shalt return." Of his ancestor, the first Baron Eames: "A favourite of James the First. Need one say more." Of the first Viscount, a General in India: "He laid about him with supreme efficiency, plundering Princely palaces from one end of the sub-Continent to the other – all in the name of pacifying the natives. He returned in triumph, a gigantic bag labelled swag over his shoulder."

Anthony (always Anthony, *never* Tony) had just turned fifty when I met him and had been living in France for twenty years. His father's suicide had left him with enormous death duties to pay and he had been forced to hand over Luddenhall Court, the family seat in Kent – an exquisite country house by Inigo Jones – to the National Trust. ("Bloody place always felt like a museum. Now it is one.") His mother still lived there and his tales of her guerrilla warfare with the Trust were guaranteed dinner-party show-stoppers.

What else can one say about Anthony? He had a habit of allotting possessive nicknames to his closest friends. Bob Pennycuick was "Our Ambassador," Betty, "Our Ambassadress," a retired Anglican priest who lived in a nearby village, "Our Padre," and so on. In due course I naturally became "Our Spook" – until he discovered that my first wife's father, Lord Airne, was some sort of relation of his, whereupon I was transformed into "Cher Cousin." He was a Catholic convert who took his religion much more seriously than one might have supposed. He was an ardent Stuart Successionist, a member of the Royal Stuart Society ("One must remain loyal to dear James The First.") He invariably referred to the present Royal Family as "those ghastly Schleswig-Holstein-Sonderburg-Glücksburgs" and at dinner would invite us all to drink the health of the Duke of Bavaria, aka King Francis II. With Joe, he ran an antiques business that always seemed to me to involve a lot of buying and very little selling – and it was through the business (to return to the point where this rather lengthy digression began) that he had come across Hélène Raget.

Her grandfather, Henri Merle-Rivière, had been a famous antiques dealer in Paris at the turn of the last century. A pioneer of ethnic art, especially African totem art, he had supplied the Trocadéro Museum with many of its finest pieces. His son, Max, Hélène's father, had inherited the business. When he died, in the 1970's, it had passed to his only daughter, Hélène. By this time Hélène was married to a man called Jacques Benoit. "An utter wastrel apparently, my dear," Anthony said. "Whistled through her money like the Flying Scotsman. Drink, gambling, women, mad business ventures – the usual. She used to recount it all in vivid detail and of course one shook one's head and tut-tutted like mad but actually the bold Jacques sounded rather amusing. One loves a rogue. Of course she divorced him. Two children left bobbing in the wake. I've met them. Absolute horrors. But I suppose it's not their fault, poor things."

Hélène had come to live in the South West soon after the divorce. "Hideous house. Built by her great-grandfather on her mother's side. She has some sort of sentimental attachment to it, spent childhood holidays there, you know what the French are. Don't know how she can stand it. She has impeccable taste." She and Anthony soon got to know each other and became quite close friends. "She adored Joe. Always the way to my heart." For some years they had seen a lot of each other, lunching and dining together regularly. Then – as Anthony put it – came The Fall. "She married that dim little man. She brought him to dinner. He bored us all into dry racking sobs. We tried to cover up but of course she twigged. I rang the next day to make peace and we had one of those polite conversations – so exquisitely polite that one realized it was the *last* conversation. Since then, *silence absolu*. Such a shame."

I gathered that for a time Hélène's marriage had been a major topic of debate among Anthony's circle. Nobody could understand why she had done it, especially when it transpired that she had met Pierre-Jean Raget in the Crédit Agricole bank in Charmeuil, where he worked as a clerk. On the grounds that he had retired from the bank soon after the marriage, Anthony deduced that he had married *her* for her money – but why she had married *him* remained a mystery. She was rich, cultivated, *mondaine*. He was, well, a bank clerk – and during that disastrous dinner party had shown no signs of wit, sophistication or education. "In the end," said Anthony, "we went with Joe's theory." "And what was that?" I asked. "A ten inch cock," said Anthony.

Those early years at Palanouard were unquestionably the happiest of my life. In the summer of 1992 both my children by my first marriage came to stay, Jenny and her husband from America, Tim and his wife from Australia, and I met my grandchildren for the first time. These summer visits became part of the tapestry of all our lives (they still are) and because life attracts life my immediate neighbours were drawn closer.

Most days Mme. Dupeyron would stagger round with a basketful of vegetables. The Cassagnaus, who had three children in quick succession, were regular visitors, especially after I – reluctantly – put in a swimming-pool. (Both Jenny and Tim had Betty-Pennycuick-type objections to river bathing and even I had to admit that for very young children it was dangerous.) Tim and Jenny's American husband, Alex, were addicted to barbecues and that attracted the Judge, Georges Ducasse, and his family, who were similarly afflicted. (I have steadfastly refused to get involved with the barbecue, my role being confined to supplying mountains of steaks, sausages and chicken legs and rivers of Saint Mont *rouge* and *rosé*.) The Barbets, Olivier and his rather beautiful wife, Marie-Yvonne, were cordial if still a little distant but then they kept very different hours, starting work at the *Maison de la Presse* impossibly early in the morning and thus, understandably, not too keen on night-time revels.

Ironically – or, with hindsight, I would say understandably – the life that had returned to Palanouard, while it attracted everyone else in the hamlet to varying degrees, repelled the Ragets. I now saw very little of Pierre-Jean, even in winter, and nothing at all of his wife. I would occasionally bump into him at the Intermarché in Charmeuil and we would chat pleasantly – he was always *pleasant* – about nothing much. I once ventured to ask him if the screams of the grandchildren, frolicking in the pool, disturbed him. "No, no, not at all," was all he said.

And so things carried on, very agreeably as far as I was concerned, until the winter of 1997. Summer visitors would often ask me what I did during the winter and the answer is that apart from my books and music, I occupied myself with what Jenny had dubbed "Dad's archives." In fact they were not, strictly speaking, my archives, but the archives of the small publishing house, Wheeler & Coates, that my father had started in London just after the war and ran until his death in 1981, when the business of winding everything up, mainly returning copyrights to authors, settling debts, and selling off the last bits and pieces to a larger publisher, had fallen to me. Wheeler & Coates had published some very interesting poets and novelists in the '50's and '60's and before my mother died, in 1984, I had made a semi-promise to her to write a short history of the firm as a tribute to my father – and indirectly to her because it had been her money that had kept the show more or less on the road. I was not so wrapped up in this task, however, that I failed to notice a change in the pattern of life next door.

One morning, as I was setting off for a walk, I saw the Ragets' Renault emerge through the gateway on the western side of the property. No great surprise there. I often saw Pierre-Jean setting off to go shopping and he was invariably alone. The mild surprise therefore was that his wife was with him in the car. The major surprise was that she was driving and Pierre-Jean was in the passenger seat.

Late that afternoon, I happened to see the car return. Again, Hélène was driving – and since they had been out all day, I couldn't help wondering where they had been and what was going on.

A few weeks later, Olivier Barbet enlightened me. Pierre-Jean, he said, had cancer. Hélène was regularly driving him to the hospital in Auch for observation and treatment. Some days after this I met and spoke to Hélène for the very first time. It was in the prosaic setting of the Intermarché car park. A thin, cold drizzle was falling. She was dressed in a rather elegant fawn mackintosh. She wore a headscarf that I thought was Hermès. We coincided at the trolleys. It was impossible to avoid some sort of conversation. I opened it (rather boldly, she commented much later, when we had become friends) by saying that I had heard of her husband's illness and that I was very sorry. "Thank you," she said. "The doctors are pleased with him. We have hopes of a full recovery." With that, she slotted a coin into a trolley and wheeled it away. I followed her slowly, allowing her to get ahead, because I sensed that she wanted to avoid further contact. In the supermarket, I kept getting will-o'-the-wisp glimpses of her in the maze of aisles. I had a mad desire to get behind her in the check-out queue because, for some reason, I wanted to know what she had bought. I resisted this. In fact, I lingered for a few minutes to allow her to make her way past the till unobserved.

I thought perhaps that, now the ice had been broken, I would see a little more of her. Nothing of the sort happened. She made no moves in my direction and I certainly didn't want to impose on her in any way. I had to rely on Olivier, at the *Maison de la Presse*, for news of the Ragets. He and his wife had become close to them and were helping them out as much as they could. Pierre-Jean's condition worsened. He was taken to Toulouse, an international centre of excellence in cancer treatment. He returned home in the early summer of 1998 and died on June 12th in the late afternoon. Olivier told me that the funeral was to be held in our little church and that traditionally close neighbours attended, however slightly they had known the deceased.

Hélène once told me that she had been amazed at the number of people who came to Pierre-Jean's funeral. And she rather grudgingly admitted that she had also been touched. Apart from the immediate neighbours, there were a lot of other local people, a sprinkling of Pierre-Jean's former colleagues from the bank and a host – I don't exaggerate – of his relations: aunts, uncles, nieces, nephews, cousins. Somehow I had never thought of him as having a family of his own, but there they were, the more elderly men in formal suits, the middle-aged in ill-fitting tweed jackets and blazers, the women in their Sunday dresses and the young in jeans and trainers. I couldn't help thinking of *les trente-cinq*. Somewhat to my surprise, Anthony and Joe turned up, and of course Maître Dulac was there. The church, which smelt of mould and damp, was packed.

Hélène sat in one of the front pews, flanked by her two children. I was towards the back so I didn't get a good sight of them until the end of the ceremony, when they and their mother followed the coffin out. The son, François, a hulk of a man, paunchy and round-shouldered, with purplish bags under his eyes, looked cross and sulky. His sister, Marie-Hélène, was tall, thin and bony, with a long neck, a receding chin and a small mouth down-turned in a permanent pout. She looked mean, peevish and rather dangerous. I learned later that at the time François was thirty-eight and his sister thirty-six. Both looked considerably older. But, to me, the real puzzle lay in trying to relate their physical appearance to their mother's. I could find virtually no resemblance. Hélène, as I think I have already indicated, was slight, fine-boned with – to use an outmoded expression – a look of good breeding about her. She possessed an inner radiance, a sort of serenity, that made her, well, beautiful. She had dignity. As one watched her follow her husband's coffin out of the church one could certainly sense her grief, very powerfully, but also the strength of character that forbade any public expression of what she was feeling.

The reception afterwards was held in the Barbets' garden. Hélène and her children did not attend. They had gone, with the coffin, to the crematorium. Anthony, Joe and I did not stay long. As soon as we decently could we slipped away to Palanouard to get mildly drunk. About an hour after Anthony and Joe had left, I was by the pool, checking the chlorine and PH levels, when a woman's voice suddenly ripped through the silence. I couldn't make out the words but the tone was unmistakable – ungovernable rage. A moment later a man's voice rose above the hysterical torrent pouring out of the woman. "Ça va pas, ça va pas, ça va pas," he shouted, over and over again. The voices were coming from Castilloux, next door and something told me that they belonged to Hélène's children. What shocked me – and I felt a physical shock – was the violence, the raw intensity of the anger in those voices. For a second I thought I ought to do something, go round there. Someone, I felt, was going to kill someone. Then the voices faded. A few minutes later, I heard a car leaving.

Next day, when I went to get my paper, I mentioned the incident to Olivier. It was mid-morning, the shop was empty and he was able to talk. "Yes," he said. "There was a big row after the funeral. She doesn't get on with her children, you know. She never has. I was surprised that they came at all. After something, I suppose. I don't know how they could treat their mother like that – on the day of her husband's funeral – it's completely unfeeling."

About a fortnight later, as I was setting out for one of my regular walks, I happened to glance through gate in the high wall. Hélène was on the terrace, dead-heading the geraniums. On an impulse, I stopped and waved. After a slight hesitation, she gave a little wave back. On a further impulse, I tried the gate. It wasn't locked. I opened it and entered Hélène's territory for the first time. She looked faintly startled as I approached. She was wearing a faded house-coat and apron. Somehow, her aristocratic air made these shabby garments seem chic. "I just wanted to say," I started, rather awkwardly, "that if you need anything, I'm next door." "That's very kind," she said. And that was all she said. There was an edgy silence. At least, it was edgy to me. She seemed perfectly at ease and unembarrassed. "Well," I said eventually, "if you need anything." I walked away with a feeling that I had made some sort of unwarrantable intrusion. At the same time I felt resentful, almost angry that my neighbourly advances had been so regally rejected. "Don't worry about it," Olivier advised me, when I took my troubles to him. "She's a very private person." Fine, I thought to myself. But why is she as thick as thieves with the Barbets but wants to have nothing to do with me? What have I done? What's wrong with me? "It doesn't matter, Dad," Jenny said later that summer. "She's obviously a bit bonkers. Forget it."

That's what I tried to do. But the situation rankled with me. For some inexplicable reason I wanted to be Hélène's friend. I wanted to be able to knock on her door in the same casual, neighbourly way that I could with old Madame Dupeyron, with the Cassagnaus, the Ducasses and the Barbets. But it was more than that. It was as if that stolid, glowering, ugly house was some sort of magical domain from which I was excluded. Absurdly, I felt like some minor courtier at Louis XIV's Versailles desperate for an invitation to Marly.

On 12th August, 1999, at about twenty past six in the evening, Anthony Eames was found dead in the woods near Harlat. He had been murdered, bludgeoned to death with a hammer. My neighbour, Georges Ducasse, the *Juge D'Instruction*, was put in charge of the case. Some days later he asked me to play a role in the investigation. He explained that under French law he had the right to appoint whomever he wished to assist the police. At the time of his death Anthony had been entertaining quite a large house-party at Harlat, including his mother, his cousin – and heir to the title – and six other friends, all English and all, of course, potential suspects. The police had already encountered considerable language problems in interviewing these people but, according to Georges, the difficulty was greater than that. The inspector leading the enquiry had no real insight into the English character and mind-set and Georges was convinced that without those elements the case would be extremely difficult to solve. "In most murder cases," he said, " it's obvious who did it. But from time to time one comes across a case where nothing is obvious, nothing is quite as it seems, when one has to be alert to the subtlest nuances to arrive at the truth. Inspector Rezet is, quite frankly, out of his depth. He needs help. With your background in Intelligence, as a friend of the Vicomte, you are ideally placed."

And so I turned into a sort of latter-day Hercule Poirot – except that I had an official position with right of access to all information gathered by the police, particularly forensics – attempting to solve a classic Country House Murder. It is not a story I propose to tell here and I mention it only because it opened the door to my friendship with Hélène Raget. Anthony's murder was, as may be imagined, a local *cause célèbre*. The regional papers were full of it and my somewhat controversial involvement became known. It was that, as she later admitted with disarming frankness, which prompted Hélène to phone me one afternoon and invite me round for a drink.

"Facts are better than dreams," Winston Churchill famously wrote. Generally speaking, I disagree. Dreams never disappoint, realities almost always do. The perfect desert island remains perfect in the imagination. Step ashore on a real one and most likely you will find it infested with sand-flies and stinging jellyfish. I had built up an image of the interior of Castilloux in my mind as a sort of mysterious treasure-house of beautiful things inherited by Hélène from her father and grandfather, of large, dim, cool rooms full of priceless bronzes, gilded mirrors, glowing tapestries, patinated marquetry. As I approached her front door, I was convinced that I would be disappointed, that the fairy-tale palace would turn out to be full of lugubrious *buffets*, irritating occasional tables and some sort of hideous three piece suite. I was quite wrong. In the hall, to the right of the main staircase hung a stunning late 17th century Verdure tapestry. Opposite, by the door into the main *salon*, was a cabinet full of the African totem art Anthony had mentioned, elongated ebony masks that normally I would have found faintly repellent but which in this setting I discovered to be both beautiful and fascinating. In the *salon* itself, over the fire-place, hung a stupendous Louis XIV carved giltwood mirror in the Baroque style. I felt I had arrived at Marly itself! But I must not be drawn into an inventory of Hélène's possessions, glamorous though they were. The thing that I remember most vividly about that first visit is the ease with which the conversation flowed. It was as if we were old friends, as if all the distance and reticence of the past had never existed.

So began a close and immensely rewarding friendship. Hélène was exactly as Anthony had described her: cultivated, sophisticated, *mondaine*. But she was more than all that. She was thoughtful, original and had a dry, sly wit that appealed to me enormously. "God, Dad, don't say you're going to marry her," Jenny said once. "I've had quite enough of all that," I replied, "and so, I think, has she." I reported this exchange to Hélène and she agreed that it just about summed up the situation.

I have said that in that first long conversation (three hours and God knows how many whiskies) the former distance between us had evaporated but in fact, as I got to know her better and better, I realized that there were still barriers between us that I could not cross, that nobody perhaps could cross. I discussed this with Olivier. He agreed. He too felt that there was a core to Hélène that she would never expose to another person, that he felt sure she had never exposed to anybody except possibly to Pierre-Jean.

By this time Olivier and I were taking it in turns to mow Hélène's grass, a job that Pierre-Jean had, of course, always done. Olivier, who was something of a gardener (I am not) also took on the heavier manual tasks outside. It was a puzzle to us that Hélène would not employ a professional gardener. Nor would she engage a *femme de ménage* to help with the house-work. I knew that Marie-Ange Cassagnau, at the farm, was keen to take on the job – the extra money would have been welcome – and suggested it to Hélène. She shook her head and stroked the arm of the Louis Seize chair she was sitting in, then gestured to all the treasures in the room. "These are my ghosts," she said. "I must look after them myself." And so she did. One never saw a speck of dust in any of the main rooms and her kitchen, which had Persian rugs on the floor and valuable paintings on the walls and looked nothing like a kitchen, was always spotless. I know, because I did most of her shopping, not that there was much to do: she ate like a bird. Very occasionally I succeeded in persuading her to lunch or dine with me in a restaurant. (She always paid her share by cheque. Interestingly, she did not possess a credit card.) But I felt that she did not really enjoy these outings and preferred the solitary seclusion of Castilloux.

Things carried on in this way for a couple of years. The only big change was that Olivier Barbet decided to retire. With plenty of time on his hands he now became more and more Hélène's *chargé d'affaires*, relieving me of all gardening and most shopping duties, helping her with her investments and taxes. (There is nothing he doesn't know about paperwork and bureaucracy.) Then came a significant development in my own relationship with

Hélène. It was in mid-December, 2002. Tim and his wife Anita had invited me to spend Christmas with them and their children (three of them now) in Australia and I had agreed – reluctantly, because it would inevitably mean spending the next Christmas with Jenny and her family in America. I was due to catch the flight from Pau up to Paris and then on to Singapore and Perth on a Thursday morning. On Wednesday evening, therefore, I strolled round to Castilloux to say good-bye to Hélène and deliver her Christmas present. When she came to the door, I saw instantly that she had been crying. All my instinctive reluctance to intrude on her returned. I held out the present and said something like: "I only came to give you this and say good-bye," and made to leave. "No, no," she said, "come in. Please."

I followed her into the *salon*. As usual, she poured me a whiskey from the decanter and one for herself. She sat down – and almost immediately burst into tears. I didn't know what to do. I wanted to hug her, give her the physical comfort I sensed she needed. But she was sitting in her armchair. It would have been awkward. At least I had the sense not to *say* anything. After a moment, I rose, stepped to her chair and took one of her hands in mine. I held it, saying nothing, until her sobbing subsided.

"It's François," she said. "My son. You don't know him."

"I think I saw him at the funeral," I replied – idiotically: this was hardly the moment to remind her of Pierre-Jean's funeral.

I was still holding her hand. She was looking away from me, down towards the floor. I didn't know whether to let go of her hand or not. She saved me from having to make a decision. She gently withdrew her hand. "He's written to me," she went on. "A terrible letter."

She paused. It seemed the moment to resume my seat opposite her, on the other side of the fire-place. I waited. I didn't want to say anything. I realized that she might, just might, be about to open up her heart to me. And I realized something else: that this was something that I had, unconsciously, always wanted her to do. I was desperate not to break the spell.

"Money," she said. "it's always money, money, money. He hated Pierre-Jean. Both of them did. They couldn't understand that he wanted nothing from me in that way. He was proud. He had his pension and his savings. He never touched a *sou* of mine. Not a *sou*. I've told them that a hundred times. They don't believe me. François is in trouble again. He's always in trouble. But I know who's behind it. It's Marie-Hélène. François is weak. He could never have written a letter like that unless Marie-Hélène had pushed him into it. What does he think he's going to gain by it? Does he think I'm going to be frightened into doing what he wants? He should realize that I'm capable of having nothing more to do with them. After what happened at the funeral I'd be perfectly justified."

Without thinking, I told her what I had heard from next-door on that afternoon.

"Then you know," she said. "Was that any way to behave to a woman who had just lost her husband – let alone to one's mother?"

Suddenly it was all pouring out of her: François's failed marriage, his disastrous business ventures, his drinking, his cocaine. But the true venom was reserved for the daughter. And as she talked about Marie- Hélène – her lack of feeling, detestable husband, two scared little children, soulless house in Antony – an extraordinary change came over Hélène Raget. I was looking at someone I had never seen before. Her beauty, which as I have tried to convey stemmed as much from her inner serenity as from any physical characteristics, was being transformed in front of my eyes into a frightening sort of ugliness by a stronger force, the force of visceral hatred. I was sitting six feet away from a hag.

It was profoundly disturbing, so disturbing in fact that

for some moments I ceased to take in what she was saying. When I, so to speak, came to, I found that she was repeating herself, as people in the grip of anger do.

"They hated Pierre-Jean, hated him. They never gave him a chance. They never understood why I married him."

She paused then. She was calming down. She took a sip of her whiskey. She gave a little laugh. The haggish look was fading. She was regaining her poise.

"Mind you," she said, "I don't think anybody understood. Everybody must have wondered. I know Anthony did. Pierre-Jean bored him and his friends. They thought he was *nulle*." Then she added: "You must have wondered."

I was disconcerted. This amused her. "What did you think? Pierre-Jean liked you. He thought you were very simpatico."

I floundered. I said something rather feeble about companionship. She looked at me directly, with a smile, a fond smile, but one that was slightly pitying, even a little patronising. "It was very simple," she said. "It was love. I loved him and he loved me." It sounds faintly absurd but I must record that as she said this there was a radiance about her that completely restored her beauty. There was a slight pause, then she added: "You're none the wiser, are you?"

All through the endless flight to Australia I thought of Hélène. I couldn't get her out of my mind. I tried to imagine what her life with Pierre-Jean had been, how they spent their days and, more to the point, their nights. But I completely failed. I simply could not conjure up any mental pictures. One thing was clear to me though: someone capable of such hatred as she had shown for her daughter must also, presumably, be capable of feeling the opposite emotion in an equally extreme form.

I was away for nearly two months. Jenny insisted that I change my ticket and come back to Europe via America and I couldn't very well refuse. The first person I saw on my return was Olivier. He had news of Hélène – and it was not good. She had developed angina. The doctor in Charmeuil had put her on aspirin, beta-blockers and statins. When I saw her later in the day she looked no different. The attack, she said, which happened a few days after Christmas, had been painful and frightening but now that she had the right medicines she was not worried. "And anyway," she said, "it was a wake-up call."

I had no idea what she meant and in fact forgot all about the remark until a few weeks later, when we were having whiskies in her salon, she steered the conversation towards her furniture, pictures and *objets d'art*. "I've decided to get rid of a lot of it," she said.

"What? Your ghosts? Why?"

"I'm tired of my ghosts."

She stood up and stepped to the fire-place. She put a hand on the intricately carved frame of the Louis Quatorze mirror.

"I want you to have it."

I was totally taken aback.

"But – I couldn't possibly."

"You've always loved it, haven't you?"

"Well, yes but–"

"I want you to have it."

Next day, Olivier helped me to take the mirror down and carry it – very carefully – to Palanouard. We propped it against a wall in the living-room and I unleashed a couple of beers. I asked him what he thought was going on with Hélène. He hesitated a moment, then said: "She is selling me the house. *En viager*."

For those who don't know I should explain that in France when you buy a house *en viager* you agree to pay the owner a monthly sum. The owner has the right to go on living in the house, or to let it, until his or her death, when the property passes to you. There is usually, but not always, a cash payment up front. Essentially it is a gamble. You are gambling that the seller will die before the total of your monthly payments exceeds the original purchase price agreed. Perhaps the most famous transaction of this sort was when Jeanne Calment sold her apartment in Arles to her lawyer. She was ninety-one at the time. She lived to the age of a hundred and twenty one – the oldest woman in the world. And her apartment must have been one of the most expensive in France! I reminded Olivier of this.

"She doesn't think she'll live long," he said. "I don't think she wants to."

I began to see light.

"The children."

"Exactly. There was more trouble over Christmas. Some phone calls. She's determined that they should get as little as possible.

"I see the logic of it," I said. "But it's – mad."

Olivier stared at me. He didn't get my drift at all. But then he *is* French.

"What about her money?" I said.

"There's not that much. People think she's richer than she actually is. What she has she's going to give to charity."

"What's she going to live on?"

"My monthly payments."

"Will it be enough?"

"Oh yes. She spends so little."

"That's true."

"The real money's in her collection – the furniture, pictures and all that."

"What's she going to do with it?"

"Auction it. The proceeds will go to Cancer research in Toulouse, in the name of Pierre-Jean."

It was a strange experience going into Hélène's denuded house after the auctioneer's vans had departed with her treasures. Stripped of all those beautiful things the rooms were revealed in all their late 19th century ugliness. I found the square and oblong patches of unfaded paint and paper on the walls, where the pictures had hung, particularly depressing. Hélène didn't seem to mind at all

– and anyway, within weeks, Olivier was spending much of his time redecorating for her. Of course she had kept a certain amount of essential furniture, including her favourite arm-chair, and in the old stables on the far side of the courtyard at the back of the house, where what she described as junk had been stored for years, she found various bits and pieces that she could bear to live with.

By a curious chance, I was in a rather similar position to Hélène. During my visits to Australia and America, I had realized that both my children could do with some financial help. In marked contrast to François Benoit and his sister, they had not actually asked for it, or even hinted, but in Perth Jenny's husband, John, had been made redundant and was clearly struggling to make a living as a "consultant," while the children were all in private schools and in America Tim's property business had run into trouble, through no fault of his own, and his wife confided in me that they were having trouble meeting the payments on their very nice – perhaps too nice – house near Boston. Unlike Hélène, I actually wanted to help them. The question was how. My second marriage, to a Czech emigrant, a moment of madness that lasted three tumultuous and agonizing years, had punched a permanent hole in my capital. The divorce from Anna had cost me the London flat and a further reduction in capital. The interest on the remnants of my mother's money, plus the balance left over from the sale of the cottage, less what I had spent on restoring Palanouard, was a useful addition to my income, but one, I thought, I could do without. Bob Pennycuick had been quite right. One could live in France very comfortably on relatively little – and of course the older one gets the less one needs or wants to buy. Nevertheless, I felt I should have some sort of reserve, in case of severe illness or other unexpected eventuality. It was then that it occurred to me that I might be sitting on a modest gold-mine.

Throughout this period I had continued to work –

intermittently – on "Dad's archive." Sifting through the mountains of files I had come across packets of correspondence between my father and various people, mainly writers, who were "names" – some of them very big names indeed. I was vaguely aware that the market in autograph manuscripts, documents and letters had taken off and that such things could be valuable. I had also discovered a cache of much earlier documents, dating from the late 19th century through to the 1920's that related to my grandfather's business. A brief digression into family history will be necessary here.

My grandfather, Alan Wheeler, was born in 1876, the fifth son of a country parson. He emigrated to South Africa in 1896 at the age of twenty. He did not, alas, make his fortune in the diamond and gold fields, but set up a modest printing and publishing business in Cape Town. At some stage, he was "taken up" by Cecil Rhodes and was able to expand his activities into the new colony of Rhodesia and later into Kenya and, after the German defeat in the First World War, Tanganyika. My father, John, was born in Nairobi in 1906. Grandfather Alan died young, in 1930, and my father inherited the business but not, unfortunately, the skills required to run it successfully. In 1933, on a trip to London, he met my mother, whose family had been in shipping, they married and I was born in Nairobi in 1934. By this time the business was already in trouble. As my mother once said: "I'm afraid your father is more Wheeler than dealer." In 1937, he decided to change his life completely, sold the company, bought land in Bechuanaland and took to farming. It was a crazy venture, doomed to failure, but it enabled him to indulge his passion for exploring the wildernesses of Africa. It was through these expeditions that images of the Okavango and the Kalahari were permanently imprinted on my young mind. When the Second World War broke out ("It saved the day," my mother used to say) he decided his duty was to return to England. Typically, he landed a hush-hush job in Intelligence and spent most of the war years flying back and forth to Africa. After the War, as I have said, he started the publishing house of Wheeler & Coates. Coates was my mother's maiden name but she took no part in the business (apart from regularly signing bail-out cheques) but my father added it on the grounds that all the best publishers bore two names: Chatto & Windus, Secker & Warburg, Weidenfeld & Nicolson and so on.

I had made only a cursory examination of my grandfather's papers but now, on delving into them more thoroughly, I made some remarkable discoveries. There were letters from Cecil Rhodes himself, from Leander Starr Jameson and several other prominent players in the Imperial Game of those times. Most remarkable of all, there were six letters from the young Winston Churchill relating to a series of articles about his exploits in the Boer War that my grandfather had commissioned from him. A phone call to an old friend in London established that the letters from Rhodes – very rare, apparently – and Churchill would certainly fetch high prices.

I made a selection of the most obviously desirable items, put them in a briefcase, drove up to Calais and took the car ferry. Following my friend's advice, I took the letters to a specialist auction house. Their estimate of what the collection would fetch amazed me.

I had said nothing to Hélène either about my intention to pass my capital on to my children or about the means of doing so. It would have been tactless in the extreme, positively cruel in fact, to have underlined the positive relationship I had with my children when the relationship with her own children was so dreadful. But somehow she found out.

I have never discovered who told her. It may have been Olivier, it may have been Marie-Ange Cassagnau, who was now helping her with the house-work. It may have been someone else. The truth is that I prefer not to know.

Because if Hélène had never heard about the sale of the letters I firmly believe that she would be alive today.

The morning after my return from London, I was out in the garden, about to mow the grass, when, as once before, I heard a woman's scream coming from Castilloux. It was a long, high-pitched scream of incredible intensity. It was not so much a scream of pain – though there was that element – as one of pure rage. Then there was silence.

I ran round to Castilloux. I could see nobody in the garden. Since the scream was unlikely to have come from inside, I headed as fast as possible round the side of the house into the courtyard at the back. Hélène was lying on her side on the ground a few feet from the door of the stables. She was crumpled into a foetal position. Standing over her, looking stricken and helpless, was Olivier Barbet. Lying between them was a small, oblong piece of paper that had obviously fallen from Hélène's hand. I picked it up. It was hand-written and dated Paris, June 18th 1906. It read: "My dear Merle-Rivière, Herewith the portrait in exchange for the masks as agreed. I hope we may meet at G's next week." It was signed by Pablo Picasso.

The following day, François Benoit and his sister came down from Paris. They stayed in the house, unaware as yet that their mother had sold it to Olivier Barbet. I was keeping well away so I can only surmise that the first thing they did was to look through the junk stored in the stable. I learned much later, through Marie-Ange Cassagnau, that they found the unframed Picasso portrait of their grandfather among a stack of other canvases, crude amateur works by some other member of the family, possibly Henri Merle-Rivière's wife.

Students of Picasso will not need reminding that in 1906 and 1907 the Spanish master went through what is now called his "Black Period," during which he made a collection of African totem art. It culminated in the seminal *Les Demoiselles d'Avignon*, now in the Museum of Modern Art in New York. In that painting – regarded by many critics as the first of Picasso's works to contain elements of cubism – the faces of the three women to the left of the picture are based on ancient Iberian sculptures (allegedly stolen from the Louvre by one of the artist's friends) and those of the two on the right, on African totem masks. In later life Picasso denied the African influence. "L'art nègre? Connais pas!" he is supposed to have said. The note to Henri Merle-Rivière would seem to show otherwise.

Exactly what had happened on the day of Hélène's death? I propose that she heard about my errand to London the night before. It occurred to her that among her grandfather's documents there might be valuable autograph material. Marie-Ange Cassagnau is almost sure that these documents had been kept in the attic. I think it probable that Hélène waited till morning to look through them. What is certain is that a large box full of documents was found on the kitchen table and that shortly before her death Hélène had been going through them because there were papers on the table, chairs, sideboard and floor. When she found the Picasso note she must have instantly realized its significance and, moreover, known where the portrait, if it still existed, was most likely to be found. She hurried into the yard, heading as quickly as possible for the stables. The excitement, combined with the sudden physical exertion, must have been too much for her heart. She felt the onset of an attack. In those few seconds she realized that she might be too late, that she could be about to die. Her children would discover the portrait. Under French law it would form part of the inheritance that she had gone to such extraordinary lengths to reduce to a minimum. My private view is that this is what actually killed her. Hatred killed her. If she had hated less she might have survived. As it was, she let out that appalling scream – and died.

One mystery remained. How was it that existence of

the portrait had been forgotten? Henri Merle-Rivière had, after all, been a dealer, as had his son. They must have known the value of a Picasso. Certainly when Henri acquired it, in 1906, Picasso was relatively unknown. But Henri did not die until the mid-1930's by which time Picasso was world-famous and his works were fetching high prices. The answer, I think lies in the picture itself. It rather resembles the *Self Portrait* of 1907, an angular, crudely executed work with the artist's features stabbed onto the canvas in sharp black lines and curves. The portrait of Merle-Rivière is in a similar but even more aggressive style. Its subject must have found it both bewildering and highly unflattering and quickly consigned it to the attic. I suspect he never mentioned it either to his wife or his son. He didn't want them or anyone else to see it. It is indeed a formidably hideous picture. But at Christie's in New York in 2004 it fetched thirty-three million dollars.

*

Editor's note: It will come as no surprise to the reader that what Michel Walrangis and I really wanted from my friend Jim Wheeler was the story of the Anthony Eames murder. He refused. Very politely, as you would expect, but very firmly, citing "issues of confidentiality" that I found somewhat unconvincing. Instead he offered us the story of Hélène Raget. When Michel read it (I translated it for him) he responded as follows: "It's so autobiographical! I like that, but I wonder if your friend realizes how much of himself he has revealed. I no longer regret the murder story. This is much better."

LA PERLE

That day, everybody I saw in the streets, on the *métro*, in restaurants and cafés, seemed to look like François Mitterand – particularly women.

To what can one ascribe this strange phenomenon? Perhaps it is not so strange. We are, after all, descended from vertebrate reptiles that emerged from the sea and evolved into various land-dwelling branches of the animal kingdom. To take a few random examples, one only has to observe the face of a hyena, a vulture, a cobra and a politician, to recognize the common origins in the primordial oceans. A week-old human embryo looks remarkably like a little fish, or indeed a tadpole. If *homo sapiens* shares certain basic features with such a diversity of creatures, one should not be surprised to find even more startling similarities among members of our own species.

In Mitterand's case, the ravages of the disease that finally succeeded in removing him from the scene, where so many plots, scandals and elections had failed, refined and subtly altered his face. The cheek-bones were more prominent, conjuring up an image of a quivering whippet. The eyes seemed to have moved in closer towards the bridge of the nose. They were still watchful but gave an impression of greater vulnerability, like those of an eland sensing the approach of lions. The nose itself was thinner and sharper, a bird-of-prey's beak. The lips were narrower, often pursed or pouting. They remained essentially pike-like but the jowls, sagging on either side of the amoebic chin, introduced an amphibian note. One had always had a sense of him as forever lurking under a stone, waiting for a young trout to swim by, but now one almost expected a

201

long, viscous tongue to flick out and whip an insect from the air.

But it wasn't just a question of age and illness transforming The Sphinx's features into some matrix of animal physiognomy. There was also the paradoxical nature of the man himself: Vichy functionary and Resistance hero; man of the Left and republican monarch; aesthete and patron of La Défense. His character was a mirror, admittedly on the grand scale, of the self-contradictions, mixed motives and veiled emotions of which we are all made up. Everyone, to a greater or lesser extent, is a Sphinx.

There was another element. I call it New Car Syndrome. I cannot be alone in having noticed that when one has decided to buy a certain make of car one suddenly seems to see nothing else parked in the streets, or bumper-to-bumper on the périphérique, or streaming past on the autoroute. After perhaps weeks of thumbing through magazines, visits to show-rooms, test-drives, the mind has become attuned to that particular model while at the same time taking on a curious ability to screen out others. Only after one has actually bought the car and driven it for a while does the effect wear off.

That day my mind was attuned to Mitterand. This was not because we had been great friends – I can claim no more than a slight acquaintance – or because he was a political hero of mine (he was quite the reverse) but because I had been invited to dinner by Dominique Vinteul and she had been a member of his inner circle – though never, I am convinced, his lover, as rumour has so persistently whispered.

I had been surprised by Dominique's invitation. We had not seen each other at all for months, very little in the past few years and then only at social occasions in other people's houses or in restaurants and concert halls. I could hardly remember the last time I had been to her apartment in the Avenue Foch. I had long since been dropped from her *galère* as insufficiently famous, influential or intellectually stimulating.

In saying this, I do not want to give the impression that Dominique was one of those tedious women who are interested only in celebrity and wealth. Far from it. She had friends from various periods in her life, especially her childhood, who were of no importance at all in the worldly sense but to whom she remained devoted.

I did not come into that category. She had taken me up when I was a very young man, after my first screenplay had been produced. Thanks largely to its director, Gaston Rumette, it had been well, in some cases ecstatically received by the critics. I should add that, outside Paris, the public had remained sublimely indifferent to its, I quote, "fantastical mingling of present and past and subtle satire."

It was Rumette who introduced me to Dominique and she invited me to one of her notorious Sunday evenings. Not long after, we spent a week together at her country house, a half-timbered *gentilhommerie* near Vernier-le-Chateau in Normandy, that had belonged to her grandfather. After an uncertain start, we made love two or three times a day, but in a somewhat mechanical way. "Perhaps a little less percussion, darling," she once said, "and let's try not to forget the String section." It was impossible to tell whether this was advice to me or a reminder to herself.

I must explain the uncertain start.

I was sixteen when I first heard Dominique's *Balbec Suite*, the piece that made her world-famous, on a live radio broadcast from the *Salle Pleyel*, three years after its first performance. It completely intoxicated me. Next morning, I borrowed some money from my mother and rushed out to buy the record. I played it over and over again until my brothers and sisters threatened to smash it.

It is almost impossible to write a description of a piece of music and avoid its coming over like one of those pretentious programme notes where, in attempting to show off his knowledge and expertise, the author succeeds only in baffling and irritating the reader. I will do my best.

In the *Balbec Suite* Dominique combines the structural elegance and elusive emotion of Ravel, the laconic voice of Satie and the rhythmic drive and dissonance of Stravinsky with a *sensation* that is entirely her own. (I feel I am already failing in my task!) In this there are elements of jazz, of Balinese *gamelin* and French folk-song.

I see I have made it sound as if the *Balbec* is some sort of many-coloured coat of borrowed plumes (some critics have said precisely that) but it is not. The Atlantic rollers of the Normandy coast surge through it and break on the sands in glistening, sunlit spray, singing of the exuberance of youth and the infinite possibilities of life. Echoes of the gunfire of the 1944 landings linger in the darker passages. Threads of folk tunes evoke the pastoral and the long, rich history of the land. The last movement delivers an overwhelming sense of a place and a nation emerging from the humiliation of defeat and occupation, reasserting its culture, its vigour, its belief in itself – which is of course why it had such an astounding success in France.

Dominique's international fame, which quickly followed, was I think largely due to the fact that America embraced both the *Balbec* and its young composer. She was twenty-three, petite, pretty in a plump sort of way, and as a woman triumphing in a field dominated almost entirely by men, headline news. Success abroad gave her an almost unique prestige in France. She became the symbol of the message of the *Balbec*. The press dubbed her *La Perle*, the pearl in the crown of French culture. She was adored, revered, almost sanctified, in spite of the scandals that whirled constantly round her. In fact, the wild spending, the fast cars, the lovers of both sexes, only added to her glamour. She was indescribably famous.

This rather long digression, for which I apologise, goes some way, I hope, towards explaining the fact that when, some eight years after first being bowled over by her music, I found myself taking off my clothes in the composer's bedroom, the effects of the foreplay we had enjoyed in front of the crackling fire in the *salon* below faded away like the final bars of a Chopin Prelude. The thought that I was about to share a bed with a national icon was the opposite of stimulating. I was not very experienced at the time – and Dominique's First Symphony had just had its premiere at the Met.

She was wonderful about it. "Damn," she said, "I forgot the fire-guard. Won't be a minute." When she returned, a few minutes later, I had got over my nerves.

Was I ever in love with her? I suppose I was in a way. She had a black humour and a self-mocking wit that I found irresistible. Her social circle was fascinating. I worshipped her as an artist. But from the first I knew there were other lovers and that a penniless, if promising *scénariste* had very little chance of supplanting them, still less of supplying the constant variety Dominique needed. And finally, I have to confess, I didn't find her particularly attractive, physically. Our affair petered out, with no acrimony on either side, and became a friendship.

I was reviewing this friendship as I walked to the Avenue Foch that evening. The Mitterand phenomenon was still active. He stepped off buses, stubbed out cigarettes on pavements, emerged from shops and cafés, shooed chattering mini-Sphinxes in and out of Macdos.

All this had a sort of *madeleine* effect on me. Suddenly I could remember with perfect clarity the first time I met him – at Dominique's, of course – in the early seventies, a decade before he became President. I could feel the firm, silky grip of his hand and remember the wariness with which I shook it. I was still a member of the Communist Party in those days and he was The Enemy. He had great charm, wit and erudition. He had the professional politician's knack of making you feel that you were the only person in the room worth talking to and that he was moving on to someone else only out of duty and with regret. But that didn't fool me, nor did he charm me.

I realized that there was a link between Mitterand's rise to power and glory and the decline and fall of my friendship with Dominique. It was not a direct link because, as I have said, she remained loyal to old friends. It was simply that her ascent into the very highest realms coincided with my descent into the relative obscurity of being asked occasionally by *France Culture* to talk on cinema-related subjects – pieces that were invariably broadcast in the early hours of the morning.

I had never quite been able to recapture what an English colleague of mine irritatingly refers to as "the first, fine careless rapture" of my debut film. (Browning is not a poet much read or admired in France.) I disappointed the small circle of producers, directors and critics who had seen me as a potential trail-blazer. I committed the crime, unforgivable in the eyes of such people, of writing for television. I made things worse by achieving certain popular successes in the detective *genre* and actually making a comfortable living.

What was so curious was that during these years Dominique's own career as a composer went into free-fall. The First Symphony turned out to have been radiant more from the after-glow of the *Balbec* than from any inherent qualities. It was rarely performed after the premiere and has vanished from the repertoire. The Second Symphony was politely panned in America and even in France received only tepid praise. Her Messiaenesque oratorio *Lazarus* was frankly an embarrassment. She never grasped that it was Olivier's deep religious faith that enabled him to infuse the great empty spaces of his mature work with the almost hallucinogenic tension and mystery that makes him the greatest master of modern French music. *Lazarus* was boring, which is perhaps a pardonable offence, but it was also pretentious, which is not. Her Third Symphony suffered the humiliation of being withdrawn from the Promenade Concerts in London, where it had been due to receive its first performance. It has never been performed.

"What you've always failed to understand, Miche," my friend Séchaux, the musicologist, once said to me, "is that the *Balbec* is music for adolescents and that Dominique has never grown up. There's nothing there. That's why she's done a Sibelius."

He was referring to the fact that Sibelius was still allegedly working on his Eighth Symphony when he died at the age of ninety-two, having started it some thirty years earlier. There is no Eighth, of course, and opinion varies as to whether the Finnish master actually wrote it and then destroyed it or whether it had been a genial ploy to ensure a quiet life in the country. In 1976, Dominique announced that she was embarking on an opera, entitled *The Dream of Alcibiades*. She intended, she said, to devote herself entirely to the work, to the exclusion of all other commissions. A quarter of a century later we have yet to hear a single note. I need hardly point out the difference: Sibelius retired behind the veil of the Eighth having given the world some of its greatest and most enduring music; from Dominique we really have only the *Balbec*. However I still maintain, in defiance of Séchaux, that it is a masterpiece and I listen to it frequently and it still moves me to tears. Perhaps there is part of me that remains adolescent. So be it!

Séchaux was among a growing number of critics and intellectuals who, during the 1980's, dared to question Dominique's position as The Pearl in the cultural crown. He did his own career no harm by heading one of his articles "In Your Dreams, Alcibiades."

Such attacks had not the slightest effect on Dominique's fame. If anything, it increased, at least within France. Her private life continued to provide the media with scandalous *gourmandises*. She was arrested – twice – for possession of cocaine, though never charged. Her dinner parties, it was said, turned into orgies. On the verge of bankruptcy, she was saved by a mysterious friend. Most people thought it was The Sphinx but I have my doubts.

In other ways, though, her close friendship with the President was productive. She was appointed to numerous public bodies concerned with the arts, chaired – very successfully – an official enquiry into the public funding of music, was a regular on TV discussion panels and a gave frequent talks on *France Culture* – in primetime, naturally.

I had been invited for eight o'clock, arrived punctually to find that I was the first, and realized how rusty my social skills had become. In the higher circles it is not *chic* to be punctual. A terrifying-looking maid, rumoured to be Dominique's current *mâitresse en titre* (unlikely I thought), showed me into the *salon. Temps retrouvé* indeed!

Everything was as it always had been: the great, brown Bechstein with its cargo of dog-eared scores heaped in perilous piles, the wall of pictures, the wall of books, the eclectic collection of furniture, some immensely valuable, some fit only for a skip. Even the little table by the piano stool was still in its place, with its jam-jars of tea and sugar and the battered electric kettle whose wire trailed dangerously past a bust of Boileau.

It was a beautiful room and expressed the essential soundness of Dominique's taste. Her chair, a dreadful product of the 1930's, its upholstery in ribbons and caked with dog-hairs, was next to a *fauteuil Voltaire* of such impeccable provenance that it might have belonged to Voltaire himself. But Dominique's chair was where it was because she found it comfortable and she and her dogs had been sitting in it for forty years. Similarly, pieces she had inherited from her family, who were of the *haute bourgeoisie* of Rouen, competed for space with objects that Dominique had picked up on her travels or found in *brocantes*, some interesting and beautiful, some banal.

I was a little surprised to see, among the familiar pictures, that the prize of her collection, a small but exquisite late Gauguin, of the Marquesas period, was still its place. I had heard that Dominique's financial problems had become acute again lately and that she had been forced to sell many of her treasures.

The royalties from her music had been reduced to a trickle over the years and would have been almost nothing if an American advertising agency had not bought the main theme of the last movement of the *Balbec* for a commercial promoting a well-known brand of lavatory cleaner. Her fees from television appearances, speaking engagements, lecture tours and so on would hardly maintain a penthouse apartment in the Avenue Foch, let alone the house in Normandy and the villa at Cap D'Ail.

I was just looking more closely at the Gauguin and discovering it to be a reproduction when the double-doors opened and the baleful maid ushered in another guest. To my delight it was a familiar face: Adrienne Deloitre (the painter not the popular novelist). Adrienne and I had lived together for a year in the late seventies. I was delighted to see her.

"Miche!" she said. "How lovely!"

"You must be surprised," I replied as we kissed.

"Not at all. Dominique told me you were coming."

I asked her if she knew who the other guests were and she reeled off a list of names, most of which I recognized. They seemed to represent distinctly the more raffish side of Dominique's circle.

"Is there going to be an orgy?" I said.

"Oh, I don't think so. Dominique's got a bad back."

"She could watch."

"Oh God, I hadn't thought of that!"

"Since you seem to know everything, have you any idea why I've been invited? I feel like Rip Van Winkle."

"Perhaps La Perle wants you to write the libretto for *Alcibiades*," she said dryly, with a lift of an eyebrow and a half smile. This subtle satire made me laugh – and feel much better. I began to long for a drink but knew there would be nothing on offer until after Dominique had made her grand entrance.

Adrienne and I chatted about common friends and revisited the past a little, as one does. A few moments later, the rest of the party arrived in one of those flood tides that are characteristic of the grand social occasion and the room was suddenly full of people and noise. Drinkless, we waited.

About five minutes passed before the doors opened and the procession appeared. First came a great wheeled chariot, jingling with bottles, pushed by the sinister maid. Then came Dominique, followed, as ever, by a minute dog on a lead.

This latest in a long line of canine companions was of a breed I could not identify. Its plump little body appeared to have been shaved to the skin. In contrast, plumes of black hair grew on its ankles, its bat-like ears and at the end of its tail. Later, when I saw it squatting to piss by a leg of the Bechstein, I realized that it was a bitch.

I hardly recognized Dominique. She was still tiny and bird-like but whereas only a few months ago she had been a plump robin-redbreast she now resembled an emaciated sparrow, but with none of the sparrow's traditional quickness and lightness of movement. She was using a stick and walking unsteadily and with difficulty. She looked a hundred.

She made straight for me and Adrienne. "Miche! How delightful!" she said as she kissed me, then turned to the room and added: "We once fucked for a whole night, non-stop."

To which the only reply I could find was: "But it was midsummer when the nights are short."

Shock tactics had always been Dominique's stock-in-trade on social occasions. It was a way of quickly establishing her ascendancy. On the more positive side, it often served to jolt people out of their usual banalities and into a more lively, open conversation. I remember a famous occasion when, during one of those lulls, when a room goes suddenly silent, she had seized the opportunity to ask an elderly Senator: "Tell me, how often do you masturbate?" To which the Senator had replied, with considerable aplomb I thought: "Only as often as is absolutely necessary for the health, Mademoiselle."

We sat down sixteen at the long, Italian table in the dining-room overlooking the floodlit roof garden. This was a relief to me because at one point it had seemed that we would be thirteen. Three late arrivals had saved the day. On the way into the room, Dominique had taken me aside for a moment and said: "We must have a little chat later, darling Miche. Business. I want to spread my wings."

As a result, during the first course, I was preoccupied. It was now clear to me why I had been invited. Some years before, I had written, for my own pleasure, a film that I thought had some merit. Unable to sell it, I set about finding the finance myself. In the process I became fascinated by the whole, vexed business. I did eventually succeed in securing backers, the film was made and was a modest art-house success. I managed to sell it in England and America and actually made money. With two younger partners I started a production company and we made more films. We developed relationships with producers in London and Los Angeles and our latest effort, a romantic comedy, shot in English, had, as they say, broken out. It was doing big box office in America and although nothing is ever certain in the movie business, it looked as if I might soon be a rich man.

In the early seventies, before creating the myth of *Alcibiades*, Dominique had written several film scores and had been paid a lot of money for them. I was now in a position to commission her. The game was obvious. Also obvious was how it would be if I did give her a commission. She would demand an enormous advance, would deliver late, if at all, and in any case the score would be unusable. On the other hand, the value of having her name attached to a project would be immense. I was weighing the advantages and disadvantages when I felt something pressing against my ankle. It was the black, olive-like snout of the dog. I looked down and encountered a pair of large, pleading brown eyes. I slipped the animal a sliver of smoked salmon which it devoured in a snap.

The dinner proceeded. The food, delivered by a local restaurant, was bland and chilly but the wines were magnificent, particularly the Yquem which accompanied the Crème Renversee au Chocolat. I suppose like everyone else I wondered how on earth Dominique could afford it.

My neighbour on the right, a very beautiful girl whose name, alas, I never quite caught, proved to be both witty and intelligent. We talked about religion. I told her about the Mitterand effect I had experienced that day. We discussed the possibility that something similar might account for Our Lord's post-Resurrection appearances. The disciples hadn't seen Jesus himself but the Jesus in other people. Dominique, always alert to a more interesting conversation than the one she was having, interrupted us with: "What are you two plotting?"

"We're talking about religion, Dominique," I replied.

"*I've* got religion, you know."

"Really? Reconciled with Rome?"

"*Kabbalah*, dear. The real thing."

After dinner we all returned to the *salon* for the ritual performance by Dominique on the piano. Like quite a number of classical composers I know, she played only jazz or popular songs for her friends. She had never been a great pianist and now, at seventy-two, the wrong notes were so many that at times it sounded as if she was playing a chromatic scale. On the other hand her voice, which had always been lovely, was as true as ever. Even so, having had an enormous amount to drink at dinner, I fell asleep.

I woke to see Dominique, in her chair, leaning over the glass-topped coffee table, snorting a line of cocaine. There were four or five other people doing the same, including my dinner companion. The air was thick with the smell of marijuana. A Miles Davis number was playing on the CD. Two men were kissing on the small sofa next to the bust of Boileau. The carpet was littered with screwed up paper tissues discarded by coke-sniffers. Some of them looked wet and soggy, as if they had been chewed. My dinner companion sneezed violently, blew her nose on a tissue and dropped it on the floor.

Then I noticed the dog. It was lying on its side under the piano. It seemed to lying very still. I watched it. More sniffing and sneezing competed with *Kind of Blue*. The dog did not move. Not the slightest flicker of a muscle or twitch of the nose or mouth.

I got up and went over to the piano. I squatted down and tentatively prodded the dog. Nothing. No reaction at all. Its eyes were wide open but they had an empty stare. It was dead.

I straightened. "Dominique," I said, "I'm afraid…"

"What is it?"

"Your dog. She seems to be…"

Dominique rose from her chair and limped rapidly to the piano. She bent down. She picked the dog up in her arms and then sat down with it on the floor. She cradled it in her arms. Tears were running on her cheeks.

"La Perle," she wailed. "La Perle."

I realized that, with that self-mockery of hers, that strain of satire that she could always turn against herself and which ultimately made her lovable, she had named the dog La Perle.

La Perle had been chewing the cocaine-impregnated tissues. She had died of an overdose.

*

Editor's note: Michel Walrangis sent me this piece with a note that its author wished to preserve a strict anonymity. I cannot resist quoting his PS. "You can't call it a shaggy dog story. The dog was bald."

Dominique Vinteul died of cancer in June, 2002.

CHINBE N'TALA

That afternoon there was a story going round the Section about former President Reagan. Apparently, in his last years he was totally out of it, didn't know who he was or where he was or anything and the only activity he had left was to scoop the leaves out of his pool. That's all he did all day, scooped leaves out of his pool. So some poor bastard of a Secret Service guy was given the job of throwing leaves into the pool when Reagan wasn't looking so the old fellow could go on enjoying life to the full and the question we were all asking was – what kind of an almighty fuck-up had this man made to be given a job like that?

So when the Chief called me into his office and told me I was being posted to Cannes, to join the team guarding the ex-President of the Bangui Republic, Chinbe N'Tala, I honestly thought it was a wind-up and I said something like: "Who's supplying the leaves? Field Resources? Stationery and Office Supplies?"

The Chief's eyes, which on a good day resemble a couple of ice cubes floating in a *pastis*, went into permafrost mode and I realized I'd made a BIG mistake. "Deveau is in charge of the unit," the Chief said. "Report to him tomorrow morning. Perhaps he'll appreciate your sense of humour more than I do."

What the fuck have I done, I nearly said. I mean, this was like being exiled to the satellite monitoring station in St. Pierre et Michelon. But I stopped myself. It would sound like a whine and whining gets you exactly nowhere in the Section. So I just said, "Yes, Chief."

"Get on with it, then."

End of conversation.

First stop was Uncle Jo, Head of Operations. He's a family friend – worked with my Dad, my sister's Godfather, my mentor in the Section.

"It's that e-mail," Uncle Jo said, lighting up a *Gauloise blonde*.

I got the same feeling in the pit of my stomach that I used to have before singing a solo in a church. (Whenever I hear Fauré's *Pie Jesu* on *Classiques* I get the same sensation.) By now, the smoke from Uncle Jo's cigarette was hitting me and Madame Nicotine was calling seductively from beyond the heaped-up files on his desk.

"Give me one, Uncle Jo," I said.

"Thought you'd quit."

"Yeah, but my life's over anyway."

He shuffled a *blonde* out of the pack and I lit it with his lighter. The office is non-smoking, of course, but Uncle Jo doesn't give a toss and nobody has ever dared say anything to him. That's his power. I took a drag and it was like the first time I ever smoked, behind the bogs at school, age eight. A moment of dizziness and slight nausea then – YES! This is for me!

"But nothing *happened*," I said.

"Nothing happened because the Chief spent a morning on the phone, calling in favours. It really pissed him off."

Here's the thing. I'm crap with computers. Always have been. I've never really worked out why. Maybe because when all the other kids were playing with their Macs my mother was dragging me across Paris to singing lessons. Or maybe there's a deeper reason.

When I was about thirteen, my Dad bought a computer. I remember he spent a whole weekend struggling with it, then on Sunday night he carried it out to the garage, literally kicking the dog out of the way, and dumped it behind the pile of rolled-up tents and camping stuff we used to dust off every year before our summer holiday. A couple of days later, my Dad went off on what was always referred to in our family as "important business for France" and never came back. Perhaps I've always associated that computer with losing him. When I was doing the Psychological Profiling course I suggested this to the woman who was running it. "Highly fanciful," was her opinion. But then she was an idiot.

Anyway, to return to the point, as the Chief always says, about a week before, a friend of mine had sent me an e-mail with this really funny attachment. It was a picture of Le Pen and you clicked on it (I admit it took me some time to work this out) and depending on where you clicked you could turn him into Adolf Hitler, or Genghis Khan or Pol Pot. I thought, I've got to send this to Gilles.

Gilles and I were at school together. While I was going off the rails, smoking a ton of dope, half killing myself at a rave every night, stacking shelves in Prisunic, Gilles was studying journalism at the Sorbonne. Now, he's got a job on *Libération*. So I sent him an e with the Le Pen attachment. Except – and I genuinely don't know how it happened – I attached the wrong file. I sent him an internal report on a surveillance operation we were doing on some mosque out in the suburbs. To make matters even worse, I used the wrong address. Gilles has a personal e address and another one, for work, which he shares with half a dozen colleagues. That's the one I mistakenly used. According to Gilles – and I have to believe him – someone else got hold of it and the shit hit the fan. But as I'd said to Uncle Jo, nothing actually happened. I assume the Section has somebody on the inside at *Libération* who tipped off the Chief and the whole thing was dead and buried in a few hours. That's the way it works in France and that's why France works.

"How pissed off d'you reckon the Chief really is?" I asked Uncle Jo.

"Frankly, if your father hadn't been who he was, if you weren't, so to speak, family, he'd have had you out on your ear. It was an unpardonable breach of security."

Another *Pie Jesu* moment. "But, Uncle Jo," I said – and even to me it sounded like a whine – "bodyguard duty. After all the training I've had. It's insane."

"Listen, Charlie, he'll get over it. Go to Cannes, keep your head down and your nose clean, and in a couple of months you'll be back behind your desk."

"You really think so?"

"So long as that evil bastard N'Tala doesn't get his head blown off on your watch."

I left the office feeling a bit better about life. I swung by the *tabac* on the corner and bought a packet of *blondes* and smoked two on the way to the *metro*. Then a really bad thought hit me. What the fuck am I going to tell Astrid? And – more to the point – how am I going to live without her for the next – fuck – it could be *months*.

Astrid is twenty-six and fit, fit, fit. I met her through Gilles. She works for this little film production company that's always on the brink of disaster. She's in charge of script development which according to Astrid entails spending day after day arguing with mad writers who can't write worth a toss. Our apartment in Billancourt is littered with scripts covered with coffee rings, many of which I have contributed myself. I tried to read one of them once. Couldn't make any sense of it at all.

Anyway, Astrid and I met at this party Gilles threw for his girlfriend's birthday. She'd just broken up with someone and so had I. I took her out to dinner a couple of times, then we went to see some art-house movie she thought she ought to catch. It was rubbish. About this middle-aged woman who dreams of making love with a young guy from *France Telecom* who fixes her phone. Then suddenly you're into some obscure story about carrier pigeons in the Napoleonic era, with all the same characters in period costume, then the two stories sort of blend together and there's Napoleon on a mobile getting Josephine to play with herself back in Fontainebleau. Ludicrous. *Communications* it's called. Avoid.

Anyway, in the restaurant afterwards, we laughed ourselves silly about it – Astrid was brilliant – and from there to Billancourt and my bed – where we spent most of the weekend – was a logical progression.

Astrid was living with a bunch of friends on a house-boat near Neuilly and it took me a month or two to persuade her to move in with me. But she did and it was great. It is great. Astrid, you're beautiful, you have the BEST stories, your cooking is a nightmare and I love you.

To return to the point. In the Section, there are strict rules governing what you can tell your wife/partner/family/friends about what you do. Basically, if you have a desk job, you say you're a Civil Servant working in a department concerned with police and security matters. If you work in the field, as my Dad mostly did, you're still a Civil Servant but your job's about foreign trade or something similar. Important business for France. So how was I going to explain to Astrid that I was about to disappear to the Riviera for an indeterminate period?

She was there when I got home, just stepping out of the shower in fact, and the first thing she said after I kissed her was: "You've been smoking. You bastard. Give me one." We'd had a pact to quit together. So over a couple of *blondes* and (on my part) a mega whisky, I broke the news. I told her I'd been given this really important assignment (yeah, well…) that meant I'd be working out of our office in Nice. She was terrific about not asking for details but naturally she wanted to know how long I'd be away, what was going to happen about weekends etc. Since I hadn't got a fucking clue myself, I couldn't really answer her.

"It's not something dangerous is it?" she said. And when I told her, *Of course not*, I didn't do that sort of thing, she didn't look very convinced. We ate at the *brasserie* round the corner, had a shedload to drink and I got up at five next morning, feeling like shit, to catch the seven o'clock flight from Orly down to Nice.

It was a clear day in June and I sat with my forehead pressed against the window watching France scroll by below, thinking about my Dad. He was a big man who always wore a black suit, a white shirt and a plain tie to work. He smoked those fat, yellow *caporals* you hardly ever see now. After every meal he'd smack his lips and say to my mother: "You're a marvel!" He helped me to build a big box-kite, a go-kart and – our most ambitious project – a tree-house in the garden in Antony.

In the summer, when we went camping, he'd barbecue steaks and shoulders of lamb that I can still practically taste today. He knew the names of wild flowers and even when he dragged us all round *chateaux* and *monuments historiques* he made it really interesting. He knew everything about the history of France. His big hero was Charles De Gaulle. (His Dad had been killed fighting in the Resistance.) "History's important," he'd say. "I don't want you thinking we named you after the airport."

I worshipped him. When he didn't come back that time, I refused to believe he was dead, that I'd never see him again. In the end, my mother had to get Uncle Jo round and he made me face the truth. I went to my room and cried for hours. When his body was eventually brought back to France and we had the funeral – shit, I'm starting to mist up as I write this.

Anyway, my mother got clinically depressed and went on pills which helped me over the bump in a way because – for a time – I sort of ran *her* life as opposed to the other way round. We got a bit closer. It didn't last long. I started getting into trouble – drugs, drink, the usual stuff, nothing very heavy – scraped through the *bac*, refused to go to University. Eventually she threw me out and then, for fuck's sake, when Uncle Jo told me (which I was already starting to see for myself) that I was headed nowhere fast and said he could get me into the Section, she went into hysterics, saying I'd end up dead like my father and how could Uncle Jo do it etcetera etcetera.

220

Anyway, there I was, on the plane, thinking about my Dad and feeling that somehow I'd let him down, betrayed his memory. I wondered if, in his career, *he'd* ever fucked up. It didn't seem possible. He was so solid, so competent. On the other hand, he'd gone on a field mission and never returned. He'd died – which I suppose you could regard as the ultimate fuck-up in our line of business. But maybe it hadn't been his fault. Maybe somebody else had screwed up. I don't know what happened to him. I'll never know. It's seriously classified information. The most I ever got from Uncle Jo was that he was in Africa and it's perfectly possible that's all Uncle Jo himself really knows. The Section is all about water-tight compartments.

Ex-President Chinbe N'Tala lived in this massive villa in Mougins, above Cannes. It stood in about two hectares of landscaped gardens, surrounded by high walls and security fences. The view from the terrace was spectacular. You looked right out over the pine-trees and rooftops of Le Cannet to the Bay of Cannes and the Mediterranean. There was a vast swimming-pool, complete with a jacuzzi and a water-slide for the kids (N'Tala had three, all under the age of six). There was a tennis court, a shaded barbecue area, even a *terrain de pétanque*. Not that anybody ever played. Or tennis. And all this fantastic luxury courtesy of *Madame La Republique*.

One of the first questions I asked Deveau, my new boss – my *temporary* boss, I reminded myself in an effort to stay sane – was why? Why was the Government going to so much trouble and expense to protect a monster like N'Tala and give him this multi-millionaire life-style.

"That is a seriously stupid fucking question," Deveau said. "Even if I knew the answer, which I don't, and don't want to, isn't it rather obvious that nobody would be going to all this trouble and expense, as you put it, unless there was a seriously fucking good reason. I thought you whiz-kids were supposed to be intelligent."

Deveau was one of those types whose career in the

Section had taken a wrong turn at some point and had ended up in a cul-de-sac. He was in his forties, a short, pudgy guy with a bushy, brown moustache and eyes like a sorrowful spaniel. He was rapidly balding but instead of getting himself a number one crop, which is the way to go, he grew what was left of his hair long and scraped it over his shiny pate in straggling strings that were held precariously in place mainly by his sweat. I'd met him a couple of times before in Paris and he obviously knew about me and resented me. I was on a fast track. He was basically off the field.

The team consisted of six men, plus Deveau. According to standard Section procedure it was divided into two groups: Perimeter Surveillance and Personal Protection. The poor bastards on Perimeter Surveillance basically spent their time staring into CCTV monitors or checking visitors in and out. Personal Protection was exactly that: bodyguarding N'Tala and his family whenever they stepped outside the villa. I mean that literally. If any of them went for a swim or a barbecue or even for a stroll round the grounds, one of us had to be there. If they went into Cannes to shop, or eat in a restaurant, it was a two-man job. Deveau's role was to supervise the team, liaise with the local police, and collate and assess information coming from the Section and other agencies about possible threats.

These threats, Deveau told me, came from three groups: Islamic extremists after revenge for N'Tala's massacre of Bangui's Muslim population; agents of the current ruling party, the People's National Movement, whose hold on power was apparently shaky and who were shit-scared of a counter-revolution; the CIA, for unspecified reasons. The latter sounded to me like paranoid bullshit.

The Section team was housed in what had been the villa's staff quarters, a squat box of a building behind the garages. It had four bedrooms and two living-rooms.

Deveau had requisitioned the largest of them for his office, the bastard. The other one was the surveillance station where the Perimeter boys sweated it out over their monitors and wrote up the day's comings and goings with squeaky felt-tip pens on a whiteboard. The only other room on the ground floor, apart from a toilet that stank, was the kitchen, which was none too big but where we had to eat, sit, watch TV etc. Upstairs there was a bathroom with a shower that dribbled like a guy taking a piss in public and four bedrooms. Needless to say Deveau had taken the best one for himself which meant that everybody else had to double up.

My room-mate's name was Yves. He was about my age (28), ex-Army, body-builder's physique, and a really good type. I should have said that Deveau had assigned me to Personal Protection which at the time I thought was the lesser of two evils (how wrong can you be!) and Yves was the same. He was on a rest period when I went into our room and dumped my back-pack on the horrible-looking narrow bed. He was lying on his bed, smoking, reading a porno mag. I thought, thank God, he smokes.

We got chatting. He told me that the third PP guy – Jean-Paul – was on pool duty, watching N'Tala's brats swim and said we weren't allowed to use the pool ourselves. Which reminds me of the heat. Inside the house, with no air-con and bugger all breeze, it was like something out of Devil's Island. It was 26 degrees that day and over the next few weeks we headed into a full-blown fucking *canicule*.

Yves produced a baggie and we sparked up a couple of spliffs. I asked him about N'Tala and he said he was a total arsehole. He reckoned that Deveau was a loser and that our colleague, Jean-Paul, was a wimp and probably gay. Great news all round! He offered to lend me his mag. and I said, What's the point, getting yourself worked up when there's fuck all you can do about it.

"Don't worry," he said. "You get a day off a week and

there's a great place in Le Cannet."

So I told him about Astrid and that there was no way I was going to be screwing some pox-ridden pro.

"Don't be a cunt," he said. "They get checked out every week. Most of them are illegals, you know, Kosovans, Albanians and, like, really cool, with, you know, degrees, I mean like in fucking Astro-Physics."

Yeah, right, I thought, then, better get it over with, so I went outside and called Astrid on my mobile and gave her the bad news. Deveau had told me (really enjoying it) that I wouldn't be getting leave for a month and then it would only be two days and not even the week-end, because that was the busiest time. She was great about it, really understanding, said the company had just landed a commission from *France 2* for a mini-series so she was going to be up to her eyes in it anyway. As I went back into the house it struck me that maybe Astrid had been *too* fucking understanding. Then I told myself, calm down, less than a day and you're already paranoid!

Around noon, Deveau took me up to the villa to introduce me to N'Tala. The place was fully air-conditioned (what was *that* costing?) and stepping into the hall was like stepping into Heaven. The Banguian butler (there were six staff in the house, all Banguian) said the family were in the *salon* and we followed him into a room full of incredibly expensive-looking white leather sofas and armchairs. The first thing that struck me was the silence. Nobody was saying anything. I mean, they were all sitting round this big glass coffee table in total fucking silence. Another servant was pouring champagne into flutes and there was a two-litre bottle of coke for the kids.

Uncle Jo has this theory that you can always tell if someone has ever killed another person because the experience sets them apart, gives them a sort of aura. If you've looked into the eyes of someone while killing him you can never again look into anybody else's eyes in the same way as before. Of course, to recognize the signs it helps to be in our business, or something similar, like the army, but frankly, until that moment, I'd never really got it.

Uncle Jo had killed in his time, I knew that, but to me he was just Uncle Jo with his gray hair cut *en brosse* and his lean, serious face that lit up like a football stadium when he smiled. The Chief, who according to the buzz had been a top assassin in his time, was another matter. But then if you had any sense you tried to avoid looking directly at him. Not easy. Which proves the point, I suppose. I'd often tried to conjure up a mental picture of my Dad. With the sort of missions he presumably went on he might easily have had to kill someone. Did he have the aura? Waste of time, of course. I just remembered him as my wonderful Dad. I even asked my mother once and she said, with a sort of hiss: "For God's sake, Charlie." Point proven? I don't know.

Well, Chinbe N'Tala had the aura in fucking spades. When Deveau introduced me as the new bodyguard and I said (as previously instructed) "Monsieur Le President," the bastard very deliberately took off the Ray-Bans he was wearing and looked directly at me and I tell you those eyes of his – big, brown, huge in fact – were a couple of death rays. He was wearing a kind of multi-coloured Batik shirt, like Mandela, but there the resemblance definitely ended. N'Tala was a fat bastard, with a massive belly on him. His hair looked like grey fluff. Need I say he was wearing a fucking great diamond-studded Rolex that must have cost half a million euros.

N'Tala replaced the Ray-Bans and that was that. Not a fucking word from him. I didn't know what to do. I felt totally stupid. The kids were staring at me. I vaguely noticed a sensational-looking girl I took to be his daughter by a previous marriage (in fact, as Yves told me later, she was his new wife, Lolli) and a couple of wrinkled old bags (his mother and aunt), all of whom were staring at the floor. Deveau did a sort of bow, the prat, and I realized I was supposed to follow suit, but was fucked if I was going to, and we left.

"Doesn't exactly suffer from verbal diarrhoea, does he?" I remarked as we trudged back to Devil's Island in the glaring heat.

"Your instructions are to behave respectfully at all times when you're with him," Deveau replied.

"Get used to anything, I suppose," I said, or words to that effect.

"Get used to it right now," said Deveau.

Cunt.

Later that day, I had my first tour of duty with Yves. Around five, N'Tala's driver, Moko, who turned out to be a really good type, always up for a chat and a spliff when he was supposed to be washing the cars, brought out this huge black American stretched sports utility vehicle and we piled in, N'Tala in the front, next to Moko, Yves next to Lolli (lucky bastard) and the two youngest kids – both girls – and me in the third row with the boy, who was called Oladulu, or something like that. I never did really get it. Destination, the Macdo in Cannes.

I'd never been to Cannes before – the taxi from the airport took the autoroute direct to Mougins – and the first thing that struck me was the traffic, especially when we got down into the old town. Narrow streets seething with cars and pedestrians, a one-way system out of hell. It was a security nightmare. And by the way, throughout the journey, which took at least half an hour, not a word was spoken.

When Moko dropped us off at the Macdo down by the Marina, close to the *Palais*, my opinion about the security situation was reinforced. There were huge posters everywhere advertising some trade fair at the *Palais* and I remembered that, the famous Film Festival apart, there was usually some international congress going on i.e. fucking *anybody* could be around.

The Allées de La Liberté was swarming with people,

heading for Vieux Cannes or in the opposite direction to the Croisette but luckily the Macdo wasn't too crowded and we found a table for the N'Talas and another one for us. N'Tala produced a five hundred euro note and handed it to Yves.

"You're the new boy," Yves said, handing it on to me. "You go and fucking queue. It's three Royale Cheese menus, with beer, for His Highness, a chef's salad for Madame, and Big Mac menus with Sprite for the kids, plus four M&M MacFlurries. I'll have a Big Mac. Anything you like for yourself. Good luck."

Well I had to queue (which I hate) for about five minutes and by the time I made it to the counter I was hazy about the order and basically fucked up on it. Plus when I handed over the five hundred the kid nearly had a baby and there was major fuss over getting change. Result, I was a Royale Cheese and a Big Mac out and I had to rejoin the queue. As I waited, I discreetly watched the N'Talas. Lolli occasionally said something to her husband, who was devouring his burgers rapidly and methodically, and got a slight nod or shake of the head in reply. The kids said nothing. I wondered if he beat them or if they were all autistic or something. At one point, N'Tala caught me looking and stared at me. But at least he kept his Ray-Bans on.

We got back and Devil's Island was unbearably hot and airless after the car's air-con. We reported to Deveau and went into the kitchen for a cold beer but it was even hotter there so we took the beers up to our room. "Don't worry," Yves said mysteriously. "Give 'em a couple of hours then…"

"Then" turned out to be creeping out of the house, like a couple of kids, when Deveau had gone to bed. We slipped through the grounds, following a route that Yves said wasn't covered by the CCTV cameras, then climbed the wall that surrounded the pool, stripped off and lowered ourselves into the cool water. As we swam about, it occurred to me that the pool area had to be covered by CCTV but Yves said not, which led a discussion about what crap this whole operation was from a security point of view. I mentioned my worries about the traffic and crowds in Cannes.

"You should have been here a couple of weeks ago," he said. "The Film Festival. Fucking chaos. But wait till you have to do a Friday."

"What's a Friday?" I asked.

"N'Tala's night out. He's got this little apartment in a block near the station. Goes there alone, only takes one of us, usually Jean-Paul. Could be something going on there."

"What the fuck are you talking about?"

"You'll find out."

I did. The following Friday. It was Deveau's day off but before he left he told me I'd be bodyguarding N'Tala that night. We went in the Merc, Moko driving, me beside him, N'Tala in the back. The apartment block looked pretty damned seedy to me, a big, run-down sixties building.

N'Tala's love nest was on the second floor. There was a little hall, then you went into the living room, which was sparsely furnished with cheap stuff and an old TV with a portable aerial on top, and glorious views of the bumper-to-bumper traffic on the rue D'Alsace. There was a kitchenette off this room, then a door that led to a short passage and the bathroom and bedroom beyond.

"There'll be someone coming in ten minutes," N'Tala said. The first words he'd ever spoken to me. "Send him in. He's OK. Then there'll be someone else. He's OK too. Send him in." He pointed to the kitchenette. "There's beer in the fridge." That was it. He disappeared into the passage, closing the door behind him. But I have to admit, his French was impeccable. He'd been a lawyer or something before going into politics.

The fridge contained a couple of bottles of "33 Export." I fished one out, twisted the screw-cap off, took a swig and nearly gagged. It was warm. The fridge wasn't working. About ten minutes later the front door buzzed and I opened it to this Arab-looking guy. It took me about two seconds to work out who *he* was. Mr Tambourine Man. In other words, a dealer. He didn't say anything, just gave me a nod, I let him in and he went straight through into the passage. About five minutes later he came back and left. Five minutes later, another buzz and I went to the door pretty well knowing the sort of type I'd see when I opened it. Sure enough, it was a boy. I was shocked. Not because of the situation, which I'd already read, more or less, but because this kid, another Arab, looked so fucking young. I mean he didn't look sixteen. When he said *bonsoir* it was a relief to hear that he had a broken voice!

Like Mr Tambourine Man, he knew his way around and went straight into the passage, closing the door behind him. Time passed. I tried the TV. It didn't work either. I drank the beer. I called Astrid on her mobile but it was on answer. I left her a stupid message. I watched the traffic start to thin out on the rue D'Alsace. Out of sheer boredom I checked my gun out, which you are absolutely not supposed to do on bodyguard duty because it wouldn't be much use to you if terrorists burst through the door and the clip was out, would it? I realized I needed to take a leak. I went to the passage door. It was locked. You inconsiderate fucker, N'Tala, I thought. Then, can I last? Then, I don't know how long I'm going to have to. So I went into the kitchenette and pissed into the sink. At least the cold tap *did* work.

About an hour later, the boy emerged, looking none the worse, I have to say, for whatever disgusting services he'd had to provide, and left. Soon after, N'Tala appeared, we took the lift down to the ground floor and there was the Merc parked outside. We drove back to the villa, you guessed it, in silence. Yves was still awake when I went up to bed. "Did you piss in the sink?" he said.

Next morning, I went to see Deveau. It didn't need a

genius to work out that N'Tala's Friday nights, moral considerations apart, constituted a breach in his security you could drive a tank through. According to Yves, the apartment was unattended during the week except for a woman who went in to clean and change the sheets. How much would it cost to buy her? In fact you wouldn't even need to do that. The entry-phone system on the street door wasn't working. Anybody could walk in. Judging from the general condition of the building, nobody was going to be fixing it in a hurry. It would take about five seconds to get past the ridiculous lock on the apartment's door, then you could pack the bedroom with enough explosives to turn the whole place into a crater. Or you could buy Mr Tambourine Man and supply him with a drug that'd kill Monsieur Le President in less than a heartbeat. Or in a few months you could train a boy in assassination, then slip him into whatever the supply system was. (Internet was my guess.) There were a hundred other ways you could eliminate N'Tala on a Friday night.

Maybe I didn't put all this to Deveau very tactfully because he got seriously pissed off. He told me that the arrangement had been cleared by Section, that I was paid to guard N'Tala not to ask impertinent questions, that I was insubordinate, out of line, and would you please fuck off out of my office. Then I made a BIG mistake.

"So how much is N'Tala paying you?" I asked.

He blew his stack. He screamed at me. I left. Thinking, was that reaction genuine? And then – a much better thought – hey, maybe he'll call Section and get me fired. Then I made another mistake. I called Uncle Jo and asked him if the Friday night arrangement had really been cleared. He replied exactly as I should have anticipated.

"You know I can't answer that," he said. And he didn't sound *at all* friendly. "What's the matter with you, Charlie? Stop acting like an arsehole." Then he hung up.

So why was I getting myself so worked up about all this? What did I care if some joker bumped M. Le

President? I was watching my back. If N'Tala did get the magic bullet "on my watch" as Uncle Jo had put it, even if I wasn't directly responsible, it would not look good on my record. Not good at all. Later on, when I made up my daily log, I put my concerns in writing. Obviously Deveau would read it but frankly I didn't give a shit. He hated me anyway and now he'd have the dilemma of whether or not to pass it on up the chain of command. That made me feel a *lot* better.

I didn't get fired (in retrospect I realize Deveau didn't have the power) and over the next couple of weeks, I surprised myself by settling into the routine. Actually, it wasn't that onerous. A few times Yves or Jean-Paul and I escorted the ladies on shopping trips to the rue D'Antibes. They were well known in all the most expensive establishments and dealt out their gold cards like poker hands. Even the old mother and the aunt. There were more Macdo runs, dinners in the over-priced, over-rated restaurants in Vieux Cannes, usually just with Monsieur Le President and the First Lady, when Yves or Jean-Paul and I would have a separate table near the door. I made a habit of ordering insanely expensive wine. Why the fuck not. The only time I really worked up a sweat was when they went to the big casino at the end of the Croisette. In a way it was irrational because casinos have security systems the fucking Section could learn from. But logically or illogically, I felt it was dangerous. Or maybe it was just the sight of N'Tala blowing scads of taxpayer's money on roulette that got me steamed up.

Funnily enough, the pleasantest duty was the pool watch. The kids actually showed a little animation, laughing and screaming as they whooshed down the water-slide. But when I tried to talk to them, they clammed up. Maybe they didn't speak French.

I called Astrid every day, or tried to. Her phone was often on answer, even quite late at night. She said she was working all hours on the mini-series. But I began to wonder. I also began to wonder how much longer I could go on without some sex. I even began to work out strategies for having what those pervy priests and choirmasters used to refer to as "a five finger exercise." But where? The downstairs toilet? Wait till Yves is asleep? At night in the garden? But the downstairs toilet was disgusting, what if Yves woke up, what if the Perimeter boys picked me up on CCTV. Ouch! Things got so bad that one night, after a really good talk with Astrid, I started to wonder whether that scene with Napoleon and Josephine was quite so ludicrous after all.

I took my days off but always ended up wondering why I'd bothered. The beaches were shit, most of the restos were tourist rip-off joints and I spent most of my time mooching about with my headphones on, listening to *Skyrock*.

Yves and I sneaked out for a swim most nights, smoked a spliff or two in the pool-house and raided the fridge for beers and half-bottles of champagne. Sometimes we talked about N'Tala and Bangui. Yves knew a lot more than I did. He wasn't so dumb.

To cut a long story short (but it's important) France conceded self-government to Bangui in the '60's, the decolonisation period. Before handing over we organized elections, no doubt fixing things so the right candidate got elected, which he duly was. But his regime didn't last more than a couple of years. Civil war broke out and (inevitably, this was at the height of the Cold War) the Marxists (People's Liberation Party) won out. By the end of the '70's, aid from the Soviet Union was drying up, the economy was fucked and the regime collapsed.

Civil War broke out again. There were three factions: The Popular Liberation Party, The New Dawn Party led by N'Tala and The People's National Movement. According to Yves, France put its money, i.e. arms supplies, some discreet help from the Foreign Legion and the Section, on the PNM. But N'Tala won anyway and became President in 1980. Two years ago, by which time our baby had massacred the Muslims and a lot of other people, while allegedly stashing the usual millions in a Swiss bank account, the PNM staged a coup and he was out.

"You know he's a fucking cannibal," Yves said one night, cupping his hands over his face to get the last bit of buzz out of his spliff.

"They say that about every African dictator, don't they?"

"Apparently he used to chop guys' balls off and eat them."

"Come on."

"Have you seen his eyes?"

I couldn't get to sleep that night. The heat was terrible, I was trying to think away an erection, but most of all I was trying to work out why, if we'd backed the PNM in 1980 *against* N'Tala and they'd finally made it to power two years ago, we were protecting the loser. If he had all these millions why didn't we just kiss him goodbye and let him pay for his own fucking security? Then I made the connection. (*Ciao* erection.) My Dad died in 1980. Somewhere in Africa. Bangui? It had to be. Working *against* N'Tala.

After that, I didn't sleep at all. At eight, when I knew Uncle Jo would be at his desk, I called him. He was furious. "What the *fuck* are you talking about?" he yelled. "What's got into you? For God's sake stop obsessing about your father. It's pathetic. Pull yourself together. I can't go on protecting you forever."

Over-reaction? I thought so.

The third Friday came round. Jean-Paul had done the previous one and Deveau called me in and told me it was my turn. About the first words we'd exchanged since the big bust-up.

It was the same routine. The silent drive in the Merc. Mr Tambourine Man. A boy – but a new face. The only difference was that the fridge was working (electrical engineer, perfect cover for a bomber!) and the beer beautifully cold. I tried Astrid. No luck. I stretched out on the sagging sofa and the next thing I knew I was waking up, feeling like TOTAL shit and N'Tala was standing over me. He went: "Tst, tst, tst, tst." Then: "Don't worry. Our little secret." Then he took off those fucking Ray-Bans and winked.

At that point I swear to God I didn't get the significance of it. It was only when I stood up and a searing pain shot through my rear-end that I realized what had happened. By this time, he was heading for the door. I looked at my watch. It was over three hours since we'd arrived at the apartment.

I fell asleep again in the Merc. I woke up to see one of the Perimeter boys waving us through the gate. I staggered into Devil's Island and up the stairs. Yves was still awake.

"What the fuck are *you* on?" he said.

"Nothing," I said. "I think I'm sick."

"You look terrible."

He suggested a swim but I said I just wanted to sleep. He went off on his own, which was a relief. I didn't want to answer any questions. I just wanted to think. The first thing that occurred to me was that maybe I was wrong. Maybe I *was* sick. Maybe the pain in my rear had nothing to do with N'Tala but was associated with some disease.

Well, obviously the first thing to do was check myself out. I was wearing jeans with a button fly and as I started to take them off I noticed immediately that one of the buttons was in the wrong hole. Evidence, but not proof exactly. I unhooked the mirror off the wall, lowered my jeans and boxers and took a look. I'll spare you the details. What clinched it for me was that I found traces of lubricant. So N'Tala had done exactly what I thought.

I took a shower, got into bed, turned the lights out. I knew a little about these date rape drugs and one of the things I remembered someone telling me once is that they can induce a sort of amnesia. The victims get confused, have gaps in their memories. I was terrified that this would happen to me, that I'd wake up in the morning and wouldn't be able to focus clearly. Maybe N'Tala was counting on something like that.

The Section runs a course called Subdivided Recall where you are taught how to access your memory in a controlled, accurate way by mentally dividing a period of time into discrete parts that can be as short as a few seconds. Even Uncle Jo thinks this is a valuable technique, though he hates the jargon. I lay in the dark and tried to apply the method to what had happened that night. I took as my starting point the moment when I touched the handle of the fridge.

White Plastic. Ingrained dirt. Warm to the touch. Pull. Door sticks. Pull harder. Door opens. Light fails to come on. Interior has two shelves. Both white plastic-coated metal grilles. Lower shelf empty. Blackish spots of mould. Top shelf. Two bottles of "33 Export." One on left lying roughly straight, cap towards the back of fridge, one on right slightly askew, cap also facing inwards. Put left hand on left bottle. Sensation of cold. Shut fridge door with right hand. Bottle is squat, pale green glass. White metal screw-cap. Red and yellow label. Yellow and black band on neck. Transfer bottle from left hand to right. Curl left hand round cap. Serrated metal at base of cap feels slightly harsh against skin. Squeeze. Slight discomfort. Twist. Cap yields. Easily. Put it down on counter. Bottle still in right hand. Not much froth in neck. Bubbles rising slowly. Yes!

That's how he'd done it. Removed the screw-cap, put the stuff in, replaced the cap. Wait a minute. When? Same day. Not too long before we arrived. Would have to be. When he forced the screw-cap back on he couldn't have achieved a perfect seal. Liquid would seep out. The beer would go flat. OK, but how did he get the bottles (obviously the other one was spiked as well) into the fridge? I was with him all the time until he went to the bedroom. Who supplies the fridge? Never thought about it before. The cleaning woman? Unlikely. Too complicated. Have to give her cash, she'd have to produce receipts. Nightmare. Moko! Obviously. He runs errands all the time. Must be Moko who keeps the cleaning woman supplied with detergents, spray polish, bags for the vacuum etc. N'Tala gets the beer delivered to the villa then he sends Moko to the apartment to put it in the fridge. Do the Perimeter boys log Moko in and out? Must do. Check tomorrow.

I went back into Recall. Put bottle to lips. Tilt head. Lift elbow. Sensation bland. No sharp feel of bubbles creaming on tongue. Think: "It's flat, been sitting on a supermarket shelf for months. Cheapskate bastard."

I remembered it all quite clearly now. The beer *had* been slightly flat but still drinkable and the heat had made me thirsty so I drank it. Naturally, I didn't think of any other explanation at the time.

I woke up late next morning feeling better, almost normal, physically. My mind was clear and all I could think about was what N'Tala had done and how I'd like to kill the bastard. When I took a dump it hurt so much I was ready to march up to the villa, shoot the fucking cannibal and claim extreme provocation.

I was on pool duty that morning. While the kids splashed about and the two old ladies dozed in the shade, I thought about what I was going to do. It didn't take me long to work out that there wasn't a hell of a lot I could do. Say I reported it to Deveau. Say he believed me. What would he do? Pass it on up the chain of command as fast as fucking possible. What would the Chief do? What would Uncle Jo – and then it hit me that I didn't want anybody to know. It was too humiliating. If it got around I'd be a laughingstock. "Hear about Charlie C? Had a tough time on his last assignment but he took it. Right up the rear."

It wasn't long after I'd come to this conclusion, feeling really frustrated and fucking angry when N'Tala showed up. This had never happened before. I'd never seen him anywhere near the pool. The kids stopped laughing and playing. But he took no notice of them anyway. He started talking to me, asking me questions in like a really friendly way except I knew what he was really doing. He was taunting me. He kept kind of lowering those Ray-Bans and looking at me over them. And then he said something like: "You were here last year weren't you?" I said no.

"But your face is familiar. I've seen you somewhere before. You've been in my country perhaps?" I said no. "Strange. Your face is familiar."

Then I got it. I knew why he thought my face was familiar. Look at the photo of my Dad on his wedding day and look at a photo of me and you can hardly tell the difference. This bastard had known my Dad. In Bangui. In 1980. He'd killed him. If not personally, he'd ordered his death. That was when I realized that there was something I could do. I could kill this murdering bastard.

But could I? How? No point in doing it unless I got away with it. Answer – make it look like a hit. The Islamists. The PNM. Was that possible?

N'Tala barked something at the kids and they scrambled out of the pool and I escorted them, N'Tala and the old bags back to the villa. By the time I left them I was calmer, I was thinking logically. One year's thinking to one minute's action, that's the right proportion, Uncle Jo says and he's right. Well I didn't have a year but I sure as hell wouldn't get far unless I did a lot of thinking.

First thing I did was to look in on the Perimeter boys. After a bit of chat, I introduced the subject of Moko. I said I thought he could be vulnerable. I casually flipped over the current sheet on the whiteboard to get a look at the previous day's record. Sure enough Moko had been logged out at six, back in just before seven, then out again, with me and N'Tala, at seven forty. I covered this by pointing out the frequency of Moko's comings and goings. By this time the Perimeter boys were getting restive.

"Why don't you try minding your own fucking business for change?" one of them said.

"Your funeral," I replied and left.

I went for a walk in the grounds – that was permitted. I considered various options. It would have to look like a genuine hit and no suspicion must fall on me. Unless I got myself another gun, shooting him was out because Ballistics would suss it in no time and anyway getting a gun, though possible, isn't that easy, especially if you can't afford to leave a trail. Plus even if I set it up right – crowded street, panic, confusion – how could I be sure of getting rid of the second gun safely?

Explosives. A possibility. As I'd already pointed out to Deveau, and recorded in my log, the apartment was wide open during the week. I could slip in on my day off, plant the stuff in the bedroom, then trigger it one Friday just after the boy left. The down side of this was that although I'd done a course in explosives I didn't remember a lot about it and would have to do some research which the lads from Internal might pick up on. Also there was the problem of where to get the stuff without leaving a wake like the Brittany Ferry. Also, I could easily be seen entering or leaving the apartment block. And if I miscalculated the charge N'Tala could survive or alternatively we could both go together. Not a good idea.

I was thinking that nevertheless explosives might be the way forward when I got back to Devil's Island and met Jean-Paul coming out. He stopped.

"You OK?" he said.

I thought, Yves must have told him something. Then a weird thing happened. Jean-Paul kind of half looked at me, then turned away as if he'd said something embarrassing. And I got it. *N'Tala had done it to him too*.

To test this, I said: "Must have drunk too much beer."

Again, he half-looked at me and seemed to be about to say something important – you know how you can tell when that happens – but he looked away again and muttered: "You'll be all right." Then he walked away.

I now had no doubt. And I also had a plan.

Phase one was a friendly chat with Moko over a spliff in the garage. Without, I hoped, being too obvious about it, I established that N'Tala's practice was to call him on his mobile ten or fifteen minutes before he wanted to be picked up. I had seen N'Tala make such calls in restaurants etc. but I had to be absolutely sure this was the system. I was tempted to ask Moko how long, if N'Tala didn't appear, he'd wait before calling his boss back, or going to investigate, or calling Deveau. But I reckoned it was too risky. I didn't want Moko remembering such a conversation under questioning by Internal.

My two-day leave was due to start the following Monday. Astrid had agreed to phone in sick so we could spend some time together, even though she was under huge pressure at work. So when I buzzed her and told her that my leave had been postponed, she was more relieved than anything. "Poor you," she said, not very convincingly. "Are you all right? You sound a bit low." Just tired, I said. Not very convincingly either, I suspect. The conversation limped along then petered out. Later, she told me that it had really worried her. I'd sounded so unlike my usual self. Yeah, well I was hardly going to tell her that there was no way I was going to sleep with her until I'd had an AIDS test oh and by the way I'm planning to kill Chinbe N'Tala.

I left the villa early on Monday morning and got a taxi down into Cannes. I went to the clinic on the rue Georges Clemenceau and they took my blood. They told me they'd have the result in a week. Then I took the train to Nice and hired a car. Plane tickets are easy to trace, ditto the TGV. But it was OK to pay for the car on my credit card because if Internal did, by any chance, check up on that month's statement, I had a story all ready for them. Plus, have you tried to pay for a hire car in cash recently? It causes hysteria. And then they remember your face.

I took the A8 to Aix then the A7 north to Lyon. I drove very carefully and didn't exceed the speed limit. How many carefully thought-out plans have got fucked up by a stupid little thing like a speeding ticket? Just outside Lyon, I found one of those "Formule 1" hotels which could have been designed by the Section itself to aid covert operations. You just stick your credit card in the machine, get a code and you're in. No receptionist. No staff. Completely anonymous. Adulterer's paradise.

I set off from Lyon around five and headed for Paris on the A6. The story I was going to tell Internal, if they ever asked, was that I'd spent Monday night in Lyon hitting the night-clubs. So when I stopped for petrol near Auxerre, I did pay cash. I got to Paris soon after ten, parked in a *souterrain* near Place Clichy (you don't want to risk a parking ticket or a tow-away), called my own personal Mr Tambourine Man from a public phone (didn't want *his* number showing up on the monthly statement) and arranged to meet him in the usual place. He sold me the stuff – it was expensive – and told me it took twenty to thirty minutes to take effect and the subject would be out for three to five hours. I was back in the car and heading out of Paris soon after eleven, which gave me just enough time to swing by the *Grange au bouc* in Vieux Lyon and buy a load of drinks on my credit card before they closed. Then back to the "Formule 1" to crash out.

I didn't have to report back for duty till Tuesday evening so I took it easy next day. I treated myself to a fantastic lunch at a little place in a village near Aix, right under Sainte Victoire. My one regret was that Astrid wasn't there to share it with me. On the other hand, I did have time to think.

My general plan of operation was fixed but I still had a problem about exactly how I was going to kill the bastard – I mean, what weapon, how do I dispose of it, what about Forensics? If I went for a hammer, for example – piece of piss to obtain, highly effective – how would I get rid of it afterwards and how much mess would there be to clean up? Answer, no way (at last no way I could think of) to get rid of it safely and probably blood everywhere. I couldn't hide it the apartment because they'd search the place down to the last fucking carpet tack. Toss it out of the window? Take them about five minutes to find it. Dump it somewhere outside? I couldn't go outside.

The same problems seemed to apply to every other possible weapon. I did think of using my hands. I'd been taught how to do it. You chop or punch the guy's Adam's Apple then break his neck with a double-arm twist. But I wasn't going to be dealing with a rubber dummy on a Close Combat course. I was going to be dealing with a six foot cannibal with a neck like an elephant. And anyway, when you do the chop there's a risk of bruising to your hand.

As I drove back through the Var, I started to obsess about the forensics aspect. I mean this was the Section. Those boys would be all over it like ants on sugar. A bit of my DNA, like a hair, or an eyelash, or a flake of skin or even a drop of sweat on N'Tala's body or clothing could fuck me totally. Similarly, if they examined my clothing and found his DNA on me, same story. I couldn't wear a face mask or protective clothing or even gloves because I had no way of getting rid of them.

I remember it was just after the last *péage* before Cannes that the answer hit me. The most ancient, traditional tool of the assassin. The garrotte. You could turn the most innocent-looking things into a garrotte – a tie, a shoe-lace, a belt, any kind of wire or thin rope. Perfect. Or maybe not so perfect. I hardly ever wear a tie, certainly not in a heat-wave. I don't possess a belt. The sort of trainers I wear don't have laces. Yes but surely I could conceal some sort of rope or wire on myself. Sew it into the waist-band of my jeans or something. And they wouldn't find it?

I was still wrestling with the problem when I got back

to the villa, having dropped off the car in Nice and taken the train and a taxi. After the usual swim with Yves, during which I gave him a highly imaginative tour of the night-life of Lyon (good practice for a grilling by Internal) I went to bed and did a bit more Subdivided Recall. You see, I'd realized that my only chance was to find something in the living-room of the apartment that I could turn into a garrotte and something, moreover, that the Scene Analysis lads might just overlook. So I closed my eyes and took a step-by-step walk round the room. I don't know how long it took – ten minutes, maybe twenty – before I found what I was looking for. But when I did, I thought, Yes. Perfect. Part of the furniture.

Friday came round again and Jean-Paul got the assignment. I'd done my best to avoid him since my return from leave. I didn't want any confessions *before* the event. On my day off, I had some things to do for a change. First stop was the rue Georges Clemenceau – with a visit to the toilet in a hotel on the way because not surprisingly I was having serious *Pie Jesu* symptoms. They had the result of the test. I was negative. I had a couple of drinks in a bar to celebrate and calm myself down then I walked about till I found what I was looking for in a street near the covered market. A discarded phone card in the gutter. Having learned a valuable lesson from the hotel toilet incident, I stepped into a *pharmacie* and bought a packet of Diaretyl pills.

As I'd anticipated, next Friday I was selected for the duty. The tablets I'd bought in Paris were in the right-hand pocket of my jeans, wrapped in a Kleenex tissue. The phone card was in the left-hand pocket. I had everything I needed.

What were my feelings as I climbed into the Merc that night, about eight o'clock? Well, yes, I was incredibly nervous and tensed up but my real worry was that the six Diaretyl pills I'd swallowed at intervals during the day wouldn't work. Was I having any second thoughts about what I intended to do? Absolutely not. He'd been involved with my Dad's death.

I couldn't prove it. I'd never be able to prove it. But now I didn't have to. I was the judge and the executioner. Just between the two of us. Like the rape. Was I scared about pitting my wits against the Section? Better believe it!

Everything went according to the usual routine. We arrived, went up in the lift, I let Mr Tambourine Man in and saw him out. I'd decided not to spike the beer till N'Tala and the boy were at it and I even waited a few minutes after the boy had gone in before I went to the fridge.

I opened it. Empty.

At first I couldn't believe it. Stupidly, I felt around inside (the light was still not working) thinking there must be *one* bottle. There wasn't. My whole plan was fucked.

That was the moment when I think I came of age. Looking back on it, I'm amazed at myself. I could have just given up, there and then. I could have made a decision to postpone the operation till another Friday. Neither thought even occurred to me. I suddenly felt incredibly calm. I knew exactly what I had to do. It was as if I had a typed list of bullet points in my head. As I walked across the living-room into the hall, another list surfaced in my mind, a list of the insane risks I was about to run. But simultaneously, as I let myself out of the apartment, leaving the door on the latch, I was devising ways to avoid or explain them.

I took the lift down to the ground floor. I had it to myself and there was nobody in the hall, nobody entering from the street or leaving the building. Risks one and two crossed off. I moved to the street door, stopped and looked. No sign of the Merc. Risk three eliminated. Then I got my second big shock. As I put my hand up to open the door I noticed (thank God for Section training) that a new lock had been installed. The answer-phone system was functioning again. Okay, I could leave the street door an inch ajar but there was no guarantee that some resident or visitor wouldn't arrive or depart during my absence in which case I wouldn't be able to get back into the building without attracting attention.

That was when I seemed to divide into two Charlies. Charlie 1 was verging on panic, telling himself to stop, go back up to the apartment, forget the whole thing. Charlie 2 took the phone card out of the left hand pocket of his jeans, snapped off a corner of the plastic and used it to jam the lock.

Charlie 2 was still dominant as I stepped into the street. I stopped again. I checked the line of parked cars. No Merc. I moved on, walking briskly, still keeping an eye out for the Merc, working out that the little old-fashioned *Alimentation*, run by Asians, a couple of streets away, was the nearest place I'd find a bottle of "33 Export."

It took me maybe three minutes to get to the shop. I went in. Just inside the door was a refrigerated unit stacked with cold drinks. I opened the glass door, searched among the various beers. No "33 Export." Charlie 1 said: "What the fuck does it matter? Just get any fucking bottle." Charlie 2 replied: "I don't know which brands have screw-caps and which need a bottle-opener. Anyway, it has to be "33 Export" because that's what it always is."

I left the shop and headed towards the covered market, where I knew there was another place that stayed open late. It took me five or six minutes to get there, during which Charlie 1 was having all kinds of panic attacks about time, about someone discovering the jammed lock and calling whoever ran the building or even worse, the police, about N'Tala finishing early with his boy. Charlie 2 was keeping an eye out for the Merc *and* for Moko, because he didn't know where Moko went or what he did while waiting for his boss to call him.

I found the shop. They stocked "33 Export." Charlie 1, who'd calmed down a bit, bought a bottle. Charlie 2, clever bastard, bought a cheap pen-knife. Ten minutes later, I was back at the apartment building. I used the penknife to prise out the fragment of plastic from the lock, then threw both the plastic and the knife under a parked car. My luck was still holding. There was nobody about to witness all this. Several more risks crossed off the list.

I took the lift up to the second floor and the final – and biggest – risk on the list. I'd been gone nearly half an hour. If N'Tala had finished early I was fucked. I entered the apartment. No N'Tala on his mobile screaming at Deveau. To make quite sure, I tried the door into the passage. It was still locked. It was OK. But it would still pay to hurry.

I went back to the front door, stepped outside, closed the door, still keeping it on the latch, and inserted the phone card between the edge of the lock and the door-jamb. I worked it in and out five or six times to make sure traces would be left so that later Forensics would draw the right/wrong conclusions. Then I stepped to the lift, pressed the button to open the door, dropped the card into the gap between the floor of the lift and floor of the passage. I didn't think even the Scene Analysis lads would think about searching the bottom of the lift-shaft.

Back inside the apartment, I unlatched the front door and closed it. Really hurrying now, I took the beer over to the counter, fished the tissue out of my pocket and shook out the two little tablets. I twisted the screw-cap off the bottle and dropped in the tablets. They dissolved very quickly. I forced the cap back on and put the bottle in the fridge. Then I went over to the TV, unplugged the portable aerial and slid it under the sofa.

Then I sat down and waited. My thoughts were entirely centred on the *very* unplanned trip I'd had to make to get the beer. My whole strategy had been based on the fact that, as N'Tala's bodyguard, I couldn't set foot outside the apartment. Had I made any mistakes? Had I left any sort of trail?

For instance, had someone in fact noticed the jammed

lock and reported it and I'd just been lucky in getting back before anybody did anything about it?

I was – not very successfully – trying to work out what I'd say to Internal if they raised such a point, when the passage door opened and the boy came out. I escorted him to the front door, then went back to the sofa and sat down again.

I was still sweating a bit from the trip outside but now I really began to stream. *Pie Jesu* was playing to my gut and Charlie 1 was having another of his panic attacks. Then N'Tala came through the passage door and Charlie 2 took over. His timing was perfect. As N'Tala headed for the door into the hall, his back towards him, Charlie 2 stood up, taking the aerial from under the sofa. He strode towards N'Tala, stretching the wire between his hands. When N'Tala was a foot from the door, he flipped the wire over the grey fluff, drew it tight round the throat, twisted hard and hung on like a cowboy on a bucking bronco till the cannibal's legs buckled under him and he fell forward onto the floor. Charlie 2 didn't let go of the wire until he felt absolutely certain that the monster was dead.

Then he unhitched the wire and carefully examined the whole apparatus. He couldn't detect any obvious damage. The connection to the aerial was still tight, ditto to the plug at the other end. The wire itself showed slight signs of stretching and kinking but nothing you'd notice in a cursory examination. If Scene Analysis suspected it could be the murder weapon they might be able to prove that there had been stress on the filaments inside the rubberized coating but in that case he'd probably be fucked anyway. Forensics was the greater danger.

He went into the bathroom, got a handful of toilet paper and used some of it to clean the wire and aerial as meticulously as he could, given the time pressure he was now under. With the rest of the paper, he cleaned the top, sides and screen of the TV. He didn't want some bright spark in Scene Analysis to start wondering why the TV was dusty but the aerial clean. He flushed the toilet paper and the tissue that had wrapped the date-rape pills down the pan, returned to the living-room, took the beer out of the fridge, drank it and, every phase of the operation being now completed, he stretched out on the sofa.

I came round in a room in a private hospital. A guy I vaguely recognized was sitting on a chair, reading a paper. I tried to remember who he was. Operations or Internal? If he was Operations I was probably in the clear. If he was Internal I was in trouble. He saw that I was awake and stood up.

"Welcome back," he said. "How are you feeling?"

His voice gave me a cross-bearing on him. I was almost sure he was from Operations.

"Like shit," I said.

He grinned. I asked him what time it was. Two in the morning, he said. I'd been out for just under five hours.

"You're OK."

"What the fuck happened to me?" It was time to start playing the role I'd rehearsed over and over again in my mind. "N'Tala!"

He shook his head.

"Fuck," I said. Then: "My life's over. What the fuck happened?"

"Look, the Chief's here. He'll explain everything."

He left. I sat up. I saw that I was wearing some kind of cotton robe. Panic. They've taken my clothes. Forensic have got the fucking fluff in my socks under the 'scopes at this moment. Then I noticed my hands. On each one there was a faintly discoloured line running from just inside the palm round to the knuckle of the index finger, where the wire had bitten in. I'd thought of everything except that. The one mistake that fucks you.

The Chief came in. He looked kind of icy and pissed off. But that didn't tell me anything. He always looks like that.

"You all right?" he said.

"I think so, Chief," I said. "I'm a bit – confused."

I wasn't at all confused, I was thinking, fuck, for him to be here they must have flown him down in a military plane then choppered him to Cannes. This is not good. I said: "I don't understand what's happened."

"A kindly assassin has saved you from a fate worse than death."

I didn't get it. He must have seen that and he said: "But I must curb my sense of humour."

Sense of humour? What sense of humour?

"Did Lagrange tell you? We lost N'Tala."

Lagrange! That was his name. He worked for Uncle Jo. He was Operations.

"You were drugged," the Chief said. "Something called Rohypnol." I contrived to look dumb. "It's a date-rape drug. Its street name is apparently *roche*." Again I managed (I assume) to look as if none of this meant anything to me. "It was in the beer you drank."

"The beer?"

"Yes. The beer supplied by N'Tala."

"You mean…" I did my best to look as if the implications were slowly dawning on me.

"N'Tala drugged you. He was going to sexually assault you." And while I was doing my best to look aghast, he added the magic words I'd been waiting for. "He had already, successfully, assaulted your colleague Jean-Pierre Meunier using the same method. Meunier told us this when he heard what had happened to you."

We talked for a bit more after that but frankly I don't remember much of it. I was too elated by the thought that good old Jean-Paul had come through and that my plan had worked out fucking PERFECTLY. And too busy making sure my elation didn't show.

They let me out of hospital in the afternoon. My clothes had been returned. I couldn't tell whether Forensics had worked on them or not. Lagrange drove me to Nice. My orders were to return to Paris and report for duty on

Monday morning. By this time I wasn't feeling so elated. In fact I was worried. It seemed odd that I was being sent straight home. The usual procedure would be an on-scene de-briefing by Operations – which I'd prepared myself for. Plus there was a loose end.

The empty fridge.

Why had it been empty? The most likely explanation was that N'Tala had simply forgotten to get Moko to restock it. That would be OK because Moko wouldn't know what had been left over from the previous Friday. Unless he'd gone in to check during the week. Shit, he might have done exactly that. If for some reason (malice?) N'Tala had specifically told Moko not to replenish the supplies, or if Moko *had* checked and told him the fridge was empty and N'Tala had said something like, Good, fuck them, then Moko would absolutely know that there couldn't have been any beer for me to drink. What were the chances that Operations or – God forbid – Internal would question Moko that closely? In the case of a major screw-up like losing N'Tala, every chance. In which case, the Chief's friendly attitude had been designed to lull me into a false sense of security. Classic Section technique.

I'd left Astrid a message telling her I was coming home and she must have picked it up during the flight because when we landed at Orly and I switched my mobile back on there was a message from her saying she had to go to a screening and wouldn't be home till after ten but wow how exciting and she couldn't wait to see me etcetera etcetera. I took a taxi to the apartment, had a shower and a drink and switched on the TV. Well, it wasn't like in the movies when someone does that and by an amazing coincidence gets the news at the very point when they're reporting exactly what we need to know to move the story along. A reality show was on that I like and I watched it for a bit before drifting off.

When I woke, the ads were playing, then the news came on. The lead story was Iraq, as usual, then something about a big strike in Bordeaux, as even more usual, then something boring about the E.U. Commission and then I found myself looking right into the death-ray eyes of Chinbe N'Tala. A full-face photo of him. It was followed by archive footage of his swearing-in back in 1980 as the newsreader announced that the former President of Bangui had died suddenly of a heart attack at his villa in Mougins. I nearly yelled out loud.

A cover-up! The Section was going for a fucking cover-up! That's why they'd bundled me out of Cannes so fast. Grill Moko? They'd already be opening a Swiss bank account for him and making plans to knock him off discreetly in a year or two if he didn't behave. I was in the clear. I was home free. And suddenly I was in a mood, which I hadn't been in before, to greet Astrid when she came home in the way both of us needed and deserved.

Life doesn't get much better than the next day, Sunday. To wake up with Astrid beside me. To stand in a shower that actually worked properly and whose temperature you could fine-tune through long experience. To stroll to the *boulangerie* and get *croissants* and *pains aux raisins* that didn't taste like office stationery and see familiar faces in the *quartier*. I was so happy I actually went to Mass with Astrid (a first) and even thought about calling my mother and casually mentioning it because I knew it would make her feel good. However, I didn't want to risk spoiling a perfect day. We had a long, long lunch, then back to bed and in the evening Astrid had to do some work on a script and I was even able to help her over one of the characters – which somewhat amazed her until I told her (discreetly) a bit about the Psychological Profiling course. She was impressed! Dinner at our *brasserie* then back to bed – perfection.

On Monday morning I was at the office at eight. Half an hour later I was with the Chief.

"Of course you've seen the news," he said. "Someone in Operations can write your report for you or you can do it yourself. I presume you've already worked out what needs to be said."

"Absolutely, Chief. I'd quite like to give it a go. Operations can always adjust it if I don't get it exactly right."

"Get on with it then."

"Yes, Chief."

And that was that. No twelve-hour sessions with Internal. Just an enjoyable few hours with one of Uncle Jo's people polishing my entirely fictional report, during which I discovered that it had been Moko who had raised the alarm about an hour after I'd done the deed. As I left the office that evening I thought, It's over.

It wasn't.

A couple of weeks later, Uncle Jo asked me to have lunch with him. That in itself didn't ring any great alarm bells because we did occasionally have lunch together, though usually on my birthday or around Christmas. We went to one of those *Hippopotamus* places. It's a chain, not expensive, excellent food , so always crowded. Plus it was highly unlikely that anybody from the Section would be there.

Uncle Jo didn't waste a lot of time. His bombshell just about dead-heated with the *aperos*.

"We know you killed him," he said, taking a sip of his jaune.

Pie Jesu domine ...

"Actually, it was the first thing that occurred to me," he went on. "You see there was never any real threat to N'Tala. Well, yes, there were a couple of *fatwas* out against him but frankly with the Middle East exploding on all sides we didn't think he was very high on anybody's list of priorities, though of course *he* did. As to the PNM, they couldn't organize a fuck in a brothel let alone the assassination of someone protected by the Section. Our political masters are disappointed in them. They aren't performing. French interests in Bangui are not being taken care of in the way we like and the way that was agreed."

"What about the CIA?"

Possibly the stupidest thing I've ever said in my life. But then I was in a state of shock.

"Can't you recognize a Foreign Office fantasy when you see one? There's a whole group of opera-loving *enarques* who are paranoid about Bush. It's extremely boring. To return to the point, we were keeping N'Tala on ice as a pressure on the PNM. I'm surprised you didn't work that one out. It's hardly rocket science."

"So the protection operation was just a front."

"Well, look at the dead-beats we assigned to it. I don't include you. But no. Not entirely a front. It was in our interests to keep a close eye on N'Tala – and it paid off. The Friday night excursions. Extremely valuable. Homosexuality doesn't play in Bangui or anywhere else in Africa much. They have – rugged views on such matters."

"You set up those boys for him."

"Not exactly. Shall we say we facilitated his natural, or perhaps I should say, unnatural proclivities."

The waitress arrived with a *pâté maison* for me and soup for Uncle Jo. I realized that there was no way I was going to be able to eat anything. Uncle Jo attacked his soup heartily.

"What makes you think I killed him?" I said after a moment.

"Your sudden loss of appetite would seem to be an indication."

"For fuck's sake, Uncle Jo, why do you think I killed him?"

"If it wasn't an assassin it more or less had to be you, didn't it? I mean, who else? The only real question was your motive. But I had an idea about that. I thought you might have got some notion into your head that N'Tala had somehow been involved in your father's death."

"Wasn't he?"

"I don't know."

"You must know."

"Charlie, I wasn't Head of Operations in those days. I didn't have access to that sort of information."

"Did he die in Bangui?"

"I don't know."

"You were friends. You must have known where he was going."

"We were friends but we were also professionals. Sometimes we worked together. But there were plenty of missions I did which I never talked about to him and plenty he did that he never talked about to me. Information can be *compromising*. You do your best to protect your friends from it. I see you don't believe me. I'll give you an example. The only two people who know for certain that you killed N'Tala – apart from you yourself, of course – are the Chief and me. We are the only two people who will ever know. And I doubt if even in private conversation we will refer to it again."

"You say you know for certain. I don't see how you can."

"Because you covered your tracks so carefully? You certainly did that. Forensics and Scene Analysis got nothing. Zero. I congratulate you. Very sincerely."

"If those boys were investigating me –"

"They weren't. Their job was to make absolutely sure that there was nothing that could compromise the heart attack story."

"Even so they must have thought I was a suspect."

"No doubt. They aren't the only ones. There's Deveau, who's not quite as stupid as you think. There's young Meunier. And your friend Yves. So what? N'Tala died of natural causes. In terms of the Section that is an undeniable fact."

"You keep saying you know for certain. You still haven't told me how."

"Meunier's statement. If N'Tala had done it to him he might well have done it to you. Suppose that was the case.

253

What would you do?"

"Kill him? Bit strong."

"Before you did anything you'd get an AIDS test, wouldn't you. Last week I paid a discreet visit to Cannes. The rue Georges Clemenceau."

I wasn't angry, I was fucking beside myself. "That's supposed to be a hundred per cent confidential." Uncle Jo just looked at me with one thin, grey eyebrow slightly raised. "What a curious mixture of cleverness and naivete you are, Charlie."

Too right. Charlie 1 and Charlie 2. But that was a later thought. At the time, I was still too angry to think straight. Angry, of course, at *myself*. The AIDS test had been a gaping hole in my plan. I could have waited. You have up to eight weeks. I'd read all the stuff. I should have fucking waited. Uncle Jo was speaking again.

"I had no doubt now. N'Tala had raped you and you believed, rightly or wrongly, that he was responsible for your father's death. If I'd been in the same position I'd have killed him. There's only one thing I haven't been able to work out. What did you kill him with? You don't have to tell me, of course."

I looked at Uncle Jo. He smiled. All the lights went up in the stadium.

"The TV aerial," I said.

"What TV aerial? None of the reports mentions a TV aerial."

"They wouldn't," I said. "It's part of the furniture." Suddenly I had my appetite back. I started to eat my *pâté*.

"The TV aerial," Uncle Joe said. "Brilliant. Truly brilliant."

"Uncle Jo," I said, "I *know* N'Tala had something do with my Dad's death." I told him about the conversation by the pool.

"That isn't proof," he said. I just looked at him much the same way he'd looked at me earlier.

"OK, OK," he said. "The bastard. Here's to you, Charlie."

Later, when we were heading for the taxi stand, I asked him why Section and the Ministry had decided to go for the cover-up. "Why don't you try to work that one out for yourself," was his reply.

The taxi stand was empty. We waited. "I lost Section a valuable asset," I said after a moment.

"We'll get over it," Uncle Jo said. "Don't worry too much. In a way you've proved yourself. You've got a great career ahead of you. Bangui's chaos. The PNM can't last. N'Tala was never the preferred alternative. Someone else will emerge – lowering his trousers. Oh. Sorry. There's always another one. Like a taxi," he added, as a taxi pulled into the rank.

There was some sort of funeral service for N'Tala. A junior Minister from the Foreign Office attended. Lolli announced that she would keep his ashes until the day that Bangui was free again and they could be interred in the soil of the beloved country to which he had devoted his life etcetera etcetera.

I slipped back into the office routine. They sent me on the Geopolitics course which was a good sign, virtually a guarantee of promotion, but I wasn't happy.

I'd thought about the cover-up as Uncle Jo had suggested and realized that it worked for everybody. The Section was saved the embarrassment of having to explain how this supposedly important person had been killed while under their protection, ditto the Foreign Office. The PNM government in Bangui didn't get accused of being behind a hit and there was no chance that N'Tala would become some sort of martyr, like Che or Martin Luther King. And if they'd picked up any rumours, like from a distressed Lolli or a stoned Moko, that all was not quite as it seemed, it would just remind them how ruthless the French government could be when it wanted and how easily it could manipulate its own media. The Islamic extremists could cross another name off a list. Allah had taken care of it.

All this was great, logical, I'd come through not only unscathed but having gained the respect of the Chief and Uncle Jo, so why was I feeling so shitty about it? Because my Dad had worked in the same line, I'd never once stopped to think about, well, the morality of it all. Or maybe not so much that – all countries have agencies like the Section, they have to, and I guess they all work in much the same way – but more whether I wanted to be part of it. The lies, the cynicism, the secrets, the water-tight compartments.

Maybe it was living with Astrid. She was so open and up-front and honest about herself. Sure, you could argue that the Section existed precisely to make sure that the Astrids of this world had the freedom to be open, up-front, honest etc., but there I was with this wonderful girl, from a good family, well-educated, who cared about other people and was truly *kind* and her boyfriend had actually killed somebody and she had no idea.

That was another thing. Sometimes when I saw kids playing I'd remember the pool and the water-slide and N'Tala's kids and it was all very well telling myself I'd done them a favour and they'd have a better life without a father like that, but the fact remained that I'd taken their Dad away just as someone had taken mine.

In other words, Charlie 1 was re-asserting himself big time and Charlie 2 was starting to be someone I didn't like at all. Of course, Astrid picked up on my mood and one night, in the *brasserie*, well into the second bottle, she got me to talk about it.

I didn't tell her I'd killed N'Tala or anything, just about the problems I was having about my work. Actually, I might just as well have told everything because she said: "You had some sort of trauma, didn't you, when you were down in Nice." Female intuition. Section doesn't have a course on *that*. "Can you get out?" she said. "I mean I don't know much about it but you're not bound for life or anything, are you?" I thought about that – a thing I'd never done before. I said, Yes, I could resign. People did.

I thought about it some more. Whenever I did, whenever I imagined not working for Section, I felt light-hearted and happy. The problem was, what would I do? At my level, if you got kicked out or resigned, a job with a private security company was about your only option. Which as far as I was concerned was crap. I explained this to Astrid. She told me to open up my horizons a bit. There was a whole world out there beyond Section, full of all kinds of opportunities.

One night, when we were driving back from some party, she said: "You know what you should do, Charlie? You should write."

"What?"

"Spy stories."

"I can't write."

"Well you can as a matter of fact."

"Yeah, reports and stuff like that."

"You read."

"Mostly crap."

"That's exactly what I'm suggesting you write."

"Thanks."

She laughed. "I mean airport book-stall stuff. You've got all the background knowledge. You could make it feel authentic." She was getting more and more enthusiastic. "You could create a character, a young guy working for the security services. I could help you." Now I began to get a bit enthusiastic myself. "Remember when you helped me over that scene when the detective starts to think it's his girlfriend? You were *good*. You've got the instinct."

By the time we got home, I was thinking, well why the fuck not? Give it a try. We set up the second bedroom as a sort of study and I moved my own Sony Vaio into it and over the next month or two, at weekends, if I was off duty, on days off, sometimes in the evening, I wrote what I'm just about to finish. The story of how I killed Chinbe N'Tala. I've done it partly as sort of therapy, to get it out of my system and partly just to find out if I *can* write and if I like it, knowing that of course I'll never be able to show it to anybody, let alone get it published.

It's been worth it. It's probably full of terrible grammar and stuff but I honestly don't think it's too bad. And I have really enjoyed doing it. Also I know what the next story is going to be. About a young guy, working in a fictional version of Section, who's searching for the truth about how his father died. I've told this to Astrid. She says it's a great idea. It's what she thinks I've been working on. Maybe that's the last lie I'll ever have to tell her.

*

Editor's note: It is now thought that it must have been in the early morning of October 4th, 2005, that the writer of this story, Charles Limogaix, on his own admission "crap at computers," attached the document, in error, to an e-mail he sent to one of his friends. The friend in question has never been identified. By late afternoon of the same day, the story was already on the Internet. It appeared on a French conspiracy-theory website called *AvertiMond*, in October 2005. The e-mail address of the author (cxlimogaix-75@wanadoo.fr) was still attached.

An article appeared next day in *Libération* which forced the Foreign Office to issue a statement. The Minister's spokesman confirmed that a Charles Limogaix had worked for the department in a junior capacity, had been suffering from mental problems and had been on the point of being dismissed on health grounds. A later statement, from a psychiatrist, confirmed this. Meanwhile Limogaix himself had disappeared. Journalists established that he had left his apartment in Boulogne-Billancourt a few hours after the story appeared on the net. His girl-friend, Astrid Leblanc, issued a statement under the auspices of the Foreign Office. She said that in the past few months Limogaix had been subject to delusions and fantasies about homosexual rape. He had been a drug-user and a heavy drinker.

In France, the story quickly died. The Foreign Office refused any further comment and the press lost interest. On the web, however, it has taken on a life of its own. At the last count there were twenty-three sites dedicated to various theories about the death of Chinbe N'Tala, the real identity of Charles Limogaix, and his true role in the affair.

On the wilder shores of speculation, it is suggested that the French security services deliberately leaked the material as disinformation/a double bluff and that Limogaix never actually existed. The fact that he has never been traced is the most measured proof offered in support of this theory. The silliest (so far) is that the name Charles is close to the word charlatan. A particularly dotty site claims that the answer lies in the references to the CIA, which both Charlie and Uncle Jo ridicule in the text. This again is said to be a double-bluff. But then the site attributes a gallimaufry of events to the sinister machinations of the CIA including the death of Robert Maxwell, the disappearance of Lord Lucan and the Second World War. For me the most telling comment has been from someone called FizzyG, in the forum of an American site. "course charlei real – they cant fnd hi cos he too fuckin clever 4 em."

In conclusion, at the request of my collaborator, Michel Walrangis, I quote from an e-mail he sent me when he received the first draft of the translation.

"Once again, chapeau. I owe you €10 for remembering to transpose MPN to PNM. You were worried about the slang but I think you have succeeded admirably though I am not sure that "mega" quite captures "hypra." I think our decision to leave the text in its raw state has been justified. In fact it works very well. One notices how once Charlie gets into his stride his prose becomes more fluent and the story moves along at a better pace. It disintegrates again at the end, of course, in the self-examination passage – but I find that quite moving. At the same time could one not remove some of the more irritating repetitions of words like "so," "anyway," "stupid," "hit me" and so on – to say nothing of the innumerable "fucks" and "fuckings." Putain is so much more mellifluous! Or would this rob it of its flavour? Also the endless parentheses. There are times when it seems that the writer is suffering from some form of alopecia and is shedding eye-lashes all over the page. Yes, his strictures on *Communication* do still make me wince (thank you for asking!) but the very intelligent-sounding Astrid's satire is more wounding. I surfed some of the sites as you suggested and I agree entirely that FizzyG has put his finger on it. I was tempted to add my own hope, that Charlie is scooping the leaves out of a pool somewhere safe and warm. I resisted."

THEO

Where does an idea come from? By what hidden process does a thought float into the mind as if from nowhere and crystallize into an idea? It is a phenomenon that has always puzzled creative artists. Sometimes it is clear enough – Proust's famous *madeleine* for instance – but usually it is obscure. The composer Malcolm Arnold used to talk about how a whole symphony could evolve from a single musical interval in a way that he found inexplicable. Poets often start with one line, a sequence of words whose meaning is at first wholly mysterious and that becomes clear only when the poem is complete. The puzzle is not confined to artists. Among the most creative minds are those of scientists, especially physicists, and they experience the same thing. The French mathematician, theoretical physicist and philosopher of science Henri Poincaré, father of Chaos Theory, conceived the idea of Fuchsian functions as he stepped onto a bus. "At the moment when I put my foot on the step," he wrote, "the idea came to me without anything in my former thoughts seeming to have paved the way for it." The most perceptive analysis, perhaps inevitably, comes from Albert Einstein. "A new idea comes suddenly," he recorded, "and in rather an intuitive way. That means it is not reached by conscious logical conclusions. But, thinking it through afterwards, you can always discover the reasons which have led you consciously to your guess and you will find a logical way to justify it. Intuition is nothing but the outcome of earlier intellectual experience."

I do not, of course, propose anything as preposterous as to compare a modest collection of short stories with an

Arnold symphony, great poetry or world-changing breakthroughs in physics. I ask myself the question only because one morning, in a house in South West France that I had bought as a ruin in 1990 and gradually restored, I sat down to write one thing, a screenplay, and found myself, inexplicably and odd though it may sound, uncontrollably writing quite another: one of the stories in this book. Even more strangely, as I wrote it, or more accurately as it wrote itself, I found ideas for other stories, along the same lines, teeming in my head and by the end of that day the idea of a collection was almost fully formed and I even had a title: *Twelve Curious Deaths in France*.

Why twelve? Thirteen might have been more ironically amusing. Seven would have had pleasing mystical connotations. Fifteen would have made for a fatter volume. But no. For some reason – and I had no idea what it was – it had to be twelve.

I continued to work on the stories intermittently, juggling them with other commitments in the way that most freelance writers are condemned to do, and the puzzle of their genesis continued to nag at me. Some time later, I can't remember exactly when, I was driving along the D 943/946, the back road that runs westward from Auch, the capital of the Gers *département*, along a high ridge. The views, especially to the south, towards the Pyrénées, are spectacular and the road runs through a series of *bastide* villages and small towns: Barran, L'Isle-de-Noé, Montesquiou, Bassoues. They were all originally designed as fortresses against the depredations of the wicked English during the Hundred Years War, the houses facing inwards around a colonnaded square, their backs forming defensive walls. They are still redolent, to the historical imagination, of the rampages of The Black Prince.

A few kilometres after Bassoues, just short of a hamlet called Armous-et-Cau, on the right hand side as you travel west, lies a small vineyard and right next to it a cemetery enclosed by a wall. I had passed this place many times. It was a sort of landmark on the hundreds of journeys I had made, back and forth, along that road. I never failed to appreciate its peculiar beauty which lay, I thought, in the juxtaposition of vineyard, symbolic of life, and cemetery, symbolic of death.

On that particular day, perhaps because I was turning over in my mind a new story in the collection, it suddenly came to me that visual memories of this tiny corner of France had entered into my subconscious and out of them had somehow grown the idea for *Twelve Curious Deaths in France*. I was certain that this was the general explanation but I still had no idea why I had fixed on *twelve* stories.

My wife Anthea and I married in 1978. She had three children by a previous marriage. Our son – my only child – was born in 1982 when Anthea was forty-seven years old. We named him Theo after Anthea's father, an officer in Naval Intelligence who had been killed on active service in France, just after the D-Day landings, and is buried in the British Military Cemetery in Bayeux.

Theo, twenty-two when I started the stories, was *the* great enthusiast for them. He read each one as soon as it was written and was constantly urging me to get on with it, to set aside all my other (paying) projects and finish the book. "I think it could be important for you, Dad," he once said. He had inherited my penchant for anagrams. The handle he used on Messenger and the World Wide Web was *smoothdelight* – an anagram of Theo Goldsmith – and he spotted instantly that the name of the mythical "collector" of the stories, Michel Walrangis, was also an anagram of the name I had been given by my birth mother before I was adopted: Michael Rawlings. Knowing my other quirks, he worked out that the poem by Irène Griffonet, quoted at the end of the story entitled *Caesar*, contained an acrostic. Because he spoke fluent French he was also able to identify and enjoy the various plays on words scattered throughout the text, for example, in the same story, the name of the minor character M. Marlièvre (*Mars* = March, *lièvre* = hare.)

In the spring of 2005, Theo was taking a short break with us in France. He had been going through a difficult time. Over-indulgence in skunk had led to a psychotic episode from which he was only just emerging. On the other hand, after a few academic wrong-turnings, he had found his path in life and had gone to Leeds University to study computer science and was loving it. I told him about the flash of insight I had experienced on the D 946.

"That's the cover for the book, Dad," he said.

We jumped into the car, drove up to Armous-et-Cau, parked by the wall of the cemetery and stumbled about in the naked vineyard in search of the right angle for a photograph. When Theo found what he judged to be the ideal spot he raised up his beloved mobile phone and took the picture that appears on the dust-jacket of this book. It was one of those moments of closeness and companionship that are the best elements in our lives and the most to be cherished.

That summer, Theo came out to France again. He was in much better shape. He had kicked the skunk. He was engrossed in his university course. He was feeling more positive about himself and could see a future. He was even discovering that spending a summer holiday with his parents was not such a drag after all. In early August two friends from university joined him. I hired a car for them so that they could be independent. Theo wasn't on the list of approved drivers because he'd lost his license a few months before when he'd been caught driving over (only *just* over, he insisted) the limit.

On the night of August 4th he and his friends went into Marciac, a nearby *bastide* town in which a Jazz Festival is held annually. They met up with some French students. Theo told us later that they had climbed onto the stage set up in the square for the Festival and sung and danced. The students had a car but nowhere to stay so Theo brought them back to the house. Anthea later wrote about how he crept into our room at around four in the morning. "Theo gently opened the door. 'Mum, we've made friends with some students, can they put their sleeping bags on the beds upstairs and stay the night?' 'Go for it,' I said sleepily."

Morning came. August 5th. We didn't expect to see anybody about much before noon. Let Anthea take up the tale again. "However, as I was sitting on my own, having another coffee, Theo came round the corner from the cottage. He'd grown his hair and it was curling round his head; he had beads around his neck which I'd given him. They were dark green and black, from South America. We both loved them. He didn't have a shirt on, but just old jeans and bare feet. He sat down opposite me and poured himself some orange juice. 'I may be only your mother,' I said, 'but you're looking good. SEXY!' 'You may be only my mother – but THANKS!'"

My niece Kate and her fiancé, Carl, were due to arrive at Pau airport for a long weekend and Anthea and I were to pick them up. The students were still asleep upstairs – as it turned out we never set eyes on them – but one of Theo's friends had appeared and they had started a game of table tennis. As we headed towards the car, I passed Theo. I remember just raising my right hand in a little in a gesture of farewell and saying "A bientôt, Théo." "A bientôt, Papa," he replied. That was the last time I saw my son alive.

We drove to Pau. As we waited for the plane to arrive, Anthea rang Theo. He said that the French students had gone and that he and his friends were going to have lunch in the restaurant in Bassoues. "Bonne idée," she said. It was the last time she spoke to him.

We met Kate and Carl. We had lunch in a *routier* outside Pau then drove back to the house through the rolling hills and rich vineyards of Gascony. The weather was perfect. The sky was an unblemished blue, the heat intense. The countryside had never looked more beautiful.

We got back to the house. Anthea said later that she had been faintly surprised that Theo was not yet back from Bassoues. We played table tennis. We swam in the pool. Kate, Carl and I had come out of the pool and were sitting at the table in the shade when the phone rang. With a towel wrapped round my waist, I walked into the dim cool of the house and picked up the phone. It was the mother of one of Theo's friends. She said that there had been a terrible accident. I thought she meant that *she* had been in an accident and asked if she and her husband were all right. She said that the *boys* had been in an accident. I asked if her son was OK. She said he was. I asked if the second friend was OK. He had been badly injured, she said. Then I said: "Theo?" "I'm afraid Theo didn't make it."

A dull pain began to throb in my guts, a pain that was to stay with me for days, weeks and months, a pain that I can still summon up by remembering those moments and the even more desperate moments that were to come. I experienced the condition that I have tried to describe in one of the stories, the division of the self into two separate entities, one able to cope with immediate practical concerns, the other howling in a dark place. The first entity managed to continue the phone conversation with the shattered voice on the other end of the line. I wanted her son's mobile phone number. I couldn't find a piece of paper or anything to write with. I stumbled about, tripping over the hem of the towel, found the stub of a pencil and a scrap of fax paper. I wrote down the number. I thanked her for her courage in making the call. I put down the phone. I walked back out into the brilliant sunshine. Anthea was floating in the shallow end of the pool. "Anthea, you've got to get out of the pool," I said. "Theo has been killed." She climbed out. She walked up and down the baking tiles saying: "No, no, no," pushing a fist into the space between her ribs.

I went back into the house to get dressed. Kate came in.

She said a Frenchman had arrived. They needed me.

I went back outside. The Mayor of our local village, Beaumarchès, was there. I shook hands with him. His manner was faultless: grave, compassionate. He said that our son was dead. The accident had happened near Armous-et-Cau. At the cemetery there. Did I know where he meant? I said that I did. He said that the police wanted us to go there.

Anthea drove. She had texted her son, Alexander. She had written: *It looks as if Theo is dead. More later.* As we headed up towards Armous-et-Cau, Alexander rang on my mobile. I told him that Theo, his half-brother, was dead. He said: "No, not lovely Theo" and choked into tears. I told him what little I knew. The significance of where the accident had happened had not sunk in yet.

We arrived at the crash site. A *gendarme* waved us through the road-block when I told him who we were. The car I had hired was crumpled against the wall of the cemetery. An ambulance had already taken the other two boys to the hospital in Auch. Theo's body, I was told, was in the hearse I could just see parked behind the eastern wall of the cemetery. Anthea wanted to see him. I asked the officer in charge. He said that Theo had been terribly injured. He felt that to see him now would be too distressing. He said that we should follow the hearse to the *Funérarium* in Auch. The people there would arrange things so that we could see Theo in a way that would not imprint an unbearable image on our memories.

We followed the hearse. The weather was still magnificent. The countryside through which we were driving is some of the most perfect in that part of France. I hated it all. I hated the blue of the sky, the green of the vineyards, the naturally sculpted contours of the hills.

We arrived at the *Funérarium*. It was in a little back street up a hill in the outskirts of the city. We sat side by side in the clinically clean waiting-room. I suddenly thought that if Theo were still alive we would be discussing the near-impossibility of pronouncing the tongue-twisting word *Funérarium* correctly. We would have had a competition to see who could come closest. I broke down then – the first tears I shed. Anthea comforted me. The young undertaker appeared. He ushered us into a little room.

Theo was lying on his back on a gurney. A blanket covered his body up to the neck. There was a very faint smile on his lips, a smile almost of contentment, of repose. I touched his cheek. It was still warm. "Oh, Theo," Anthea said. Then she buried her face in his neck and kissed him. We talked for a little – I can't remember what we said – then Anthea left the room, went out into the street. She told me later that she wanted to get away, right away, from everything, from the whole situation. She felt she couldn't cope with it. She underestimated her own inner strength.

Alone, I knelt down by the gurney and prayed. I said the Lord's Payer to myself, that's all, then rose and traced the sign of the Cross on Theo's forehead and said: Rest eternal grant unto him O Lord; and let light perpetual shine upon him.

We drove to the hospital. Images of the crash site kept invading my mind. I was beginning to realize that the last thing that my son had seen on this earth was the vineyard and the cemetery that he had photographed for the dust-jacket of my book. I felt that there was a doom about the thing, that I was somehow responsible. But I knew that I had to drive such thoughts out or I would go to pieces, that I had to hold onto myself as Anthea, with a marvellous courage, was holding onto herself.

We arrived at the hospital. The boy who had been injured didn't know that Theo was dead. We had to tell him. The other boy, who had been driving, said that the *gendarmes* in Bassoues wanted him to make a statement.

We drove to Bassoues. The sun was setting. It kept blinding Anthea, at the wheel. We got to the Gendarmerie. The *gendarme* on duty tapped out the driver's statement with two fingers on a computer keyboard. I acted as interpreter. It was surreal.

That night I couldn't sleep. Just after dawn I got up and walked over the ramshackle cottage which is part of the property. It contains a study, a games room and the makeshift bedroom where Theo had been sleeping. I did what I suppose many people do in the first stages of bereavement. I lay in Theo's bed and talked to him. I got up, went into the office and wrote him a long letter. Alone, I was able to give way to my grief in convulsive weeping.

I had agreed with the *gendarme* in Bassoues to return that morning so that the driver could complete his statement and sign various documents. My niece Kate came with us. Her presence was immensely comforting to me. Without her, I don't think I could have gone through with it. Neighbours had agreed to collect the driver from the *gendarmerie* and take him to Pau. His parents were flying in, as were two of Anthea's children, Alexander and Cressida. Her third child, Joanna, was on holiday with her husband and children in America. At the *gendarmerie*, the same officer took me aside and said that he had rung the *Procurateur* in Auch who had advised him that since I was the father of the victim of the accident, and might want to take legal action against the driver, I should not act as interpreter. They had found someone else, an Englishman in the village, who had agreed to take my place.

Anthea and I drove to Pau to pick up Alexander and Cressida. Cressida had cried throughout the flight from London. I must quote Anthea again: "Cressida, Alexander and I went into a corner and wept. The howling, for me, was to come much, much later."

We drove to Auch, to the *Funérarium*. We saw Theo. Then we were ushered into an office. On the wall was a sort Argos catalogue of coffins. Elements of black comedy started to creep in as the undertaker tried to edge us towards mahogany and brass handles and we determinedly steered the discussion back towards plainness and simplicity. As we left, Anthea, who is blessed with an invulnerable digestion, said she had to go to the loo, adding that since Theo's death her system had gone completely haywire and that she had seen the inside of a great many very peculiar public lavatories. "You should write a book called *Twelve Curious Lavatories in France*," I said.

We went back to the house. It was late afternoon now. Our immediate neighbours came to see us. The French don't shy away from death. They bring you flowers, food, wine and most precious of all, fellow-feeling. Another close neighbour arrived, a true son of Gascony called Alban, a widower from whose *potager* we had for years received countless gifts of fresh vegetables. He had a copy of the local newspaper, published that day. It contained a report of the accident. The final paragraph read as follows:

"It fell to Gérard Castet, mayor of Beaumarchès, alerted by the gendarmerie, to convey the terrible news to the parents of Theo Goldsmith, *the twelfth person to have been killed* on the roads of our department since the beginning of the year."

The twelfth person. Twelve. Not thirteen, not seven, not fifteen. Twelve.

See John Goldsmith's other titles and biography on
Amazon

http://viewAuthor.at/JohnGoldsmith

Connect with John Goldsmith and Marble City Publishing

http://www.marblecitypublishing.com

Join Marble City's list for giveaways, news of upcoming
releases and competitions.

http://eepurl.com/JoCm5

Follow on Twitter:

http://twitter.com/MarbleCityPub

www.ingramcontent.com/pod-product-compliance
Lightning Source LLC
Chambersburg PA
CBHW031957190626
46808CB00018B/1603